D1827488

The Malice of Angels

WENDY PERCIVAL

First published in 2017 by SilverWood Books, Bristol
This edition Independently Published 2019

Copyright © Wendy Percival 2017

Cover Images © Stokkete/Dreamstime.com | Scandinavian Stock |
Maksym Chornii | Marina Strizhak/123RF.com | Wendy Percival |
Westland Lysander Photo © Nigel Ish, August 2012. Creative Commons
Attribution-ShareAlike 3.0 Unported License. Commons.wikimedia.org.

The right of Wendy Percival to be identified as the author of this
work has been asserted in accordance with the Copyright,
Designs and Patents Act 1988 Sections 77 and 78.

All rights reserved. No part of this publication may be reproduced,
stored in a retrieval system, or transmitted in any form or by any means,
electronic, mechanical, photocopying, recording or otherwise,
without prior permission of the copyright holder.

This is a work of fiction. Names, characters, places and incidents either
are products of the author's imagination or are used fictitiously.
Any resemblance to actual events or locales or persons,
living or dead, is entirely coincidental.

ISBN 9781070787640

British Library Cataloguing in Publication Data
A CIP catalogue record for this book is available from
the British Library

Page design and typesetting by SilverWood Books
Printed on responsibly sourced paper

WENDY PERCIVAL was born in the West Midlands and brought up in the Worcestershire countryside. After training as a primary school teacher she moved to North Devon in 1980 to take up her first teaching post and remained in teaching for twenty years.

An impulse buy of *Writing Magazine* inspired her to start writing seriously. She won *Writing Magazine*'s Summer Ghost Story competition in 2002 and had a short story published in *The People's Friend* before focusing on full-length fiction.

The time honoured 'box of old documents in the attic' stirred her interest in genealogy and became the inspiration for the Esme Quentin Mysteries – *Blood-Tied*, *The Indelible Stain*, for which she received the indieBRAG medallion (Book Readers Appreciation Group), and a novella, *Death of a Cuckoo*

When she's not writing fiction, Wendy conducts her own family history research, sharing her finds on her blog, www.familyhistorysecrets.blogspot.com. She's also had articles published in Shropshire Family History Society's quarterly journal and in *Family Tree* magazine.

Wendy lives in a thatched cottage beside a thirteenth-century church with her husband and a particularly talkative cat.

You can find more on her website www.wendypercival.co.uk.

Truth doesn't always heal a wounded soul
Maxim Gorky

Acknowledgements

Many thanks to all those who have helped me during the writing of this novel. Thank you to Margot Seabrook for sharing her childhood memories of Germany, to Lorna Manton for her intuitive comments on the final draft, to Michelle Kelley for her invaluable editing and to Kath Middleton for her meticulous proofreading. Thanks also to Helen Hart, Annie Broomfield, and the rest of the SilverWood team for another great production – it's a joy to work with you again! And, last, but never least, my love and huge appreciation to Brian for his stoic support as I battled my way from initial idea to completed book!

1

It wasn't until she turned into the narrow medieval passageway of Fish Street that Esme Quentin suspected she was being followed. He – if it was a he, it was difficult to be sure, encased as the walker was in a hooded trench coat – seemed to be keeping his distance. He slowed as she slowed, held back if she paused, as though biding his time before approaching her. Perhaps she should grab the initiative and challenge him? Demand to know who he was and what he thought he was doing creeping up on a middle-aged woman in the dark?

She stopped and deliberately looked round, but he must have pulled back out of the halo of the street lamp as he'd disappeared into the shadows.

She shook her head and carried on down the cobbled street with a greater sense of urgency. Had he been in the records office? There was something vaguely familiar about the way he walked, a loping manner which she felt she should know. Thinking about it, she may have seen him before. He'd been watching from across the road as she'd hurried into the archives that morning. Had he been admiring the architecture of the old half-timbered building? Waiting for someone? Waiting for *her*? So why not come right out and seek her out? Why hover on the perimeter with intent only to follow her at the end of the day? And what did he want? To engage her genealogy research services? Perhaps he was shy or had a dark family secret he needed her help to uncover and was coy about explaining it. She'd been engaged by a couple of eccentric clients in her time but not one who'd used stalking as their modus operandi. At least, not that she'd noticed.

But she had no time to waste speculating. She had more than enough to do getting ready for the morning. She'd already cut it fine by staying so long in the records office – she should have been heading home ages ago. But despite telling herself that she was merely tying up loose ends of this case before tomorrow's deadline, she'd succumbed to her usual habit of being sucked into a story as her research unfolded. Once hooked she always found it so difficult to drag herself away.

Today it should have been just an hour or two adding a little local information to the story of her client's great-aunt, a member of The Queen Alexandra Nursing Corps who'd served in Singapore during the Second World War. The nursing sister had survived a shipwreck due to enemy attack and subsequent massacre of survivors in the water, only to be picked up days later by the Japanese Navy and suffer the inhumanity of a prisoner of war camp.

She paused at the corner of the street to glance behind her. All was quiet and she could see no one. Perhaps she'd imagined the whole thing. Perhaps he'd been merely taking the same path as her and had now arrived at his destination. She'd passed a small hotel a moment ago. He was probably staying there.

She let out a long sigh and allowed herself an indulgent giggle at her imagined melodrama, blaming her oversensitivity on an afternoon of reading first-hand accounts of wartime traumas.

The street narrowed into the passageway which exited on to the high street. As Esme plunged into the shadow between the two buildings, someone stepped out in front of her and grabbed her arm.

2

Esme yanked her arm out of the stranger's grasp and recoiled. He spoke.

'Esme?'

'What?'

'It *is* you, isn't it?' The interloper stepped backward out into the high street, where the light was brighter.

'It's Max, Esme. Don't you remember me? Max Rainsford. Mate of Tim's. You can't tell me you've forgotten. I won't believe it.'

Esme stared, breathing heavily, her body rigid and her thoughts a muddle of recollections, images of people in a busy office, sounds of telephones, voices yelling across the room, hurrying between desks in a scruffy communal space.

'You've been following me,' she managed, eventually, as her breathing became more controlled.

He shook his head. 'Yeah, sorry about that. I had to be sure it was you, didn't I?'

She did recognise him, of course she did, now she could see his face. Bespeckled, with the same short spiky hair, although grey now, not black, and with a beard to match.

He shrugged and gave an apologetic laugh. 'I mean, it's been…what, over fifteen years since Tim… More, I guess. Time moves on so quick, you know.'

'You could have phoned. I'm in the book.'

'Yeah, so I saw. Genealogy, isn't it? Digging up skeletons in people's cupboards.'

'As I recall, digging was something you specialised in. Dirt mostly, wasn't it?'

He laughed. 'You haven't changed, I see. Still as sharp as you ever were.' He lowered his head and peered into her face. 'Hey, what say I buy you a drink? Catch up on...'

'Old times?' Esme shook her head and began to back away. 'I don't think so, Max. Not now. Sorry, but I can't. I've got –'

'Please. I want to ask you something. It's about Tim.'

A surge of alarm shot through her and she felt herself go tense. 'What about Tim?'

Max rubbed his palms together. 'Hey, look. We could be having this conversation by the fire in The Loggerheads, rather than freezing our balls off out here.'

Esme stared at him, suspicious that he'd used Tim's name merely to get her attention.

Max nodded his head down the street. 'Shall we? Won't take long.'

She let her shoulders slump. It had been a long day and suddenly she was too tired to argue. Besides, she'd earned a drink to celebrate completing her last assignment. She sighed, lifting her arm to take an exaggerated look at her watch. 'OK,' she said, shoving her hands in her pockets. 'You've got twenty minutes.'

3

The pub was quiet with only one other customer. Max made small talk with the barman while he pulled their pints giving Esme a few moments to gather her thoughts. She tucked in a strand of her unruly hair which had escaped its fastening and speculated as to Max's motives for turning up announcunced. She was fairly certain she'd not set eyes on him since Tim's funeral.

But then it was easy enough to lose touch. She'd been somewhat of a nomad during those early years. Her family struggled to keep up with her, never mind old work colleagues, through the myriad of bed-sits she'd inhabited in more small towns than she could now recall. Perhaps Max had assumed that she no longer wanted any connection with Tim's world of investigative journalism and had left well alone. He would have been right.

They took their drinks into the small snug which had at one time not allowed women inside its walls.

'You still haven't answered my question about why you didn't phone,' Esme said, as she put down her glass. She slipped off her duffel coat and draped it over the bench seat before sitting down. She wondered how he'd found her and felt her stomach flip when it occurred to her that he might have been following her since she left her cottage that morning. Under-cover journalists were well practised in the art of covert surveillance. What worried her was his motive.

Max pulled out a stool from under the table and sat astride it. For the first time, he looked her in the eye and she felt conscious of the scar across her face. She wrapped her hands around her glass and resisted the urge to put her hand to her cheek to cover the puckered skin tissue. It should serve as a reminder to Max as to why she'd turned away from Tim's journalistic past. 'Well,' he said, 'it just seemed to make more sense –'

'You thought I'd turn you down. Refuse to see you.'

'Something like that.' He pulled his gaze away and stared into his pint.

'Hey,' said Esme, with a smile. 'Don't go all coy on me now we've made it this far. Come on, out with it. I'm not stupid enough to think you've tracked me down, followed me down dark alleys and frightened me half to death just to persuade me to have a drink as though we met up regularly.'

He looked up and grinned. 'I'm not usually so transparent.'

'I should hope not or you're in the wrong job.'

He pushed his pint away from him and, reaching inside his jacket, pulled out a folded sheet of paper which he opened out and slid across to Esme. 'Remember this?'

'What is it?' asked Esme picking it up. It was a photocopy of a newspaper cutting. The headline ran, MAN SHOT DEAD ON DOORSTEP.

'Victim's name was Gerald Gallimore,' said Max. 'They believe it was the killer who called the emergency services and gave them the poor guy's address. Right location but the name of the house was wrong.'

'Oh, yes. I do remember. Bugged Tim for weeks. He was convinced if he could only work it out, the story would launch his career.'

'Doubt that. We were barely allowed to make the tea back then, let alone write copy. Even if he had cracked it, it wouldn't have been his name on the byline.' Max picked up his pint and drank down almost half of it.

'And this is relevant to me because?' asked Esme.

Max leant towards Esme, resting his elbows on the table. 'Before the whole thing got shoved into touch by the editor, I was sure Tim was on to something.'

'Which was?'

'That's just it. Never got a chance to tell me. Ronald Reagan got shot and we were up to our ears in US conspiracy theories. After that...well, it never really came up again.'

She frowned at him. 'Surely you're not asking me if I remember something he might have dropped into a conversation over dinner back in nineteen...' she glanced at the news cutting. 'Eighty-one?'

'No, of course not. But you were his researcher back then. Did you do any digging on it?'

'Not that I recall, no. As you say, all eyes were elsewhere. I doubt I'd have had the time to get sidetracked.'

'What about those scruffy little notebooks of Tim's he used to keep religiously...'

'Forget it, Max,' said Esme, anticipating where this was going and desperate to stop it before it went any further. She picked up her drink and avoided his gaze. 'I didn't keep anything. Not a thing. Sorry to disappoint you.' She shrugged. 'Anyway, even if I did have them, you know he used shorthand. Which I don't read. So I wouldn't even know if there was anything significant anyway.'

'I read shorthand.'

She put down her glass. 'Yeah, well. Like I say. The question's academic. Anyway,' she said, folding her arms and resting on the edge of the table, 'why the interest now?'

He rubbed his eyebrow with his thumb, dislodging his glasses. 'Just after some background, really,' he said, pushing them back up on to the bridge of his nose. 'Right up your street, if you're interested. Family history, past connections. You know the sort of thing.'

'Stop changing the subject, Max. You still haven't told me, why now?'

Max scratched his bearded cheek with a forefinger. 'Something I'm working on.'

'Like what?'

He shrugged. 'Like a change from the day job. Not getting any younger, Ez. Thought I'd take a look at the wider view. Might even have a publisher sniffing around, if I play my cards right.'

'You're writing a book?'

Max laughed. 'You make it sound like a heinous crime.'

'And the subject of this literary adventure? I assume you're anticipating a nice fat six figure advance from this pet publisher snapping at your heels?'

He ignored the jibe. 'I just said, didn't I? Looking at the wider view. Getting away from the same old cronies at Westminster. Casting the net around, looking to the future.'

Esme narrowed her eyes. Either she was missing something or Max was being deliberately vague. 'I'm not seeing the connection with Gerald Gallimore, Max. You'll have to enlighten me.'

Max took a sip of beer before answering. 'Gallimore's son, Lloyd, keeps popping up on the radar. There's talk of him being the next Tory leader. He's not even an MP yet, but they're working on it.'

Esme threw him a scowl. 'Oh, I get it. You're on a fishing trip. See what mud you can rake up.'

'Hey, don't be like that, Ez. Wouldn't you like to be sure that your country's potential prime minister didn't have anything nasty to hide?'

Esme pressed her lips together. Max made his motives sound so ethical but she wasn't fooled. Even if the discovery turned out to be minimal, it was easy to present it as worse than it really was, to compensate the writer for time consumed with little result. But she didn't want to waste her breath getting into an argument.

'Look, Max. Even if I was willing to help, the timing's all wrong. I'm moving house tomorrow.' She made a point of looking at her watch. 'And the removal lorry is due to arrive in a little over twelve hours. I've got to get back and –'

'Move? Where to?'

'North Devon.'

'Devon?'

'Yes. Got a problem with that?'

'No, just surprised, that's all. Thought you'd stay put here. So why North Devon? Family ties?'

She shook her head. 'Not exactly. Old friends. Ruth and Pete Gibson. Used to go to Ruth's parents' farm on family holidays as a child. All on a bit of a whim, if you must know.' She gave a half-laugh. 'Had a sudden urge to live by the sea.'

'So you're selling up?'

'No, not immediately. I'm renting to start with. See how it goes.' She shrugged. 'But what the hell. Got to grab your chances when you can. There's enough of life you've no control over as it is.' She lowered her gaze and stared at the table top, feeling she'd said more than she needed. Max, of all people, knew what she meant. He'd been Tim's closest friend once upon a time.

'Don't blame you. Go for it. After what you went through –'

'Yes.' She picked up her drink and took a sip, needing all her concentration to stop her hand shaking.

Max cleared his throat. 'Did you ever find out any more?'

Esme put down the glass and shook her head. Did she really want to go over it all again? But then she'd hardly spoken to Max since it happened. She owed him that, perhaps. She focused on her glass on the beer mat, lining it up exactly so that it covered the logo in the centre. 'In a word, no.'

'You still reckon it was about pharmaceuticals?'

'Something like that. Whether underhand deals below the radar or turf warfare on the streets, I never found out. Though, as you know, I've always assumed the former.' Even now it was hard to talk about her failure.

'You were probably just as well to walk away, given what happened to Tim.'

She looked up, her stare challenging. 'What are you saying?'

17

'Sorry,' said Max, lifting his hand in apology. 'I didn't phrase that very well. I'm not blaming you for getting the hell out of it, Ez, you had no choice. I guess they assumed you knew something, too.'

She felt his eyes on her scarred face. 'I don't think that was the reason. Wrong place, wrong time. Going to look for him was my mistake.' Though what else could she have done? And she knew she'd have done the same again. Who wouldn't, if there was the slightest chance of preventing it? She swallowed. *If only* was a phrase she'd trained herself not to utter any more.

Max took a gulp of beer before adding, 'I wish we'd managed to convince them to dig deeper. The official line was always it was a random act of violence.'

Esme shook her head. 'Not your fault. Too much riding on it to blow it open. Trade agreements between nations are so much more important than the death of one journalist, don't you think? Can't afford to rock the boat by suggesting one of the party has blood on their hands.' She rubbed her eyes. 'Look, I don't really want to –'

'Yes, of course. I just wanted to say, you know.'

Esme nodded and forced a smile. 'So,' she said, taking a deep breath, 'you're done with investigative journalism, then, and branching out into the melee of the political world?'

Max shifted on his seat. 'Maybe. I'm still in two minds. Though in this case, it isn't the politics which interests me. It's the suspicious murder. From what I gather, it's an area you've taken an interest in yourself in recent years.'

Esme gave him a wary glance. 'Not by choice, it isn't.' What had he heard?

'No? Well, be that as it may, when this came up, I thought you might be interested. Especially given it was one Tim flagged up.'

'No, Max. It's not going to happen. When I was Tim's researcher, I might have helped you out from time to time, but those days are long gone.' Esme stood up. 'Thanks for the drink but I really must go. As I told you, the removal firm is booked for first thing in the morning and I've still got a million things left to do.' She slipped on her coat.

Max pulled out a card from his pocket and handed to her. 'You better take this.'

'I've already said…'

He took her hand and pressed it into her palm. 'Take it. Just in case you change your mind.'

'I won't.'

'Humour me. You never know.'

She sighed and shoved it in her coat pocket. 'Good to see you again, Max. Best of luck with everything. See you again.'

Max grinned. 'Counting on it.'

4

Esme dropped her car keys on the hall table, deliberately turning her back on the pile of boxes which were due to be collected by the removal firm the following morning for storage. She took off her coat, threw it over the newel post at the bottom of the stairs and went into the kitchen to brew a mug of tea. As she sipped the hot liquid she wandered back into the living room and stood on the kitchen threshold, staring at the cardboard mountain.

If she'd been braver and thrown in her lot with the move idea, it would have made things so much easier. But this way, this halfway house of renting out the cottage while she trialled her decision, had made more work. Instead of being able to move furniture from A to B with the minimum of fuss, she'd not only had to empty every drawer and trunk of its contents but decide what to take and what to put into storage.

Well, at least it was almost done now after weeks of deliberation, and tomorrow everything changed. She felt a tingle of excitement and allowed herself a moment's indulgence before the image of Max and his speculation loomed up in her mind again. She let out an exasperated sigh and slammed down her mug on a packing box, slopping tea everywhere and forcing her back into the kitchen for a cloth to mop it up.

Why did he have to turn up now? If he'd have sought her out tomorrow, she'd have been long gone and she'd know nothing about his investigation or his questionable motives. Despite what he'd said, she wasn't sure he wasn't really looking for a thorn to jab in Lloyd Gallimore's side. She had no wish to be part of such a campaign, let alone assist in getting it started.

She dealt with the spillage and returned to the kitchen, chewing her lower lip as she swilled out the cloth under the tap. There was no doubt the murder had intrigued Tim. Despite her casual reply to Max, she remembered it very well. Tim often recalled it. Had it ever been solved? She didn't think so. Was it possible that Tim *had* turned up something of vital importance that really should be brought out into the open, something that the public had a right to know?

So what was she going to do about it?

As she came back into the sitting room, her eyes fell on the small wooden trunk at the bottom of the stairs in which she kept old photograph albums. In the bottom were Tim's old notebooks. She wondered if Max had guessed she'd been lying.

It wouldn't take a moment to look at March 1981. Although she wouldn't be able to read the shorthand, if copious notes were scrawled around the relevant date it would suggest something of significance was recorded.

Her thoughts drifted back to Max's parting comment. *Counting on it*, he'd said in response to hers of *see you again*. Meaning, she supposed, that he'd expected her to be back in touch the moment she'd rushed back home and searched Tim's files. She snorted. She didn't intend to give him the satisfaction of being right, but it didn't mean she couldn't look for the sake of her own curiosity. At least, when she found nothing, she could focus on tomorrow with a clear head and without Max's words reverberating in her head.

She knelt down and opened the lid of the box, slowly unpacking the photograph albums and putting them down on the carpet. Tension and a feeling of agitation churned around inside her. She decided it was because she was annoyed with herself – first of all, for wasting time when there was so much to do and, secondly, allowing Max to goad her into doing exactly what she'd had no intention of doing. But it was too late now. Get it done and move on.

Towards the bottom of the trunk, Tim's notebooks were stacked in neat piles. She felt a flutter in her stomach at the sight of Tim's untidy handwriting, scrawled on the front identifying the dates each journal covered. She'd asked herself many times why she'd never thrown them out. She'd never looked inside them. What would be the point? As she'd told Max, they were written in shorthand and she didn't read it. And she had no need to be reminded of a life that had passed on.

She squeezed her eyes tight. For goodness sake, stop wasting time. If she was going to do it, she should just do it and be done with it. She quickly flicked through the pile, unloading them on to her lap, until she found the one which covered 1981.

She sat back on her heels, clutching the notebook against her, trying to clarify her feelings. Why was she even doing this? Was she being completely honest about wanting to find nothing? While it would mean she could thrust the past back into the box and breathe a sigh of relief, maybe part of her wanted to uncover some tantalising clue, forcing her to reconnect with an event which brought her closer to Tim. Was that why she'd been unable to ignore Max's request?

She became aware of numbness in her legs from kneeling, cutting off the blood circulation in her legs. She stood up and walked around the room to relieve the pressure, still hugging the notebook to her. The long case clock chimed eight o'clock, reminding her that the evening was slipping away and she still had much to do.

She fingered the cover of the notebook, and wandered to the window, pulling the curtains to shut out the muted street light in the lane. How would she feel if there *was* something in Tim's notes suggesting he'd stumbled upon clues for Gallimore's murder? What would she say to Max, having told him she didn't have the notebooks any longer?

She turned away from the window, telling herself to stop prevaricating. She could make that decision if there was anything to find. She sat down on the edge of the armchair and began leafing through the book, her heart rate quickening.

When she found the page, it was clear that the notes Tim had made were insignificant. There was one short line on the date the murder took place and nothing in depth until a couple of weeks later, when she recognised her own scribble in the margin, indicating she'd be involved in the research when they must have moved on to something else. While she'd not been honest with Max about keeping the notebooks, she'd not been lying when she'd told him that Gallimore had definitely not been the subject of any investigation in which she'd been involved. She laid the book down on her lap and allowed her shoulders to relax. Well, that was that. End of mystery.

She returned to the wooden trunk and piled the notebooks back inside in chronological order, her eyes resting on the final one, dated 1991, the year he died. For a moment her thoughts drifted back to that traumatic day – confusion as to why the contact Tim had gone to meet was talking to her on the phone unaware of their appointment, her realisation that someone had set Tim up and the panic when she couldn't find him in the pub where he'd been headed. The scene of the half-drunk pint on the bar and the landlord explaining how Tim had suddenly got up and hurried out, played over in her head like an old black and white movie.

She gave her head a shake and slammed the lid of the trunk closed with an irritated sigh. What did she think she was doing, allowing Max to stir her brain with such memories?

She slid the trunk into the corner of the room to join the rest of the items going into storage and, forcing all thoughts of her meeting with Max out of her head, she turned her attention to what was needed in readiness for her move in the morning.

5

The day started early and Esme had little time to think anything more about Max and Gallimore's murder, busy as she was instructing removal men with what was to be stored and what she planned to take with her.

The cottage she was renting in Devon was furnished and her own home in Shropshire was being let unfurnished. The bulk of her furniture was to be loaded into the larger removal lorry to go into storage for six months, initially. Going with her, into the smaller van, were the contents of her office – including her desk, typing chair and IT equipment – some smaller items of furniture, such as lamps, an occasional table and a footstool, along with clothes, a selection of books, several framed photographs, cushions, a couple of paintings and a few knick-knacks to make the place feel like home. She'd agonised for weeks over what she'd need to take with her and what to leave behind. She hoped she'd not forgotten anything.

With the furniture loaded on the lorry, there remained the two final piles of boxes in the corner of the living room, one to accompany the furniture into storage and the other for the smaller van going with her to Devon.

She made the workers tea and while they drank it, she wandered around the empty property, hoping she'd done the right thing in succumbing to what had been a sudden urge for a life change. At first the idea had seemed reckless and self-indulgent. Why uproot and move again when, after years of moving around from place to place following Tim's death, she'd felt finally settled?

But her visit last September had reminded her of the particular joy she'd always experienced at being near the coast. Why not recognise that draw and act on it? There was nothing stopping her. She was in the enviable situation where she could work from anywhere. Her clients stretched across the UK and beyond, and recently, she'd had several enquiries in the southwest with local connections.

Ruth had been particularly enthusiastic about her decision. Following the traumatic events of the late summer, when Esme had become caught up in the mystery of Bella Shaw's tragic death, Esme had promised Ruth she'd not leave it thirty years before visiting again. During the visits she'd made to Devon since, the idea of relocating had grown, bringing her to this day.

The final decision was made when Ruth telephoned in high excitement to tell her of a cottage not far from the farm, and seductively close to the sea, advertised for a winter let. It seemed fate had declared its hand. Esme hadn't hesitated.

She heard the workmen's voices coming up the path into the house. She swilled her mug under the kitchen tap and went into the living room to meet them.

'So it's just this lot, then, and we're done?' said Stan, the senior of the team.

'That's it, guys. Thanks.' She took their empty mugs from them and they each grabbed an armful of boxes to ferry out to the lorry. Esme returned to the kitchen to wash up the mugs and slip them inside the picnic bag of food which she'd be taking with her.

When she returned to the living room, there was only one box left standing on the carpet, waiting to be loaded. She felt a sudden lurch in her stomach. Tim's box of childhood mementos, swimming badges, exam certificates, newspaper articles he was proud to have written and two treasured journalist awards. Why was it still there? She'd deliberately put it back on the very top so it would go in first and wouldn't remind her of Max and his mad-capped ideas.

'Last one, lads,' said Stan, reaching down to pick it up and handing it to his colleague. Esme watched as the man took it from his boss and walked out of the front door.

'Well, that's it, then, love,' said Stan, turning to Esme. 'I'll just get you to sign the paperwork.' He headed down the path towards the lorry, opening the door of the cab to reach inside for a clipboard.

Esme followed down the path, her eye still fixed on the box as it was loaded on board and the doors were slammed shut.

'In the box at the bottom.'

Esme blinked. 'Pardon?'

Stan pushed the clipboard and the pen towards her. 'If you could just sign in the box at the bottom, love, then we'll get out of your way.'

Esme took the clipboard and stared down at the form. She looked up at Stan. 'Actually, Stan,' she said, with a sheepish smile. 'That last box. I think I may need it after all. Would you mind?'

6

The day felt as though it had lasted twice as long as normal by the time the removal van bumped its way back up the track and away from the cottage. Esme closed the door and leant back against it, closing her eyes with a mixture of relief and excitement. When she opened them again, she marvelled at the stack of boxes in front of her, waiting to be unpacked. She rubbed a finger along her scar. How could a short spell in rented accommodation – and furnished at that – require so much stuff? And there was even more in the bedroom, though that consisted mainly of clothes, bed linen and towels.

The cottage, built of whitewashed stone with a wonky, slated roof, its interior modestly furnished and plainly decorated, had everything she'd need for the next few months. The kitchen consisted of a large farmhouse table, covered in a brightly patterned oil-cloth, dominating the room. In the far corner stood a large Rayburn, for cooking and heating. Along the adjacent wall was a glazed sink with painted cupboards beneath. Above, framed with gingham curtains, was a window with a view to the sea. Open shelves and more cupboards hung on the walls to either side. The next room was a large sitting room with a deep sofa, large armchairs and a settle beside the generous inglenook fireplace. Esme planned to set up her temporary office in the space in the opposite corner. Upstairs, two bedrooms – one twin, one double – and a bathroom completed the accommodation.

Esme moved away from the door and regarded her new home. She really ought to make a start on the boxes or she'd not be able to get through to the sitting room door or use the kitchen. But what was the rush? Why not enjoy the last couple of hours of daylight by walking down to the beach, only a few yards from the cottage, and rejoice in being here? She'd tackle the unpacking later.

She snatched her waterproof coat from off the hook beside the door and headed out into the wind, hands thrust deep in her pockets and breathing in the wild sea air. On the coast path to her right, a couple of walkers strode up the steep hill, out of the valley in which the cottage sat. To the left, the path towards Warren Quay wound through the gorse away from the stream and up on to the opposite headland. Esme walked straight ahead, the sound of the rising surf becoming louder as she approached. She stepped off the grass, down the steep steps hewn out of the rock and on to the huge pebbles below. She stood on the edge of the beach and gazed around, breathing in her new environment.

On the horizon, a large tanker chugged its way across the expanse of water and the island of Lundy appeared like a farmhouse loaf in the distance, clear enough today to distinguish the green grass on its top from the dark grey cliffs rising out of the sea. On the beach in front of her the tide rushed in between the strata of rocks running from sea to shore.

As she embraced the breeze on her face, she heard her name on the wind and turned to see her photographer friend, Maddy Henderson, in a lime-green ski jacket and black leggings, waving from above. Esme waved back and trudged across the stones to meet her. 'Maddy!' she cried, hugging her. 'I didn't expect to see you so soon. I thought tonight was your running night.'

Maddy shook her head. 'I couldn't ignore your big day, could I?'

They walked back towards the cottage and Maddy paused to reach into her campervan for a bottle of wine. She thrust the bottle towards Esme. 'Welcome to Devon!'

'Oh, thank you! Come on in and I'll find some glasses. You'll have to compete with a sea of boxes, though. The removal men have only just left.'

'I know. I had to back-up for them.'

They went inside. Maddy scanned the heap of unpacked belongings cluttering up the room. 'Travelling light, I see.'

'Oh, don't. I can't imagine why I've brought so much.' Esme put the bottle on the kitchen table and looked around. 'Let's move some of these boxes and make some space to sit down.'

'I know I'm seeing you tomorrow at Ruth's,' said Maddy, grabbing a large cardboard carton and putting it on the floor. 'But I thought you might like a hand getting straight.'

'That's sweet of you.' Esme looked around. 'Though I'm not sure where to start.'

'We could always start with wine,' Maddy said, moving another box out of the way. 'Amazing what a glass of Merlot can do.'

Esme laughed. 'Sounds like a good plan.' She squeezed round the table and searched the cupboards until she found the wine glasses. She opened the bottle and poured them each a measure. 'There you go,' she said, handing Maddy hers.

'Cheers,' said Maddy as they chinked glasses. 'Welcome to your new home and let's hope this time your stay is less fraught than last time.'

'I'll drink to that,' Esme said.

Maddy took a sip and looked at Esme. 'You're sure you don't mind being isolated all down here on your own?'

Esme leaned against the kitchen worktop. 'No, I like the peace and quiet. Going to sleep to the sound of the sea. Waking up to it. Brilliant. I've always wanted to live on the coast since we used to come as kids.'

'And if you don't do it now...'

Esme smiled. 'Precisely.'

Maddy wandered around, appraising. She stopped to peer down at the top box beside her.' *For Esme. Tim's things* she read. She looked up at Esme with a raised eyebrow.

Esme shook her head. 'Mistake. It was supposed to go into storage. I think it was bumping into Max that did it. Put me completely out.'

'Max? Who's he?'

'An old journalist colleague of Tim's. Looked me up just before I left. Bad timing really. I haven't seen him in well over twenty years.'

'So what prompted him to seek you out now?'

Esme sighed. 'Oh, just something that piqued Tim's interest years ago. He wanted my take on it. But inevitably we went over everything again, as you do. You know. What happened, what didn't happen.'

'That can't have been much fun.'

'No. But Max was a good friend of Tim's at one time. We didn't keep in touch. I guess it was some sort of catalyst for him to go through it all with me.'

'So what was it that piqued Tim's interest?'

'Oh, nothing important,' said Esme. 'It was years ago. Look, can we change the subject? I've had enough of poking around in that particular closet.'

Maddy held up her hand, palm outward. 'Fine by me. Whatever you say.'

Esme walked over to Tim's box. 'And this,' she said, tapping the lid, 'is going under the spare bed. And it can stay there until I move out of here.'

'Good for you,' said Maddy, grinning and raising her glass. 'I'll drink to that.'

7

Peter Gibson took a bread roll from the basket his wife held out to him. It looked tiny in his large weathered hands. 'So Esme,' he said, tearing the roll in two and looking at her from under his dark mop of a fringe, 'Ruth tells me you might choose to become a permanent neighbour if we're nice to you.'

Ruth flapped a hand against her husband's shoulder. 'Don't be such a tease, Pete.' She winked at Esme across the kitchen table, her tiny blue eyes shining below her blonde fringe. Her hair was, as always, pulled into a high pony tail and Esme was struck by the contrast of her petite frame to that of the tall bulk of her husband.

'You're always nice to me, Pete,' said Esme, laughing. She split her own roll and breathed in the aroma of freshly baked bread, before turning to Ruth's mother sitting beside her. 'You used to bake us rolls just like this for the start of our holidays, do you remember, Bea?'

'I certainly do. And by my own fair hands, too, I might add. No home bread-makers in those days.' The old lady looked well, if a little tired, Esme thought. Her hair, though silver now, was set, as always, in a short wavy 1940s style. Tonight she looked elegant in a dark long-sleeved dress and a set of white beads. The outfit couldn't be more different to what she usually wore – and had done as long as Esme could remember – full tweed skirt and baggy jumper, a wax jacket and wellingtons on her feet. She used to tell the girls that if it wasn't for the headscarf on her head, wool in the cooler seasons, silk in the summer, she'd have been bald years ago, losing her hair to the wild wind which blew on to the coast and across the moorland behind the farm.

'These smell gorgeous, Ruth,' Maddy said. 'I really should get into bread making but living in the town makes me lazy. It's all too easy with the bakery a couple of streets away.'

Ruth ladled steaming soup into bowls and handed them around. She returned the soup pan to the Rayburn stove before coming and sitting down. 'Don't wait on ceremony. Eat up.'

'Surprised you wanted to come back after last September's fiasco,' Pete said, picking up his spoon. 'I would have thought it would have put you off.'

'My sentiment exactly,' Maddy said, smiling at Esme. 'But she tells me the good outweighs the bad.'

'Too true,' Esme said. 'I have many, many happy memories from way-back-when to compensate for anything that happened in September. I wouldn't be here, otherwise, would I?'

'That's what you've always said, isn't it, Mum?' Ruth said. 'About coming back to Devon after the war.' She looked at Esme across the table. 'You knew Mum was an evacuee, didn't you Esme?'

'I expect you told me before, but I'd forgotten.'

'Crossways Farm, over Four Lanes way,' Ruth said.

Esme smiled. 'So Devon pulled you back, then, Bea?'

'As you see, Esme. Much like yourself. Despite the war, my time here was happy, on the whole.'

'Where did you come from originally, Bea?' Maddy asked.

'I was born in London.'

'Must have been a shock coming from an urban background to a rural one.'

Bea nodded. 'Oh, it was. But I landed on my feet, at Crossways Farm. Old Mrs Beer was a lovely woman. But there's plenty that did suffer, though. Some people resented us kids being there or saw it as an opportunity for some handy unpaid labour. But you probably know about that. Things have come out about it in recent years.'

32

'Particularly with the various anniversaries coming up,' Esme said. 'And now with it being on the primary school curriculum.'

'Mum used to go into the local school to talk about her experiences, didn't you Mum?' said Ruth. 'How you practised being evacuated in lessons until one day it actually happened and you didn't have time to say good-bye.' Ruth glanced between Esme and Maddy. 'They always look shocked at that part. Even the teachers.'

'Watching old film of mothers waving their children off from the station platform is emotional enough,' Esme said. 'I can't imagine what it would be like to go without seeing your parents, Bea. It must have been heart-breaking. Did you have sisters or brothers who went with you?'

'A sister.'

'Older or younger?'

'Older. This is delicious soup, Ruth, thank you. You'll have to give me the recipe. There's nothing like a good homemade soup on a chilly day. Don't you agree, Esme?'

'I do, yes.'

'We all have our favourites. Tomato was yours when you were younger, Ruth. Do you remember?'

'And still is, Mum. But then you know that.'

Esme glanced up at Ruth. Was Bea trying to make a point about Ruth's choice of soup? Perhaps they'd disagreed about the variety to serve. But Ruth kept her focus on the bowl in front of her and Esme couldn't catch her eye.

She turned to Bea instead. 'I assume you and your sister were both evacuated to the same farm?'

But it was Ruth who answered. 'Yes, they were. Auntie Viv was a land girl there. She was much older than Mum, you see.'

'That must have been helpful, having your older sister with you,' Maddy said. 'Less likely to be homesick, I'd have thought.'

Bea focused on rearranging the napkin on her lap and made no comment.

They finished their soup and Ruth collected their empty bowls.

Bea stood up. 'Can I help with the washing up, Ruth?'

'Don't be daft, Bea,' Pete said. 'Why d'you think we've got a dishwasher?'

'Sit down, Mum. We've got beef and ale pie next,' Ruth said. She added, laughing, 'I'd be a poor hostess if I only served a bowl of soup for Esme's welcome dinner, wouldn't I?'

Ruth took the pile of crockery over to the worktop before snatching up the oven gloves from off the rail of the Rayburn. She opened the oven door and lifted out a large steaming pie which she placed on the table to murmurings of appreciation from Pete, Maddy and Esme. Bea sipped her wine and seemed lost in her own thoughts.

Ruth added several dishes of vegetables on to the table. 'You know, Mum, I've been thinking,' she said as she sat down. 'Perhaps you should pick Esme's brain while she's here.'

'What about?' Esme said, turning to Bea.

'About Auntie Viv,' Ruth said.

'Oh, I'm sure Esme's got plenty to keep her busy, Ruth,' said Bea. 'Please don't bother her with something else.'

'No, not at all,' said Esme. 'I'd be happy to help.'

'Auntie Vivienne didn't stay at the farm, you see,' Ruth explained. 'She joined up and became a nurse. The Queen Alexandra's Army Nursing Corps – have I got that right, Mum?'

Bea stared at the table. 'Yes.'

'The last assignment I did before moving here involved a QA nurse,' Esme said. 'She served in the far east.'

'I've no idea where Auntie Viv served because, tragically, she never came home.'

'Oh, that's so sad,' Maddy said, reaching out across the table to Bea. 'You must have been devastated.'

'We'd really love to know what she did in the war,' Ruth continued. 'Mum only knows the bare bones.'

'My friend Mel is quite an authority on the Second World War,' Maddy said. 'Both her grandparents served and she's done heaps of research. She'd be more than happy to give you some background, I'm sure. Point you in the right direction.'

'I've not done much military research,' Esme said. 'I've never been able to get my head around all those battalions, regiments and brigades. But I'm happy to help with the leg work.'

Ruth looked across at her mother. 'That sounds like a good idea, doesn't it, Mum?' Bea didn't answer. Ruth looked around the table. 'The saddest thing is that Mum doesn't even know what happened to her sister.'

Bea's head shot up and she glared at her daughter. 'Of course I know what happened to her, Ruth. I don't know what you're talking about. Now please let's change the subject before we bore poor Esme and Maddy to death.'

Esme saw Ruth and Pete exchange glances, as though some unspoken message of *I told you so* had passed between them. Pete cleared his throat and rubbed his hands together. 'Come on woman!' he said, giving Ruth a broad grin. 'Enough with all this chatter. On with the food. I'm hungry.'

The rest of the meal passed without further mention of Bea's wartime experiences. She joined in with the conversation but Esme sensed Bea wasn't completely relaxed. As they all helped clear the table, Bea declined coffee and said she was ready for her bed. Esme volunteered to give her a lift to her bungalow a short way down the lane from the farmhouse.

As Bea went to find her coat, Esme managed a quiet word with Ruth as they loaded the dishwasher.

'Is Bea OK?' she asked, her eye warily on the door in case Bea walked back in.

'It's my own fault,' said Ruth. 'I shouldn't have pushed it. Pete's always on at me.'

'Her sister, you mean?'

Ruth nodded. 'And the war in general. She seems to find her war years difficult to talk about these days. And yet you heard her say it had been a reasonably happy time. Perhaps it's as she gets older, I don't know.'

'It's not always been like this, then?'

Ruth shook her head. 'No. When we were kids she'd often talk of it. So I don't understand why it's almost become a taboo subject all of a sudden.'

'So has something changed?' asked Maddy, handing Ruth the next pile of plates.

Ruth shrugged. 'No idea. Perhaps it's not so sudden. Perhaps it's been a gradual thing and I've just not noticed.'

'Well, as you pointed out, Esme,' Maddy said. 'All this wartime reminiscing in the media must have brought back painful memories. It could be just that.'

Ruth nodded. 'You may be right.'

*

They said their goodbyes and thanked Ruth and Pete for the meal, Esme adding her extra thanks for securing the cottage rental on her behalf.

After waving Maddy off, Esme helped Bea into her car. In the days when Esme and her family visited the farm on holiday, Bea and Ruth's father lived in the farmhouse. Bea had moved out after her husband died, so that Ruth and Pete could live in the farmhouse and take on the farm.

Esme pulled into the gateway and turned off the ignition. 'I'm sorry about earlier,' she said. 'I should have realised I was being insensitive. I didn't mean to pry. Ruth explained it's a difficult subject.'

'You probably think that's ridiculous after all these years.'

'Who am I to say, Bea? Living through wartime can't have been easy. It's not uncommon to want to try to forget the pain.'

'It isn't my evacuee days, Esme. Don't get me wrong. As I told you, I was one of the lucky ones. Once I'd got over the shock of how different it was living in the country, I took to it like a duck to water.' She turned to Esme and smiled in the gloom of the car's interior light. 'Otherwise I wouldn't have come back to live here, would I?'

'No,' Esme said with a smile. 'I suppose not.'

Esme got out and came round to the passenger door to help Bea out of the car.

'I shall be fine from here,' said Bea, patting Esme's arm. 'Thank you for the lift.'

'You're very welcome.' She stood for a moment, watching as Bea walked away and up the path. 'Bea?'

Bea stopped and looked round. 'Yes, dear?'

'You said your evacuee times at the farm were happy ones. Do you ever go back and visit the family you lived with?'

Bea said nothing for a moment. Then she shook her head. 'They aren't there anymore, dear. The farm was sold after the war.'

Bea turned away and disappeared down the side of the bungalow. As Esme watched her go, she felt sure Bea had been about to say something else but changed her mind.

8

Esme was kneeling on the floor in the sitting room, unpacking a box of books when Ruth arrived.

'Come on in here, it's warmer, 'Esme said, leading Ruth into the sitting room. 'I've lit the wood-burner. Thought I might as well be cosy while I go through this lot.'

Ruth unzipped her jacket and perched on the edge of the armchair beside the fireplace. 'First of all, I want to apologise,' she began.

'What on earth for?' said Esme, dropping on to the opposite chair.

'For Mum and her prickly behaviour. I shouldn't have pushed it.'

Esme shook her head. 'Don't worry about that. We made it up on the way home. She's fine about it, honestly.'

'I know Mum resisted the idea of finding out more about Vivienne but I wonder, maybe it would actually help her. You know, deal with things better. I'm sure half her problem is she doesn't really understand what happened.'

'But last night she said she knows what happened.'

'Only up to a point. That she was serving as a nurse and was reported missing, presumed killed. It's embarrassing when I think about it, that I don't know any more than that. But you don't think to ask when you're a child, do you? All I really understood was that she died in the war.'

'You said Vivienne was much older than Bea,' Esme said.

'Yes, by ten years. Mum would have only been about nine or ten when Aunty Viv was reported missing.' She reached in her pocket and pulled out a photograph. 'I found this. It's Aunt

Viv in uniform.' She handed it to Esme. 'Pete found it in the loft when he was putting in some extra insulation. I assume it fell out of one of Mum's photo albums.'

'I can see a likeness of Bea,' Esme said, studying the black and white photograph. A smiling young woman stared back at her, looking coyly into the camera, her hair set in the style of the era, her fringe flicked neatly over the edge of her cap and a shoulder bag hanging by her side. The young woman's smile suggested a sense of fun and Esme warmed to her.

Ruth leaned forward, resting her elbows on her knees. 'How do we go about finding out any more? I'm sure Mum would come round if we had something tangible to look at.'

Esme wrinkled her nose. 'As I said last night, military isn't really my area of expertise but The Queen Alexandra Nursing Corps would have information on her. That might be the best place to start. It's quite straight forward to apply to the MOD for her World War Two service record.'

Ruth shook her head. 'Pete's already been down that route a few years ago and got nowhere.'

'No? OK. Well, what about that friend of Maddy's she mentioned last night. She said she was pretty knowledgeable. Why don't you go and speak to her?'

Ruth frowned. 'Perhaps it would be better if you go.'

Esme gave her a half smile and flashed an accusing look over the top of her reading glasses. 'Trying to get me into trouble instead of you, then, eh?'

'No, I didn't mean that, Esme, honestly.'

Esme laughed. 'I'm only teasing, Ruth. I'm perfectly happy to go on your behalf. Then you won't feel you're going behind Bea's back.'

'Except I am, aren't I?'

'But with the right intentions.'

'Mmm. The road to hell and all that.'

Esme reached over and touched Ruth's hand. 'I'll only do it if you're sure, Ruth.'

'I just feel there's something,' Ruth said, twisting her fingers in her lap. 'Perhaps if I understood more then I could help, you know?'

'I do know. But don't worry. I won't say anything to Bea until you're sure you want me to.'

Ruth nodded. 'You might as well hang on to the photo for now,' she said. 'Meanwhile, I'll go and have a look for the album.'

Esme stood up and propped the photograph on the beam above the fireplace. She turned back to Ruth. 'You said last night that it was a new thing and she'd not always been so affected by it.'

'She hasn't. She was quite forthcoming when we were kids. She'd often tell me and my brother stories about her life as an evacuee. How cold the school was and how they suffered from chilblains in the winter because they'd warm their icy-cold feet on the stove, having got them wet walking home.'

'I suppose that was in a time before Vivienne was killed, so perhaps happier memories?'

'If it was just that, then I'd agree. But she's even funny about talking about that, these days.'

'But you've no idea why it changed?'

'None. And I can't even be sure *when* it changed. I mean, life happens, plenty going on. It's not as though talking about her childhood is an everyday event, is it? Then, as you remarked last night, with lots of things going on in the media about the anniversary of D-Day or the Battle of Britain, or whatever, it sets conversations going but she's vague and unresponsive, when you would have expected her to revel in all those stories she shared with us as kids.' Ruth shook her head.

'Perhaps, like Maddy suggested, something happened?'

'Like what?'

Esme shrugged. 'I don't know. Someone from the past got in touch? She reached a significant birthday?'

'Mmm, maybe. Anyway...' she placed her palms on her

knees and stood up. 'I'll leave it with you then and get out of your way. No rush. You've plenty else to do, I'm sure.'

'Not especially,' Esme said, as she showed Ruth out. 'I'm allowing myself a bit of free time while I settle in.'

Ruth laughed. 'Well, you don't need me giving you a bus man's holiday, then, do you?'

'Don't be silly, Ruth. You know me – always love a good mystery.'

As Esme returned to the sitting room she picked up Vivienne's photograph and studied it again, frowning. From her limited experience of the work for her previous client, she didn't recognise the uniform Vivienne was wearing as that of a Queen Alexandra's nurse. But then, what did she know? Perhaps Maddy's friend Mel would put her right. She picked up the phone to call Maddy.

9

Esme closed the front door behind her as Maddy's campervan bumped into the parking space.

'Everything OK?' asked Maddy, as Esme climbed into the passenger seat.

'Yes thanks,' Esme said, slamming the van door. 'All boxes unpacked, folded flat and consigned to the spare bedroom.' She turned to Maddy with a smile. 'I think I can safely say I'm officially in residence.'

'Well done you,' Maddy said, with a nod. 'Right, let's go and see what Mel can tell us about the mysterious Vivienne.'

She turned the van around and they headed back to the main road. A couple of miles further along, Maddy took a left fork and Esme noticed a faded sign, lying askew in the hedge pointing to Bleakmoor Airfield.

'The place operated as an aerodrome for years,' Maddy said, as they sped down the lane, the high Devon banks on either side flashing by. 'Lots of the old buildings are still there and Mel rents one as a workshop.'

'Workshop for what?'

'She's passionate about old planes. She's been restoring one for years.'

'How did she get involved?' Esme asked.

'Oh, she's always been a mechanic nut – old engines, tractors, that sort of thing. Then she discovered her gran served in the Second World War helping to maintain the planes. That was it, then. She says it's in the genes.'

Maddy slowed the van and turned off the road on to a bleak

flat overgrown area of concrete. She pulled to a halt and rested her arms on the top of the steering wheel, the engine idling as she gazed out of the windscreen. 'Isn't it amazing?' she said. 'Most people don't even know it's here.'

'Me included,' Esme said, scanning the vast area of hardstanding which seemed to stretch away in front of them and almost disappear over the horizon. 'I was aware of the moor on the seaward side, of course, but not this.'

Maddy pointed into the distance. 'Mel's workshop's over there. You can just make out her van parked out front.' She slipped the campervan into gear and they bumped towards a long grey hangar built of corrugated iron where Maddy stopped the van and turned off the engine.

Esme climbed out and stood on the tarmac, getting her bearings. Mel was right about it being remote. The wind blowing in from the sea created a sense of isolation and was the only sound she could hear. She looked around. To the seaward side were the remains of a tall concrete structure, desolate and eerie, daubed in graffiti and under threat of being overrun with ivy. It almost seemed as though it was watching them. She shuddered.

'The old control tower,' Maddy said.

Esme nodded in acknowledgment. Even its title gave it sinister overtones.

Maddy turned towards the grey building in front of them. 'Come on, let's find Mel.'

They walked across to a wall of corrugated iron broken only by the narrow opening of an inset door. As they approached, Esme could hear music. Maddy pulled open the door and they stepped over the raised threshold to the sight of the half-stripped-down body of an aircraft in the centre of the hangar.

The music echoing around the huge open space of the building Esme now recognised as a big band instrumental from the 1940s. Her knowledge of big bands went no further than the renowned musician Glen Miller, who'd lost his life over the English Channel during the Second World War.

She followed Maddy around the front of the plane. At the back end a woman in overalls was standing on the wing, leaning into the cockpit.

Maddy called out Mel's name above the sound of the trombones.

The head popped up and Esme found herself looking up at a woman's face, smeared with oil smudges and her hair tied back with a bandanna. She grinned and waved, before dipping out of sight. The music died as Mel reappeared and jumped down from the aircraft.

'Maddy!' she said, dropping a large wrench into a canvas tool bag. 'Great to see you.'

She turned to Esme. 'And you must be Esme.' She held up her hands palms outward. 'I won't offer you my hand or you'll get covered, but welcome to Bleakmoor.'

Esme smiled. 'Thank you. Good of you to see me.' She turned to admire the aircraft. 'This is fantastic. What is it?'

'A Lysander V9312,' Mel said, laying her hand on it affectionately.

'I assume it doesn't fly at the moment,' Esme said.

'Not yet, but hopefully it will do. One day.' Mel pulled out a cloth from her pocket and wiped her hands. 'Once all the pieces are in place.'

'How do you even know where to begin?'

'Fortunately I'm not the first person to get hooked on this sort of thing and I've got to know a few experts whose brains I can tap into. I've spent the last few years rebuilding the framework. Now it's a case of locating all the necessary mechanical bits and pieces.'

'Where d'you get them from?' Esme asked. 'I can't image there's much call for manufacturing components for old World War Two planes.'

Mel grinned. 'Off eBay, mostly. Engine parts made popular

mementos for the wartime generation. Many of those I've got hold of once adorned someone's mantelpiece. The next generation's house clearing has proved to be a pretty useful source.' She dropped the cloth on to the top of a tool box. 'Let's go to the office, shall we? It's a bit warmer in there.'

They went back outside and around to the side of the hangar where a small porta-cabin stood up against the side wall.

'Well you've got the perfect location here to indulge your passion,' said Esme, as they walked over to the office building. 'You're not bothered by developers wanting to get their hands on it, then?'

'There's always somebody mooting ideas for something, isn't there Mel?' Maddy said.

'Everything from housing estates to waste incinerators over the years.'

'I was just telling Maddy that I'd no idea it existed. Has it been here long?'

'Since World War Two. Built specifically for the purpose.' She stamped her foot on the tarmac. 'There's over fifteen feet of concrete under here.'

They retreated into the cabin out of the wind, Mel leading the way. The smell of oil and dog was overwhelming, the latter explained by the presence of an old Labrador lying on the floor in front of a portable gas fire. 'It's OK, Oscar,' Mel said. 'Friends.'

Oscar lifted his head briefly to look at them, decided it wasn't worth the effort to get up from his cosy spot and went back to sleep.

Mel wheeled the heater closer to an area of unit seating and gestured for them to sit before going over to a small sink in the corner to wash her hands.

'So what was this used for during the war?' Esme said, sitting down. 'I thought all the RAF fighter squadrons were based in East Anglia and Kent.'

'Yes, they were. Tangmere or Tempsford are the names

45

most people think of if they know any places at all. Very few people knew about the Black Squadron.'

'The Black Squadron?' Esme said, with an involuntary shudder. 'Sounds mysterious.'

Mel nodded. 'It was. And it was black. Literally. The aircraft were painted black and without insignia specifically to carry out secret operations – clandestine missions collecting spies and secret agents from occupied France, that sort of thing. Few people knew what went on here, even when it was fully operational. Some missions weren't even logged.'

'So how come we know about them?' Maddy asked.

'We don't. Not all of them, anyway. Other information turns up in Canadian officers' memoirs. The Canadian Air Force was based here from 1944.' Mel grabbed a towel to dry her hands and walked over to a series of low cupboards against the sides of the cabin. She reached down and pulled open one door. Inside, Esme could see shelves stacked with bulging lever arch files. 'I've amassed a fair amount of information over the years, most of it volunteered by people who have a connection with the base, perhaps having family members who helped build it or who flew aircraft in and out of here during the war. Photographs, letters from family members, old charts, diagrams of how to dig a hideout with location maps, instruction manuals – anything and everything World War Two, basically.'

'Quite an archive,' Esme said.

'Certainly is,' Mel said, closing the low cupboard door behind her. She leant her back against it. 'Maddy tells me you're after help with some research.'

'Yes, please. If you can.' Esme fished in her bag and pulled out the photograph of Vivienne. 'It's about this young lady here. The family was under the impression she was a QA nurse,' she said, handing it to Mel. 'But I don't think it's the right uniform.'

Mel looked at the photograph, shaking her head. 'No,

I agree with you. This isn't a QA uniform. She was a FANY.'

'That's First Aid Nursing something, isn't it?' Esme said.

'Yeomanry. Originally set up before the First World War, apparently, when they still used horses – hence the name.' Mel turned and jerked her head towards a photograph hanging on the wall. 'There's a group of them in that shot there.'

Esme got up and went over to where Mel indicated. Immediately she recognised the women in the photo as all wearing the same uniform as Vivienne. Beside the framed picture was another, a different group of women dressed this time in overalls, standing beside an aircraft. 'Is this your gran?' she said, turning to Mel. 'Maddy said she maintained aeroplanes.'

'Yes it is.' Mel came over and pointed to a woman on the back row, smiling broadly at the camera. 'She was in the ATA – the Air Transport Auxiliary. Some women actually flew the planes but she was ground crew.'

'Oh, I always assumed she was in the WAAF,' Maddy said, joining them.

Mel shook her head. 'No she wasn't military. ATA was a civilian organisation – a sort of Territorial Army, like FANY.'

'So Vivienne wasn't army, either, then?'

'But she was a nurse,' Maddy said. 'That at least checks out. I expect the actual details got a little hazy over the years.'

'Not all FANYs were nurses, though,' Mel said. 'Obviously some were attached to the Red Cross, as it sounds like your girl may have been. Others became drivers, personal assistants, radio officers, decoders, radar operators and so on, as well as SOEs, of course.'

'SOEs were civilian?' Maddy said. 'I assumed all secret agents were military?'

'Not the women. Women in the forces weren't allowed to carry weapons.' She gave a wry smile. 'Most unladylike.'

'Oh you're joking,' Maddy said, pulling a face. 'But they did, though, didn't they? They must have done.'

'SOEs did, yes. They'd be trained to kill, just like the men.

47

Ungentlemanly warfare, they called it. Which they'd need to be, if they were going to be dropped in occupied Europe.'

'Hang on,' Maddy said, frowning. 'Are you saying by using civilians it got around the "no weapons" rule?'

Mel nodded. 'Something like that, yes.'

'With that attitude, it makes you wonder how women were allowed to be SOEs in the first place,' Esme said.

'Oh, there were plenty who didn't agree with the idea, as you can imagine,' Mel continued. 'It was only because Churchill recognised the advantages women could have that they were recruited at all. It was much more difficult for men to have a legitimate reason for being there, given most had been rounded up by the Germans for war work. Women, on the other hand, had the perfect cover in being wives and sisters back home caring for family.'

Esme turned back to the FANY group photo and stared at the women who looked as unlikely killers as Mel's grand-mother's ground crew colleagues. 'What motivated them to put themselves into such a dangerous situation, I wonder?' she said, almost to herself.

'Revenge, in some cases. Indignation in others. Or just straight forward patriotism. But they were under no illusions about the risks they were taking. They were told they only had a fifty-fifty chance of survival. In the event the survival rate was better than that. But even so, many of them were tortured and other suffered terrible ordeals.'

Esme turned away. Was it likely that Vivienne had been an SOE? Was that the reason for the secrecy and confusion? Then again, as Maddy said, she could easily have been a nurse with the Red Cross and the confusion of her being in the military could explain why Pete had failed to get information from the MOD.

'Your memorabilia collection's growing, isn't it?' Maddy said, wandering over to the other side of the room where two display cabinets stood facing one another in opposite corners. Esme followed, peering inside at the shelves crammed full with a hotchpotch of items – a gas mask, dog tags, medals, rusting tins labelled dried egg or powdered milk and piles of leaflets encouraging *Dig for Victory or Make Do and Mend.*

'I keep telling her she needs to set up a museum,' Maddy told Esme.

'Looks like you might have to,' Esme said.

'It's been gathering dust for years,' Mel said. 'A friend gave me the cabinets when he closed his shop but that's as far as it had got. But the local history groups are now in the process of getting lottery grant funding to get it off the ground.'

'What a great idea,' Maddy said.

'Yeah. Only down side is that word's getting around about the plan so I'm getting even more donations. So they better get a move on or there'll be no room in here for me and Oscar.'

Esme turned to look inside the other cabinet, her gaze falling on a curved length of metal like a bent knitting needle lying on a shelf inside the cabinet closest to her. One end was wrapped in faded string. 'What's that?' she said, pointing through the glass.

'A tine dagger,' Mel said. 'Made from the prong of a pitchfork. Primitive but effective. The short knife with the scabbard next to it, which looks like the end of a tent peg, is a thumb dagger. Small enough to hide in clothing and hellish sharp.'

Esme flushed and turned away from the cabinet, her hand instinctively touching her cheek. Of all the wartime roles Bea might imagine her sister to have undertaken as a FANY, she guessed that of a trained killer wouldn't be one of them.

*

Esme asked Maddy to drop her off at Ravens Farm. 'Might as well strike while the iron's hot,' she said. 'And bring Ruth up to date with what we've learned so far.'

'How much will you tell her?' Maddy asked as they drove away from the airfield. 'About Vivienne being a FANY rather than a nurse, I mean.'

'Just because she was a FANY doesn't mean she wasn't also a nurse,' Esme said. 'As you said yourself, it might be just a minor detail that's got lost over time. She could easily have been with the Red Cross rather than the Queen Alexandras, that's all.'

'What if she did something else, though?'

Esme turned to look at her. 'You think I should admit to Ruth she could have been SOE?'

'I don't know. What d'you think?'

'It might account for all the secrecy and confusion in the family. Then again, wartime and confusion go hand in hand. The family could easily have been told the wrong information in complete innocence. Perhaps I'll wait to see what else I come up with so we know for sure one way or the other.'

'Mel said the National Archives might have a file on her, if she was an SOE.'

'She also said to be prepared not to find one, thanks to a fire in 1945.'

*

Maddy swung into the yard and pulled to a halt.

'Thanks for the lift,' Esme said, opening the door and jumping out.

'I hope Ruth's right about this,' Maddy said.

Esme turned back and leaned into the cab. 'Right about what?'

'That Bea finding out the truth about her sister will be a good thing.'

'Why d'you say that?'

Maddy rested her arms on the top of the steering wheel and looked down at Esme, her mouth in a grim line. 'Something I read the other day. *Truth doesn't always heal a wounded soul.*'

Esme frowned. 'Do you believe that?'

Maddy gave her a cheerless smile. 'Guess you never know until you've uncovered it,' she said, putting the van into gear. 'And by then it's too late.'

10

Pete was in the yard, his head buried under the bonnet of the Land Rover. He straightened up at the sound of Maddy's van and waved as Esme walked towards him.

'Problems?' she said, nodding at the engine.

'No, just topping up the oil.' He pulled out a rag from the pocket of his overalls and wiped his hands. 'How'd you get on? Ruth said you were seeing this friend of Maddy's today.'

'That's right. And I think I know why you didn't have any luck with the MOD looking for Vivienne's Queen Alexandra records.'

'Oh? Why's that then?'

'Turns out Vivienne wasn't a military nurse but part of an organisation called the First Aid Nursing Yeomanry, or FANY for short. It was a civilian organisation. Well – still is, actually. We might get some more information through them.'

'So they won't need a certificate? Is that what you mean?'

'A certificate?'

He nodded. 'Perhaps Ruth didn't explain. It wasn't that the MOD didn't have anything on Vivienne – as far as we know, anyway – it's because they needed us to supply a death certificate.'

Esme frowned. 'Why? I thought that if she'd died on active service – or whatever they call it – there wouldn't be a civilian death certificate.'

Pete laughed. 'Well, if you're in the dark, Esme,' he said, clipping the wire stay back into its holding and slamming the bonnet shut. 'I've not got a hope in hell. Have a word with Ruth,' he added, climbing into the vehicle. 'Maybe I've got it wrong.'

*

Ruth was in the kitchen, wielding an iron at speed. Next to her on the table sat a tower of folded laundry. On seeing Esme, she switched off the iron and invited Esme to sit at the table. Esme relayed the information she'd told Pete about the difference between the QAs and FANYs. She also told Ruth what Pete had said about Vivienne's death certificate.

'Yes, that's right,' Ruth confirmed.

'So did you try to get one?'

Ruth looked sheepish. 'Well, no. I never got around to it. Busy season. Life. You know how it is. It's only since this has flared up with Mum that I've even thought about it again.'

'Well I could do it, if you like?' Esme said. 'Point me in the direction of your PC and I'll get what you need to apply for a copy.'

'That'd be great, Esme. Thanks.'

Ruth showed Esme into the farmhouse office and returned to her ironing.

Esme booted the computer and found the relevant database. It didn't take her long to establish that no one called Vivienne Lancaster appeared on the death registers for the wartime period. Just to be thorough, she extended her search to dates beyond 1945 and found two Vivienne Lancasters. But both had died in the 1950s in old age. Clearly not Ruth's aunt.

Esme sat back in the padded black leather chair and swivelled slowly left and right, chewing her bottom lip. What did it mean? A clerical error? Or that Vivienne didn't die in the war after all?

'No luck?' Ruth said from behind her, a mug of tea in her hand. She put it down on the blotting pad on the top of the desk.

'Nothing so far, no. I've tried every variable I can think of.'

Ruth leaned against the desk, looking troubled. 'Does that mean she could have survived the war?'

'It seems odd that the MOD had no record and neither is

she listed on the civilian register. But I can't be absolutely sure one way or the other.'

'But if she survived, she would have contacted her family, wouldn't she?'

'You would think so. But perhaps they had a falling out. Remember Bea was a child living away from home during the war. She may have been completely unaware of any rift. If the fall out was acrimonious, they may have allowed Bea to think her sister had died rather than admit to what had happened, especially if they were ashamed of Vivienne for some reason and had disowned her.'

'Ashamed of her?' She pulled a face. 'I know what you're driving at. You mean if she had a baby, don't you?'

'Only because I've come across some desperately sad stories of girls being kicked out when fathers, in particular, found out they were pregnant. Some families found it similarly shocking when their daughters fell in love with overseas servicemen, considering them unsuitable husbands. Though it was probably the knowledge that they'd go abroad and they'd probably never see them again that hurt them most.'

'So she could have married a GI and left England all together.'

Esme swivelled back to the screen. 'Now that's an idea. If she married before leaving the UK, the marriage will show up in the records. Got to be worth a try.'

Ruth disappeared back into the kitchen as Esme found the marriage database and entered Vivienne Lancaster in the search engine. As the screen refreshed, Esme wondered whether, rather than be ignorant of any rift, Bea was fully aware of what had happened and it was that which was causing her distress. She recalled Maddy's comment about truth and wounded souls. What were they stirring up?

But Bea didn't need to know about their search until Ruth decided the time was right to tell her. And that time may never be right. But at least Ruth would understand and knowing the truth may help her support her mother.

The search engine declared it had found nothing. She tried Viv Lancaster with an option for variants to the name. The closest match was Violet Lander.

Just on the off-chance, she went on to the National Archives website to see if Vivienne's name came up on their SOE database. But she didn't strike gold there, either. Though, from what Mel had told them, that didn't necessarily rule out that Vivienne had been one of Churchill's angels. Her file could have been one of those lost in the fire.

She left the office and went back into the kitchen.

'No luck, I'm afraid,' she said to Ruth's questioning expression.

'I'm not surprised, to be honest,' she said, flicking the shirt she was ironing off the board and slipping it on to a hanger. 'Not with the fiasco Mum had.'

Esme frowned. 'What fiasco?'

Ruth shrugged. 'Of course at the time, I thought it was all just a con so I didn't get involved. Mum said not to worry, she'd dealt with it. That's what she said, anyway.'

'Ruth, I have no idea what you're talking about.'

Ruth shook her head. 'Sorry. Take no notice. I'm just cross that we're having to do this all over again.'

'Do what all over again?'

Ruth picked up a pair of jeans from the washing basket beside her, gave them a vigorous flick and laid them on the ironing board. 'Prove that Auntie Vivienne was dead.' She snatched up the iron and smoothed the jeans, enveloped in a burst of hissing steam.

Esme blinked as she processed Ruth's words. 'I thought you said you were too busy to do anything about it before?'

'We were. That time. I'm talking about when Auntie Vivienne was remembered in someone's will, and they were trying to track her down.'

'Who was?'

'One of those heir hunter companies. Exeter, I think they

came from. You know the sort of thing. They search out beneficiaries to unclaimed money and take a cut for processing a claim on their behalf. Obviously when they tracked down Mum she was able to tell them Vivienne died in the war.'

'In that case the legacy would have come to your mum, I assume?'

'I suppose. But without the proper paperwork that was the end of it.' She turned over the jeans and began ironing the other side. 'To be honest, I took the whole thing with a pinch of salt, anyway. It all seemed too far-fetched to me. When they went away, I thought Mum was well out of it. You know what these things can be like. Cause no end of heartache, people getting obsessed with who's entitled to what money.'

'So whose will was it supposed to have been?'

Ruth shrugged. 'No idea. Mum didn't recognise the name so we both put it down to mistaken identity. You see this sort of thing on the television, don't you? They make mistakes following a particular blood line and end up with the wrong person. I reckon that's what happened. We never heard any more, anyway.'

'You said Bea sorted it out? The question of Vivienne's death?'

'Well, I assume she did. She said it wasn't a problem anymore so I took that to mean she'd done something official.'

'How long ago was this?'

'Goodness, I'm not sure. Years. You'd have to ask Mum.'

'I can hardly do that without letting on what we're up to. I didn't think you wanted to do that.'

Ruth put down the iron and rubbed her hand over her eyes with a sigh. 'No, of course you can't.' She folded the jeans and added them to the pile and bent over to rummage in the basket for another item. The room fell silent. Esme rested her elbows on the table and considered, the hiss of the iron oddly restful.

'This heir hunter outfit who came searching for Vivienne?' she said, after a while.

'What about it?'

'Can you remember anything about them? You said they came from Exeter?'

'Yes, I'm sure they did.'

'Not just an ordinary solicitor, definitely a specialist firm?'

'Almost certain. You're not thinking about contacting them? Not after all this time?'

'If I can track them down. Why not?'

Ruth frowned. 'They wouldn't tell you anything, though, would they? Even if they did remember after all these years.'

'How many years is it? Can you recall?'

Ruth laid down the iron in the rack with a clatter and thought about it. 'Goodness knows.'

'How old were the kids?' said Esme. 'Were you doing B&B then?'

'OK, let me think. We're probably talking...what...fifteen years ago? Bit more perhaps? More like twenty, thinking about it. Yes, that's it. We'd only just moved into the farmhouse.'

'OK. Well that's a start.'

'Are you really going to follow it up?'

'As you said, they were actually looking for Vivienne. They didn't find her through your mum, but who's to say they didn't turn up something else in their search which could help us now.'

11

The list of potential probate researchers in the whole of the South West was short. The other possibility, Esme reasoned, was that the search had been done in-house by the solicitor acting as executor. But Ruth had been sure it was a specialist outfit so if she'd remembered correctly that the company was based in Exeter, and assuming the company still existed, there were only two potential candidates. If they drew a blank here, the alternatives were much further afield – Cornwall in one direction and Somerset in the other.

The first firm on Esme's list had only been in operation for five years so she moved on to the second outfit, Wordman & Son, which looked more promising. Their entrance was on the first floor of a narrow building, reached via a flight of stone steps between black railings.

Esme climbed the stairs and pushed open the inner glass door. She gave the woman behind reception a broad smile, introduced herself and explained her problem.

The receptionist, a middle-aged woman with a voluminous head of hair in various shades of russet, glanced at Esme's business card and looked at her doubtfully over the top of a pair of over-sized glasses.

'I'm not sure that would be strictly ethical,' she said.

'No, I realise it's not exactly an everyday situation, said Esme. 'But my client has been unable to establish her aunt's death. If it was your company who investigated, you may at least be able to confirm that the matter was resolved satisfactorily. That's all she's asking to know. There are no confidences to be broken, I wouldn't have thought?' The woman continued to peer at Esme, clearly unconvinced. 'She's very anxious for her mother to get closure, you see,' added Esme. 'And we've had such problems in the past trying to resolve this.'

The woman got up off her seat. 'Wait here a moment.' She disappeared into a room behind her, separated by a glass divide. Esme could see her talking to a man in shirt sleeves at a computer terminal. The receptionist was gesturing towards Esme and the man kept nodding and glancing over the top of his screen.

'It'll be a bloody miracle if you get anything out of old Wormface. He's a tight-arsed bugger.' Esme looked across the room at a young skinny man in black trousers and an ill-fitting white shirt. 'And he's not in the best of moods, neither. We've just lost a race.'

'A race?'

'Yeah. Been working on it solid for two days since the list came out. Big outfit in Bristol beat us to it. So he's well pissed.'

'Oh, I see,' said Esme, finally working out what he was talking about. 'You were hoping to sign up a potential claimant and someone got there first.'

'In one. And it was a biggie. Would have earned us a tidy sum.' He cocked his head towards the inner office. 'So don't hold your breath.'

'It was a bit of a long shot,' admitted Esme. 'It was over fifteen years ago as well, so...' She smiled. 'Before your time, anyway.'

The door to the inner sanctum opened and the receptionist returned to her post. 'I'm sorry, Mrs Quentin,' she said, handing back Esme's card. 'We do recall the case, but it's exactly as I explained. Mr Wordman is of the opinion that we'd been treading dangerous ground, ethically speaking. And in any case, there's a matter of resources. We're very busy as is it...'

'I could have a look for her, Mrs D?'

Esme and the receptionist both looked round.

'Be a change to see you getting on with the work you're meant to be doing, Perry,' said Mrs D, through tight lips. 'And you can start by going and seeing Karen. She's got some post for you.'

Perry pulled a face and sloped off.

Mrs D turned back to Esme and switched on a smile. 'Sorry we can't be of more help, Mrs Quentin.' Esme nodded, thanked her for her time and retreated down the stairs. Back out in the street, she sighed. So much for that idea. Now what?

She headed left and began walking back towards the city centre. As she turned into cathedral close, she heard someone come up beside her. She looked round to see Perry's grinning face, his arms full of padded bags.

'Told yer,' he said.

'You did indeed.'

He sniffed. 'You said this was twenty years ago?'

'Something like that.'

'I got an idea how I could help.'

'Hey, look. I know you said you could take a look but I wouldn't want you to get in to any trouble. Best you forget all about it. I'll think of something else.'

'Nah, that's not what I meant. Your case would have been in old Crombie's time. He's retired now but he's all right, is old Crombie. Betcha he'd be happy to help. He's sure to remember something odd like that.' He shifted the bundle higher up his body and bent closer to Esme, conspiratorially. 'And I know where he lives.'

12

Frank Crombie lived in Topsham, a few miles downriver from Exeter. Esme parked her car beside the Quay Antique centre, a brick box with a surfeit of windows and a flat roof, and set off on foot in search of the retired probate agent.

She wound her way between the picnic tables of the quayside pub and out on to Ferry Road, the narrow street running between the water's edge on her left and a terrace of smartly converted former wharf buildings. As the road opened out and the buildings gave way to a high pale terracotta stone wall, she came to a boat yard, its iron gates thrown wide open. She followed her instructions on to a pontoon and peered out the end, calling out Frank's name when she could see no one around.

A head, wearing a tatty baseball cap, popped up from behind the boat. 'Who wants him?'

'Me,' Esme shouted, looking around for a way down into the basin.

'Stay there,' called Crombie. 'I'll come up.' He leant over the side of the boat and dumped a bucket and brush into the bottom before trudging across the beach towards her.

'Sorry to disturb you,' said Esme, as he emerged on to the pontoon. 'Your wife said I'd find you here.' She held out her hand and introduced herself.

'One of your former work colleagues suggested I have a word with you. Perry.'

'He's still there, then. I wonder he hasn't moved on by now.'

'Yes, I did get the impression he wasn't in awe of your former boss.'

'No. They didn't exactly see eye to eye. How I can help you, Mrs Quentin? If I can, that is. There are confidentialities in this game as I'm sure you're aware.'

'Yes, I appreciate that. I'm hoping what you can tell me is already in the public domain, once I know where to look.'

He rubbed a stubbly chin and peered at her. 'Well, you've certainly tickled my interest. OK. Fire away.'

'I'm doing some family research for a client. I've stumbled on a problem which I believe stumped you as well about twenty years ago.'

His eyebrows disappeared under the rim of his cap. 'Now you really have got my attention. What are we talking about?'

'You were looking for a beneficiary called Vivienne Lancaster and tracked down her sister, Beatrice Wood, over in North Devon. Does that ring any bells?'

'I spent many a happy hour trawling the lanes of North Devon in my time, Mrs Quentin. I'm not sure there's any particular case which has stuck in my mind.'

'Mrs Wood', continued Esme, 'believed her sister had died during the war but had nothing official to confirm her death. Obviously with no death certificate, you couldn't pursue any claim and you went away.'

'I do have a vague recollection. Are you saying she's now in a position to pursue her claim?'

Esme shook her head. 'No, it's not that. It's just that the issue of no proof of death has come up again. She wondered if you'd managed to establish anything at the time of your investigations which could help her now.'

'You're asking if we'd found the lady in question?'

'Well, obviously, if you had –'

'If we had, that would be a matter for the beneficiary to decide if she wanted to make contact with her sister. Not a decision for me or the firm.'

'So you do recall the case?'

Crombie tugged his earlobe. 'Oddly enough, I do, as it happens. Lovely stretch of coastline, I remember. It was a wild day when I went to see Mrs – what did you say her name was?'

'Mrs Wood.'

'That's right. Nearly blown off my feet, I was. They get some savage weather over there, that's for sure.'

'So, what was the outcome?'

'Well, I'm sorry to disappoint you but we never did track her down. It was all pretty inconclusive. I was sent off to another case so I've no idea where they went with it in the end. I guess it was just dropped.'

'I don't suppose you remember the benefactor's name?' she asked, wincing at the audacity of the question. She only had his memory to rely on without access to the company's files.

He laughed. 'Sorry, Mrs Quentin. That really is asking a bit too much.' He tapped the side of his head. 'I filed everything away and locked the cabinet the day I retired.'

Esme thanked him and shook his hand.

She walked back to the car park with a growing sense of frustration. Now what? With no record of Vivienne at the MOD and nothing in the National Archives she was running out of options.

Her eyes strayed across the water and tracked a flock of avocet rising from the reed beds on the opposite side of the estuary. It seemed she had hit the proverbial brick wall.

13

As the cottage came into view, Esme could see Ruth heading for the front door. She drove into the parking bay and got out of the car.

'That was good timing,' called Esme, walking round to the back of her car to open the boot. 'I was going to come and see you later. Tell you how I got on yesterday.' She took out two bags of shopping, slammed the boot closed and carried the bags towards the back door, stopping abruptly when she saw Ruth's fringe plastered against her face. 'What are you doing?' Esme said, seeing that Ruth's coat was wet through. She glanced round, realising she'd seen no sign of a vehicle. 'Did you walk here?'

'Have you seen Mum?' Ruth said, a deep frown of worry on her face.

'No. But I've been out.' She dumped the bags on the doorstep and regarded Ruth. 'Is everything OK?'

'I can't find her.'

'Come inside out of the wet and tell me what's going on.' She pulled her key out of her pocket and unlocked the door.

Ruth followed her inside. 'She hasn't been home all morning.'

Esme put the bags on the table and grabbed a towel from off the rail of the Rayburn. 'Get yourself dried off,' she said, handing the towel to Ruth. 'You're soaked through.' She took off her coat and hung it on a hook at the bottom of the stairs. 'Perhaps she's just gone for a walk. She'll head home smartish now the rain's started.' Ruth did have a habit of fretting over nothing. She started to unload her shopping bags on to the table.

'That's what I thought at first,' Ruth said, rubbing her hair with the towel. 'Then I wondered if she'd driven over to see you.'

'Me?' Esme stopped unpacking. 'What's this about, Ruth? Has something happened?'

Ruth dropped down on to a kitchen chair, abandoning the towel on the table. 'She caught me red-handed.'

'Doing what, for goodness sake?' Esme said, with half a laugh.

'Looking through her photograph album. You know. The one I told you about.'

'You found it, then?'

Ruth nodded. 'In the loft where Pete thought. Anyway, she wasn't happy. We had words. She accused me of prying.' She looked up at Esme. 'Much the same tone as her outburst when you and Maddy came for dinner.'

'Oh, I see.' Esme sighed. 'Well then, she's probably gone off for some peace and quiet to think things over. I wouldn't worry. She's probably already back there now. Either that or she's gone to a friend's to tell her how horrible her daughter is.'

Esme's light-hearted comment earned a disapproving look from Ruth, her mouth turned down.

Ruth stood up. 'Look, I should get back. I'm supposed to be seeing Maddy about the holiday cottage photos for next season's brochure.'

'Let me run you home. Pete'll start worrying about you next.'

'I left him phoning around to see if anyone had seen her.'

'Do you want to give him a call and let him know where you are? She might be home already and you're worrying unnecessarily.'

Ruth nodded. 'OK. Thanks.'

But as she handed Ruth the handset, it rang. Esme put

it to her ear. 'Hello? Ah, Pete. Yes, she's here now. She's just told me.' She winked at Ruth. 'So has she turned... She what? Where?'

Ruth's eyes widened. 'What's happened?'

'Yes. Of course. OK. Will do.' Esme disconnected.

'What did he say?' said Ruth, standing up. 'Where is she?'

'One of the bar staff from the Quay Hotel saw her on his way into work.'

'Where?'

'That's the weirdest thing. She was walking along the main road.'

'What?'

Esme grabbed her car keys and her coat off the hook. 'Pete's gone off to look for her. Come on. We need to find her. The silly woman's not wearing an outside coat.'

14

As Esme drove into the yard at Ravens Farm she saw Maddy's campervan. Maddy was standing next to the farm Land Rover, talking to Pete through the driver's window. When she saw Esme's car she ran across to speak to them.

'I'm so sorry, Maddy,' Ruth said, getting out of the car.

'Don't be silly. We can do this any time. Look, why don't you go with Pete. I'll stay and man the phone in case Bea comes back here.'

'Good idea,' Esme said. She stretched over the passenger seat and looked up at Ruth. 'And don't worry. We'll find her.'

'Pete's going to search in the Bideford direction,' Maddy said. 'That's the direction she was headed. He thought perhaps you could head inland and try the side lanes, just in case she's turned off the main road.'

Esme nodded. 'OK. Fine. Between us, it should be fairly easy to locate her. She can't have got far on foot.'

She swung her car around and sped out of the yard, a quick glance in her rear-view mirror confirming that Ruth was climbing into the Land Rover and Maddy was heading indoors to begin her vigil by the telephone.

Esme took the first right-hand turn, slowing down to ask a couple wearing backpacks if they'd seen an elderly woman walking without a coat along their way but they shook their heads. She threw the Peugeot into gear and continued down the lane which ran round a long series of bends before coming to a fork. Esme stopped to read the familiar Devon finger-post place sign, wondering which route to take. As she considered, something about the name on the sign pointing down the narrower of the two routes resonated in her head. Four Lanes. Where had she heard the name recently? Then she remembered. Ruth had mentioned it in connection with the farm where Bea had grown up as an evacuee. *Over Four Lanes way* she'd said. Had Bea gone there?

But given the distress Bea's wartime past seemed to cause her, the farm on which she'd lived seemed an unlikely bolt-hole. Besides, hadn't she said the family no longer lived there?

On the other hand, perhaps a visit might serve as a catalyst to deal with whatever problem Bea had. Seeing Ruth with the photograph album and the difficult conversation of the other evening may have been enough to shake Bea into addressing whatever issues she needed to address.

Esme decided that as she was so close, she may as well take a look. It could do no harm and it was worth crossing off the list. She threw a left and drove cautiously down the lane, the windscreen wipers whining rhythmically as she crept along. After about half a mile, the lane widered at the entrance to a farm and she slowed to a halt. Was this where Bea had lived? A crooked wooden plaque attached to a wall on the corner was too faded to read, even if Esme had been able to recall the farm's name.

She pulled off the highway and got out her phone. She should let Ruth know what she'd got in mind and find out the name of the farm at the same time. And Bea may have returned by now. But the screen showed there was no mobile signal. So much for that idea.

She slipped the phone back into her pocket and got out of the car, flicking the hood of her jacket over her head against the rain. She slammed the car door and looked around.

A woman was coming down the lane, a large red setter straining the lead ahead of her. Esme walked towards her, saying hello and making the obligatory comment about the weather. The dog pushed his nose towards her and wagged its tail.

'D'you know the name of this farm?' said Esme, fondling the dog's ears and nodding towards the sign. 'I can't make out the sign.'

'Crossways Farm,' the woman said, lifting her chin and peering out from an overlarge hood. 'Is it Jimmy Beer you're after?'

'Beer?' said Esme. 'I thought they sold up after the war?'

'Goodness, no. Been here since forever.' She glanced over to the farm. Esme followed her gaze to the dilapidated buildings in the distance and the overgrown grass which edged the entrance. 'Used to be a lovely place, so I'm told, though I've only ever known it run down and tatty. Makes you wonder how he makes a living.'

'Is there only him, then?'

'Apparently. Not that I've ever clapped eyes on him. Very much the "keeps himself to himself" sort of neighbour. Word has it he doesn't like strangers.'

'Right. I'll bear that in mind.' She began to pull away. 'Oh, you haven't seen an elderly lady walking around here without a coat, by any chance, have you?'

'No, sorry. I've only just come out.' The dog gave a tug and yanked the woman's arm. 'Cut it out, Bramble, for goodness sake.' She looked up at Esme and smiled. 'Sorry I'd better go or he'll have my arm out of its socket.'

Esme laughed. 'Yes, he's a bit keen, isn't he?'

As the woman was yanked away, she looked back over her shoulder. 'Good luck!' she called.

'Thanks,' said Esme. Did she mean in her search for Bea?

She shrugged and turned back towards the farm, troubled as to why Bea had lied about the farm being sold.

*

The front entrance to the farmhouse didn't look as though it had been used for decades. The path was barely visible but there was a narrow route through and as Esme could see a letterbox in the door, she assumed the post must arrive that way so it was worth trying there first.

Thorns of dying brambles, arching across the path, caught on her sleeves as she pushed through to rap the door-knocker. It was caked with rust and heavy to lift but she managed to make a loud enough hammering to echo within the house.

But no one responded, as she'd half expected. Most farmers used the house's rear entrance, anyway. She was sure to have more luck around the back.

She hurried back down the path and up the muddy track into the yard. Her approach disturbed a dog somewhere, as the sound of furious barking reverberated around the buildings. It didn't sound too friendly and she hoped it was tethered somewhere or, at least, shut in one of the many barns.

A rusting tractor sat against the corrugated wall of a large building to her left. The undergrowth surrounding it suggested it hadn't been used in a very long time.

She understood now about the woman's questioning how Jimmy made a living. Nothing suggested there was any farming activity. There were no signs that he kept any livestock, other than the dog she could hear barking and, she noticed, as a scrawny cat sprinted across her line of vision, the odd feral tenant. Perhaps he lived on the rental of his land to surrounding farmers. But it couldn't amount to much. And the farmyard itself looked abandoned. Perhaps it was, and was the reason why the woman with the dog had never seen Jimmy Beer. So Bea could have been partly telling the truth. The farm might still be in the family's ownership but no one lived there anymore.

She pressed on, conscious of the rustle of her sleeve against the side of her waterproof jacket as she stepped into the cauldron of the courtyard, surrounded by buildings of a variety of materials, from stone, to block, to corrugated iron sheeting. The place could do with a bucket load of TLC and several gallons of paint.

The dog, which she was now reassured wasn't roaming free, had begun to howl. The eeriness of the sound made her wary and the dog walker's cheery 'good luck' took on a new and ominous meaning the further she advanced.

She stopped walking. This was futile. If Bea was here, it was unlikely she'd be hiding in one of these barns. She turned and retraced her steps, passing a half-opened wooden door at the end of the row. Unable to resist, she peered around the open door, the sweet smell of hay filling her nostrils. As she blinked into the gloom she saw the glint of an axe blade buried in a large block of wood.

She backed out into the yard, feeling a little foolish. It was ridiculous to think Bea would have come here. She'd no idea if Bea had even set foot on the farm since she'd returned home after the war. She was probably sitting down in Ruth's kitchen at this very moment, wrapped in a warm towel and sipping hot tea, apologising for upsetting everyone. Ruth would be looking up at the clock and asking where Esme was. Well, she'd better get back or they'd be sending a search party out for her, next.

She spun round to leave and stopped with a jolt. Her exit was blocked by an old man standing on the opposite side of the yard in an oily pair of overalls. And he had a shotgun trained directly at her.

15

Esme didn't move. This had to be Jimmy Beer. She felt a moment of irritation at the lady with the dog. She might have clarified what not liking strangers actually meant.

Esme held up a hand. 'Sorry. I didn't mean to trespass. I was looking for someone. I thought they might have come here.' The man took two steps towards her, peering at her through a tendril of greasy white hair.

'Look, I'll get out of your way, OK? I hadn't meant to upset anyone.' She risked a side-step but the man tracked her with the gun. 'Oh, this is ridiculous,' she said, fear making her angry. 'You can't just wave a gun at someone because they lost their way!'

'What you doing 'ere?'

Esme took a deep breath. At least he spoke. There was a chance for dialogue, perhaps.

'I told you. I'm looking for a friend. I thought she might be here.' Should she mention Bea, explain her connection with the farm?

'How do I know you b'aint be here spying on me?'

Oh, great. Paranoia. That's all she needed.

'Look, if you'll just let me get on my way –'

A door banged in the distance. 'Oh for pity's sake, Jimmy. Put the gun down!' Bea said, emerging from the farmhouse.

'Bea! Thank goodness!' She glared at Jimmy, willing him to respond to Bea's instruction. After a moment longer holding her gaze, he lowered the gun, still scowling.

Esme let out a long sigh, and called out over his shoulder. 'Everyone's out looking for you, Bea,' she said. 'Are you OK?'

Bea tossed her head. 'Of course I am. Can't a person call in on an old friend without sparking a major man hunt?'

Esme glanced back at Jimmy who looked as though he was itching for a word from Bea to resume his stance with the gun.

'It's all right, Jimmy. Esme's a friend. We'll talk about it later, all right?'

Jimmy glared at Bea for a moment as though she'd spoiled his fun before dropping the weapon down by his side and trudging away across the yard.

'You need to let Ruth know you're safe,' said Esme. 'She's really worried about you.'

Bea pressed her lips together. 'Quite unnecessarily. I've not lost my marbles yet.'

'You had a falling out, I understand.' Bea narrowed her eyes and Esme held up her hand. 'I'm not taking sides. But you really should speak to her.'

Bea sighed. 'Oh, all right. If you insist.' She jerked her head back towards the farmhouse. 'You'd better come inside. I'll use Jimmy's phone.'

Esme followed Bea into the dim interior of the farmhouse kitchen, a noticeable contrast to the warm, friendly embrace of Ravens Farm. Unstable piles of discarded post in the form of numerous brown envelopes adorned a large grubby dresser against one wall. More paper junk filled the window sills, reducing whatever remaining light might have pierced the grimy panes which looked out on to the yard. Dirty plates and half empty mugs of brown liquid covered the table in the centre of the room.

'Have a seat,' Bea said, reaching for the phone hanging on the wall next to the back door. 'I won't be a minute.'

Esme was about to decline until she realised that coming face to face with the wrong end of a shotgun had left her a little shaky. She pulled out a chair, its seat piled high with a heap of *Farmers Weekly* magazines. She dumped them on the floor, sat down and looked around.

Stacked saucepans with blackened bottoms filled the sink. The draining board was hidden under a collection of what Esme assumed to be engine parts, spread out on sheets of newspaper. Given the state of the rest of the room, she was amused that Jimmy had given such consideration to protecting the draining board, until she realised it was indicative of the esteem in which he held the engine parts, rather than any concern for damage they may have caused the kitchen surface.

'Hello?' Bea said into the phone. 'Oh, Maddy, hello… yes, I'm fine, thank you…yes, please, if she's there.' There was a pause while the phone was passed to Ruth. She and Pete had obviously returned to the farm.

Esme watched Bea's face flush and imagined what Ruth was saying to her wayward mother. After a few moments, Bea looked over to Esme. 'No, it's all right, she's here with me now.' Esme held up her car keys and jangled them in the air. 'She'll give me a lift home. Yes. Yes, I know. See you in a little while, then.' She dropped the receiver back on its hook with a sigh.

'Well, that told *me*!' she said.

'She was beside herself, Bea. In the rain, no coat.'

'I mightn't have been wearing a waterproof but I was hardly in my nightdress.'

'Yeah, well, that's as may be but it was still a worry.' She stood up. 'Come on. Let's get you home.'

*

As they drove away from Crossways Farm, Bea said little, her head turned away, looking out of the side window.

'Does Jimmy always greet his visitors so forcefully?' said Esme, as they reached the T-junction.

'I'm sorry, Esme,' said Bea, looking round. 'I didn't apologise for his behaviour, did I?'

'It's hardly your fault, is it?' She turned on to the A39

'I should have known you'd think of going to the farm,'

said Bea after a while, 'given your interest in my life as an evacuee.'

'Is that why you made out that the Beers had sold up after the war?'

'It was a whole lot easier than telling you what reception you'd get if you turned up unannounced. You'd only want an explanation and –'

'And there'd be questions.'

Bea let out an irritated huff. 'Why does everyone need to ask questions? Can't a person's life be private?'

'Ruth thinks you'd be better off sharing your past, you know that don't you?'

'So she tells me. An idea put into her head by my trendy university granddaughter, as I understand.'

'You don't agree.'

Bea rubbed her hand across her eyes. 'I don't know what to think, if I'm honest. I mean, look at Jimmy –'

'Yes, what *is* his problem? Is it about isolation? How come he's so mistrustful of everyone? At least, that's what I assume is at the heart of it?'

Bea stared, unfocused, out of the windscreen. 'He's been like it for years, Esme. He worshipped Vivienne, that's the problem. That's how it started.'

'How what started?'

'His crush, I suppose you'd call it.' She paused, allowing Esme to concentrate on overtaking a tractor and trailer. 'Of course, Vivienne was older than him,' Bea continued, when Esme had completed the manoeuvre. 'She was the sophisticated young woman and Jimmy was an impressionable young lad. She came to the farm with me at the beginning, you see. She was going to be a land girl but before long she announced she wanted to do more, to be a nurse and go and tend to the wounded soldiers.'

'And Jimmy didn't want her to go?'

'No, nothing like that. I think he imagined when she came

back he'd be old enough for her to see him as a man, rather than a boy.' Bea looked at Esme. 'Don't misunderstand me. Vivienne wasn't unkind to him. She didn't mock him for being a flustering young man in the first flush of love. But in being kind she probably gave him hope that she felt something for him that was more than a sister-brother relationship.'

'So what happened? Did she finally have to tell him and he took it badly?'

'She didn't get the chance. When she was reported missing Jimmy wouldn't accept it. He was convinced that things were being covered up. It became an obsession with him. What is it they say? Denying it?'

'Being in denial.'

'Yes, that's it. Of course I sympathised for a while, even when I came back, years later, long after the war had finished. He was still consumed with grief and anger about her loss. I tried to encourage him to accept it as so many other people had to. *She was my sister, too, you know*, I used to say to him. But it was hopeless. Over the years he became – well, entrenched, I suppose you'd say. Eventually I had to back away.'

Esme slowed the car and turned off the main road down the lane towards Ravens Farm. 'Do you think he has any good reason to question Vivienne's death?' she said.

'No of course not,' said Bea. 'The whole thing is completely in his head. I just feel sorry for him, all lonely up there in the farm. It's not helping his state of mind, that's for sure.'

They pulled into the farmyard and Esme stopped the car.

'You'd better go and get warmed up.'

'I'm fine, Esme, don't you worry,' said Bea, opening the door and climbing out. 'A little rain never hurt no one.'

Esme sat in the car and watched Bea head over to the farmhouse, wondering whether Jimmy knew more than Bea thought he did. But dare she go back and ask him? He might be more trigger-happy the next time, especially given his comment about her spying on him.

She sighed and got out, slammed the car door shut behind her. As she crossed the yard, it occurred to her that Bea had not explained what had prompted her to go over to the farm, after all these years.

16

Esme walked into the kitchen to find Maddy leaning against the rail of the Rayburn, arms folded, deep in thought. There was no sign of Ruth and Bea.

'Where is everyone?' Esme asked.

Maddy jerked her head towards the ceiling. Bea and Ruth's raised voices filtered down from upstairs. No doubt Ruth was making it quite clear the anxiety Bea had caused her.

'Fell out over an old photo album, so Ruth tells me,' Maddy said, turning to address the boiling kettle behind her.

'So I gather. One with all her wartime pictures in.'

Maddy grabbed a teapot, warmed it and dropped in a couple of teabags from the jar on the shelf. 'Why is Bea so adamant about not going there, d'you suppose?'

Esme shrugged. 'Ruth's still thinks it's because the loss of her sister is still a painful subject.'

'And you don't buy that?'

'Not exactly. I just think there's more to it.'

'Like what?'

Esme shook her head. 'Don't know. Not yet, anyway.'

Maddy pulled her phone out of her back pocket and looked at the screen. 'I'm going to have to get going. I'm meeting a client.' She put the phone back in her pocket and headed for the back door. 'Tea's in the pot. Tell Ruth I'll be in touch about rescheduling, will you?'

'Sure,' Esme said, nodding. She remembered Ruth had mentioned a photo shoot for the new season's holiday rental brochure.

As Maddy disappeared through the door, Esme heard the sound of running water from above and Ruth came into the kitchen. She dropped down at the table with a sigh of exasperation.

'She just doesn't get it,' said Ruth, throwing her hands out.

'I'm sure she does,' said Esme. 'Just not admitting to it. Imagine how you'd feel if you thought your daughter implied you weren't capable of going for a walk on your own.'

'That's not what this is about, Esme, as you well know.'

'I'm just saying. She's an independent lady. She's probably just a bit embarrassed at your reaction at what she sees as just getting caught out by the weather.'

'Maybe. Well, at least she's agreed to a hot bath and a change of clothes. Oh, and of course, that was wrong too. I grabbed the first thing I saw, didn't I? She's not about to meet the Queen, for goodness sake. Just not catch pneumonia.'

Esme walked over to where Maddy had left the tea brewing beside the Rayburn. 'Let me pour you some tea,' she said. 'Maddy set it up before she left. She'll be in touch about the brochure, she said, by the way.' Ruth gave a vague nod, her focus aimed at somewhere in the middle-distance as Esme took a mug, sloshed in some milk and filled it from the teapot.

'There you go,' she said, sliding the mug towards Ruth. Esme sat down on the opposite side of the table.

'She's never done anything like this before,' Ruth said. 'Do you think it's the onset of dementia?'

'No, definitely not.'

'Then what in God's name was she doing?' Ruth flashed Esme a look. 'And don't say she just got caught out in the rain. She'd have turned round and come back home.'

'Have you asked her why?'

Ruth frowned. 'Of course I have.'

'And?'

'She won't say. Or can't. That's what made me think that

78

perhaps she genuinely couldn't. That she wasn't responsible for her actions.'

'Well, perhaps she's just feeling uncomfortable at the reception I got at the farm.'

Ruth sat up straight. 'Oh, goodness, Esme. I completely forgot. How are you? I'm so sorry, I was so worried about Mum. You must be feeling terrible.'

'Don't be silly, Ruth. I'm fine.'

Ruth looked down at her mug and stood up again. 'I ought to take Mum up a cup.'

'You sit down and drink your own first. I'll pour it.'

Ruth sat down and pulled the tea towards her, wrapping her hands around the mug. 'All because of a few old photos. What's the matter with her, Esme?'

'I don't know. Was there something particular in amongst them that set her off?'

'Not that I was aware of.' She nodded towards the dresser. 'The album's over there. Take a look yourself. They all seemed pretty ordinary to me. It was the fact that I was prying that annoyed her. So ridiculous.' She drained her mug and took it over to the sink. 'Thanks for the tea. You not having any?'

'No, save the one in the pot for Pete,' Esme said, hearing noises in the boot room. 'Sounds like he's back.'

'I'd better take this to Mum,' Ruth said, picking up the mug Esme had poured and disappearing out of the kitchen.

The back door opened and Pete came in, pulling off his damp beanie cap and giving it a shake before dropping it on to the rack above the Rayburn. 'How's the runaway?' he said, heading for the sink.

'Rebellious, from all accounts,' Esme said, with a grin.

Pete laughed and turned on the tap. 'And what about you?' he said, squirting washing-up liquid over his hands and rubbing them together under the flow of water. 'I hear Jimmy wasn't the most welcoming of hosts.'

'You could say that. There's tea in the pot, by the way.'

'Handsome. Must make a phone call first, though.' He gave his hands a shake and reached for the towel. 'Jimmy's always been a bit off his head. Don't take it personally.'

'I won't. Being out there on his own must be like living in a parallel universe. Hardly surprising he feels threatened when someone turns up unannounced.'

Pete nodded. 'Been like that since the old lady died,' he said, heading for the hall door.

'So Bea said. I'm not surprised she doesn't go over there anymore.'

'What gave you that idea?' Pete said, his hand on the door knob. 'Bea goes over regular. Has done for years. Might've cottoned on that's where she'd gone if that barmaid hadn't said she'd been walking the opposite way.'

Pete disappeared into the hall, leaving Esme to ponder the anomaly of Bea's account. Had she misunderstood? That was the second time she'd wanted to believe she had nothing to do with the farm – first that the Beers had sold up when they hadn't and now that she didn't see Jimmy regularly.

Esme's gaze fell on the photograph album that Ruth had been looking at when Bea accused her of prying. It had a dark green cover and was bound with a matching coloured cord. She fetched it from the dresser to the table and opened it up. Could there be any clues in there which explained Bea's behaviour?

She wondered why Bea hadn't kept it with her when she moved to the bungalow. Ruth said it had been in the loft. Perhaps Bea had forgotten it was up there. If she didn't already know Bea's reaction, she might have suggested that Ruth show it to her and look at it together. But clearly that wasn't going to help establish what Bea's problem was. It had only made it worse.

Esme opened the first page. On it was a picture of a small girl in wellies. Was this Bea at Crossways Farm? A border collie stood beside her, dwarfing her. A taller boy stood behind. Jimmy Beer?

The hall door opened and Ruth returned. 'Guess we better get that out of sight before Mum comes down,' she said.

'Tell me who's who, first,' Esme said. 'I assume this is Bea on the farm? And the boy's Jimmy Beer?'

'Yes,' said Ruth. 'And that's Jessie, the sheepdog.' She shook her head sadly. 'I really don't get this, Esme. I've looked at these photographs countless times with Mum in the past. So why is she getting in such a state about them now?' Ruth pointed to a photo of a group of children. 'I think these must be other local evacuees but I don't remember their names.'

Esme sighed. 'Such a shame we can't get Bea involved. She probably doesn't appreciate how valuable her knowledge is. If we don't win her round, everything she remembers about these photographs, and about the people in them, will be lost forever.'

Esme flicked through the rest of the album. Most photographs were scenes of Bea around the farm, carrying a bucket across the yard, sitting on a bale of hay wearing a large sun hat, or kneeling in a field hugging Jessie the dog. Jessie featured regularly.

'Did she keep in touch with any of the other children at all?'

'Not that I know of.'

Ruth stood up. 'Well, I'd better hide this away somewhere before we set off another crisis.' She picked up the album and turned away. A slip of paper fell out and fluttered to the floor.

'Hang on,' said Esme, sliding back her chair and reaching down. 'You've dropped something.' She picked it up.

'What is it?'

Esme opened it up and looked at it. 'Looks like the end of a letter. Probably stuck behind one of the photographs.' She laid it on the table and they both pored over it. 'Please don't hesitate to contact me,' Ruth read out loud. 'Once again, please accept my condolences.'

'It must be the letter sent to your grandparents to tell them about Vivienne,' Esme said. 'But there's only half of it here.' She turned over the meagre scrap of paper but there was nothing written on the other side.

Ruth dropped down at the table. 'Well that's that, then. Mum was right. She *did* know what happened to Vivienne.' She turned to Esme, holding up the scrap of paper in her hand. 'So why not just come right out and show me this?'

But Esme couldn't offer an answer. She was trying to make sense of what she'd seen at the bottom of the letter. The signatory was Lieutenant Colonel Gerald Gallimore.

17

Esme drove back to the cottage and brought the car to a halt. She turned off the ignition but remained sitting while she continued musing of seeing Gallimore's name on the letter. Was Bea aware that her sister's commanding officer had been shot dead on his own doorstep? Was it even relevant?

She was thankful that Ruth had been so busy hunting for a hiding place for the photo album she'd been unaware of any outward sign of the turmoil going on in Esme's head, allowing Esme to be saved from having to enlighten her. And until she'd properly appraised the implications, Esme had no intention of telling Ruth that Gallimore had been the victim of an unsolved murder. Somehow she didn't think the information would do anything to improve Ruth's anxieties about the current situation with Bea.

She scrambled out of the car and hurried inside to boot up her laptop and remind her of the basic facts of Gallimore's death. But the effort bore little fruit. The online newspaper report revealed no more than she knew already – no witnesses came forward and no one had heard the shot which killed him. Neither could she find any mention of a suspect or any subsequent arrest, much less a conviction.

She decided eventually that it was highly unlikely that the circumstances of Gallimore's death had any connection with Vivienne Lancaster and her wartime experiences. Vivienne died before the end of the war. Gallimore had been killed in 1981. The gap was surely too great to link the two events.

She wandered over to the coffee table and picked up

Vivienne's photograph. She wondered when it was taken and who'd taken it. Vivienne looked fresh-faced and eager. Perhaps it had been taken as a celebration on completion of her training.

It reminded Esme of the photograph her father had taken of her and Elizabeth in turn as they'd donned their smart new uniforms to start secondary school.

Elizabeth, being older, had been the first to undergo the process. She'd stood holding the handlebars of their old three-wheeled scooter, her brand-new satchel (a present from their grandparents) proudly draped across her blazer. By the time it was Esme's turn some five years later, the scooter had rusted away and been replaced by a much larger two-wheeled model. Esme had never liked her own photograph. Her satchel strap had been too long and knocked against her legs as she'd struggled to balance the scooter convincingly, while maintaining a confident smile. In the final photograph the scooter looked overlarge next to her and she'd looked harried. No one else thought so, though, and she'd been chided for making a fuss.

As she gazed at Vivienne, her mind drifted to Max. Should she talk to him? He may know, or have since learned, something about Gallimore which could be useful in finding out more about Vivienne. She'd be a fool not to speak to him, just because of being embarrassed at misleading him about Tim's notebooks. Besides, even if Max knew nothing relevant to Vivienne's case, information on Vivienne might be useful to Max.

She dug around in the bottom of her bag to find the card Max had given her. She remembered dropping it in there as she'd left the pub. She found it screwed up at the bottom, a clear indication of her determination not to get drawn in.

She picked up the phone handset, her thumb hovering over the keypad. Did she really want to involve Max?

But how else was she going to help Ruth get to the bottom of what was bothering Bea? Gallimore was Vivienne's commanding officer, after all. It didn't make sense to ignore him as a potential source.

She took a deep breath and dialled his number. As it rang, she imagined the conversation with Ruth, explaining who Gallimore was and the nature of Gallimore's death. She could hear Ruth's shocked and horrified voice, her face pale and anxious. 'Murdered? But what's that got to do with Vivienne?'

Esme cut the call and dropped the phone on to the table. Exactly. Nothing. She didn't need to alert Max. It would get too complicated. She had to find another way to find the information they needed.

She threw Max's card into the bin. Whatever Max may or may not know about Gerald Gallimore was probably irrelevant anyway.

The phone rang, making her jump. 'Hello?' she said, her mind still on Ruth and Bea.

'You rang me,' said a familiar voice. 'Changed your mind, then?'

Esme swallowed. 'Max. Hi. I er –' Gallimore's name raced around in her head, chased closely by Vivienne's. How stupid she'd been. Her number would have shown up on his phone as a missed call.

'How did the move go?' Max asked.

'Good. Thanks.'

'So? What did you call me about? Found those notes of Tim's, did you?'

Esme pounced on his words. 'Yes, that's right. At least that's what I was phoning to tell you. With all the packing and sorting – you know how it is – I came across those notebooks we talked about. But, sorry to disappoint you, Max. There was nothing. Just a one liner. So he couldn't have found out any more. Dead-end, I'm afraid. Sorry I couldn't help, Max.'

'You can, actually. Help, that is. I could use a genealogist. How about we meet up?'

'Meet up?' Esme laughed. 'I'm in Devon now, Max. Remember?'

'Of course I remember. That's why your timing's perfect.

I'm coming down to the South West tomorrow.'

'You're coming down here?'

'It's not as difficult as you think, Ez. They've built the M5, you know.'

She sighed. 'Very funny.'

'I'll buy you lunch? Can't say fairer than that, can I?'

'Well, I don't know…' She scouted around helplessly for an excuse to put him off. Having made a conscious decision not to get drawn in, she was determined not to cave in.

'I thought you'd be intrigued to hear what I've unearthed about Gerald Gallimore.'

She tried to keep her voice neutral. 'Oh yes?'

'Turns out Gallimore was in the Special Operations Executive during the war.'

Esme felt her stomach flip. 'He was SOE?'

'Could be fertile ground to find a potential murderer, don't you think?'

18

Esme wound down the lane, marked as a no-through road, which seemed to be heading to the end of the earth. As she began to wonder whether she'd taken a wrong turn, the lane opened out to reveal a large grassy area and a cluster of stone buildings with slate roofs. Confident she'd found the right place, she pulled on to the grass and parked alongside the only other vehicle there, Max's silver-grey Nissan Qashqai.

It was inevitable that she'd agree to meet Max once he'd dropped in the tantalising mention of Gallimore's association with SOE agents. It seemed likely now that Vivienne, in her FANY uniform, had not been the nurse the family had understood but had been one of Churchill's "angels."

But Esme wanted to understand much more as to where Gallimore fitted into Vivienne's story before telling Ruth. She wasn't yet clear how much she'd need to disclose about Gallimore and the circumstances of his death. Hopefully, that side of the story would prove to be irrelevant. After all, as she'd already considered, Gallimore's death was so long after Vivienne's that any connection must be unrelated. She pushed aside the gnawing question that Vivienne's death had not yet been proven. But as she'd said to Maddy, wartime and confusion were common bed fellows. Facts did not always emerge as clearly as they should. It didn't mean they didn't happen.

Despite her interest in what Max had to tell her about Gallimore she'd yet to make up her mind whether to work for him. Or whether to admit she now had her own reasons for digging into Gallimore's past.

She got out of the car and looked around. Wooden picnic tables stood on the rough lawn of the pub garden encircled by low hedges, allowing alfresco diners to take in the spectacular view of the sea on the far horizon. She must remember to revisit in the summer months and join the anticipated bustling throng of holiday makers enjoying such a pleasant location.

But first, she must find Max. He had something to show her. She threw her bag over her shoulder and carried on down the lane, in accordance with Max's instructions, passing a large imposing building on the left surrounded by a high wall on which was hung a sign offering cream teas, qualified by a closed sign underneath. The opposite side of the road was lined with trees, unusually tall given their proximity to the coast. She spied the signpost to the church and crossed over the road.

A wooden gate marked the entrance into the churchyard. Esme opened it and walked through, letting it swing closed behind her. She walked towards the church, past an ancient yew tree listing heavily to one side and throwing mottled shadows on to the gravel path. As she reached the stone porch, she spied the sea in the distance across the fields and stopped for a moment to enjoy the view and feel the wind in her face.

The door to the church opened and Max emerged. 'Church before pub?' she said, turning towards him. 'Must be important. The pub's usually at the top of a journalist's list.'

He gave her a guarded grin. 'Wanted you to see something first.' He jerked his head, indicating the path where she'd just walked. He strode ahead of her, stepping off the path about halfway along and through the wet grass to a grave beside the hedge. Esme pulled up her collar and followed him, bending down to read the plain pale headstone.

'Gerald Gallimore?' she said, looking up at Max. 'I didn't realise he was buried here.'

'Yeah, interesting isn't it? Though, not so surprising, given its proximity. OK. Done my church bit now. Pub next. I need a pint.'

Max strode back across the grass to the path, leaving Esme a little baffled. *Close by?* Close by to what? She assumed he'd explain everything over lunch. She hoisted her bag on to her shoulder and followed him down the path and back on to the lane.

'So does Gallimore have a family connection with this place?' Esme asked, as she caught him up.

'Could be. That's where you come in. Be interesting to see what you find, digging into his family history.'

Esme stopped walking. 'Hey, hang on. I don't remember agreeing to anything yet.'

Max halted ahead of her and turned round. 'So why are you here?'

'You invited me.'

He scowled. 'You didn't have to come. Last time we met you couldn't get away fast enough. So what's changed?'

'We all have to make a living, Max.'

Max narrowed his eyes. 'Do you treat all your potential clients with such suspicion?'

'Only those who have a reputation for being hard-nosed,' she said, with a little laugh. 'Oh, come on Max. All I'm saying is that I need to establish the ground rules, first.'

He stared at her for a moment before carrying on up the lane. They walked the rest of the way in silence.

Esme wondered why she felt the need to be so defensive. Was it because Max reminded her of times past, of painful past events? Because she didn't trust him entirely? Because she wasn't being completely honest with him? Or perhaps, despite what she kept telling herself – and Max – she knew she was being sucked into Max's agenda and she didn't seem to be able to stop herself. Was she really that easy to hook?

19

The entrance to the pub, in a corner of a large cobbled court-yard, opened into a flagstoned hallway. On the right was a low-ceilinged room, furnished with settles. A wood-burning stove gave out a welcome glow of heat from a large inglenook fireplace.

They ordered their drinks at the bar, taking them through into a second room to a table in the corner. Max straddled a stool and Esme sat down opposite him on the settle against the wall, throwing her coat on the end.

'Cheers,' Max said, lifting his pint. 'Here's to our new partnership.'

Esme frowned. 'There you go, jumping the gun again.'

'Oh, come on, Ez. Quit playing hard-to-get. I know what you're like when you've got your teeth into something.'

'Only once I've taken a bite. I'm still studying the menu. Talking of which,' she added, turning her head to read the chalkboard headed FOOD which was hanging above the fireplace, 'hadn't we better order? And you're buying, if I remember.'

While Max went to the bar to place their order, Esme considered her position. Should she mention Vivienne? If she did, would that put her under some sort of obligation and tie her in with Max? But if she didn't, how could his knowledge be of any use to her?

'So,' Max said, retaking his seat, 'what say we lay our cards on the table.'

'Meaning?'

Max laughed. 'I don't flatter myself it's my company you came for. You're curious about Gerald Gallimore, aren't you?' He folded his arms and peered at her, narrowing his eyes. 'So I'm thinking, maybe you did find something amongst Tim's notes?'

'No, Max. I promise you I didn't. You said you had a job for me. I've already told you. I have to make a living, same as you. Look, why don't you give me some idea what this is really all about. Then maybe we can establish those ground rules.'

Max stared at her for a moment before taking a long draught of beer. 'OK,' he said, setting down his glass. 'I'll tell you what I know about Gerald Gallimore and see what you make of it.'

'OK. Sounds reasonable.'

Max reached inside his jacket and pulled out a grainy photograph. He slid it over to Esme. 'Our man in his halcyon days.'

Esme put on her reading glasses and studied the black and white print. Gallimore stared back at her under heavy dark eyebrows. His hair was pulled off his high forehead in a quiff and he held a cigarette nonchalantly between his fingers. He reminded Esme of a young Dirk Bogarde, one of her mother's favourite actors from the 1940s. She held the photo up to the light to peer at it more closely. 'One eye looks darker the other,' she said, looking up at Max.

'Heterochromia, if I've got the term right,' Max said. 'Blue and brown, in his case.' He took the photo and slipped it back in his pocket. 'As you know, there was brief speculation at the time that his murder was an old army grudge of some sort. But, like you said before, there was other more pressing news around at the time so no one gave it much interest. And let's face it, who cares a shit about investigating some small-bit army back-biting. So the thing went cold.'

Esme picked up her drink and took a sip. 'So have you come across something that suggests it was more than small-bit army back-biting?'

'As I said on the phone, Gallimore was SOE.'

'And you think that's significant? It's hardly the deadly secret it used to be, though, is it? Agents' memoirs are all over Amazon and you can access their files in the National Archives. '

'Not all of them you can't. Some are still classified. Including Gerald Gallimore's.'

'Two fish and chips?' Esme sat upright, pulling back out of the way as the young waitress put their food on the table, warning them the plates were hot. Esme thanked the girl, who blushed and scurried off to fetch their cutlery.

When the table was set, and they'd assured the waitress they had everything they required, Esme resumed the conversation.

'So why can't you access Gerald Gallimore's files?' Esme said, cutting into the crispy fish batter.

Max chewed for a moment before swallowing his mouthful. 'Great food. Didn't realise how hungry I was. I always say,' he said, reaching for the vinegar. 'That you can tell a good pub from the way they do fish and chips.'

'Stop winding me up, Max. Tell me about Gallimore's files.'

Max leaned his elbow on the table and waved his fork in his hand. 'Gallimore wasn't a career soldier. He joined up at the start of the war and when the SOE was set up in 1940, he became part of it.'

'You keep coming back to his being an SOE.'

'Both secret and ruthless in its time.'

'Yes, but not now. That's my point. So what's this about his files still being classified?'

'It suggests he got transferred to something else in intelligence.'

'After the war?'

'Yes.'

'What about during it? Did he have a desk job?' said Esme, thinking of the letter written to Vivienne's family.

'Not initially. He worked with the Resistance in F civision. The French sector. Why d'you ask?'

'No reason. Just wanted to clarify. So he was a bit of a hero, is that what you were saying?'

'Got an MC.'

'The military cross wasn't reserved for active service, though, was it? Didn't the code-breakers at Bletchley Park get the same accolade?'

Max scratched his cheek. 'And your point is?'

Esme shook her head. 'Nothing. Sorry. So how are you able to find out about him, if you haven't got sight of his file?'

'I've got a guy collating what he can from other files mentioning Gallimore. He's been going through various letters, diaries, memoirs, that sort of thing.'

'So military decorations aside, what's he come up with so far?'

'That Gallimore was suave, good looking, charming. Bit of reputation for breaking hearts. Spoke several languages. Athletic. Keen tennis player. Trained in the use of explosives. Underwent several successful sabotage missions in France. Organised secret landing operations, getting agents in and out of France. Spent the latter part of the war involved with SOEs at home.'

Max put down his knife and fork and pushed his plate away. 'See, the thing is, pretty much everything I've told you is about his wartime years – everything that's in the public domain, anyway. What I'm interested in is his family history. Which is where you come in.'

Esme frowned. 'One minute you're saying his murder is connected to the war and the next you're suggesting the answer lies in his family history?'

'Looking at every angle, Ez. One thing might lead us to another.' He leaned towards her. 'I only need his basic family history. Will you do it? Usual rates. I'm not calling this in as a favour.'

'I don't owe you one, as I recall,' said Esme, suddenly irritated and not sure why. She speared a chip with her fork. Was it because, in order to find out more about Vivienne, it meant exposing herself to Max's agenda? She still wasn't convinced he was more interested in exposing family skeletons than solving a murder.

But if researching Gallimore's past shed light on Vivienne's story, she might as well get paid for it. She only need pass on what she uncovered that was relevant to Max and her involvement would end with her invoice.

Esme sighed. Perhaps she was being over cautious. 'OK. Tell you what. I'll think about it.'

'Well don't take forever. You've got till tomorrow.'

'Fine.'

They returned their glasses to the bar and thanked the barman, before heading out to the car park.

Esme fished out her keys from her bag. 'What you meant earlier about Gallimore's grave being in close proximity?'

'Still intrigued, then? Despite the will-I, won't-I, message you keep giving out.'

Esme pressed the button on her key fob and her Peugeot's lights flashed. 'Cut it out, Max. Close proximity to what?'

Max grinned and jerked his thumb inland. 'Dunsford House. It's a couple of miles that way.'

'Dunsford House? Isn't that the name of the place –?'

'That the murderer mistakenly gave to the emergency services, yes.'

Esme turned as though sight of it would loom up from behind the cottages. 'You think there's a family connection with the place? Is that what you want me to establish?'

'Now that's an added layer I'd not considered before.'

'Then I don't see what you're getting at.'

'Sorry, I thought you knew.'

'Knew what?'

'Dunsford House was commandeered during the war as

94

a secret training location for SOE.' Max rested his arm on the roof of his car and looked across at her. 'Perhaps the murderer was trying to make a point.'

20

After Max drove off, Esme sat in her car digesting his parting comment, before fishing out her phone and tapping 'Dunsford House' into the search engine. As Max had said, it seemed it was only a few short miles away. She chewed her bottom lip and debated. It wouldn't be too much of a detour to drive home that way.

She dropped her phone into her bag and buckled up her seat belt. Why not? It was all part of the research on Gallimore. Maybe the house had a connection with his family history. The family home? It might have been the reason he'd become involved in the SOE at the outset.

According to Max, Dunsford House was now a partial ruin, following a fire some years ago. It now lay abandoned, awaiting a developer's vision to convert it into a viable alternative.

She found it easily, even though it was all but lost behind an overgrown laurel hedge. The long drive up to it was barred by a series of mesh fence panels, adorned with 'Keep Out' signs, warning of an unsafe structure and against trespassing. She pulled on to the verge in front of the hedge and parked the car, conscious of the silence when she turned off the engine. She opened the car door and climbed out on to the grass, looking round for any other properties nearby. But of course, as an SOE training base, it would have been chosen for its isolation. Inquisitive locals would be most unwelcome. Even so, she guessed there would be plenty enough speculation within the area. Easier to hide clandestine operations in cities. There may be fewer people in the countryside but they were generally more aware of their neighbours. And more suspicious.

She closed the car door and walked along the road to the drive entrance, the sound of her footsteps unnaturally invasive in the quiet lane. At the fence, she hooked her fingers in the mesh and peered in. Only part of the front of the building was still standing, and that had been blackened by the fire. There wasn't much left of the roof but the remaining walls appeared intact.

She looked along the panel. There was a gap between this and the next which looked wide enough to squeeze through. She experienced a frisson of excitement as she pushed her way in and a moment later she was on the other side, viewing Dunsford House in clear sight.

As she approached the front facade, she looked up, wondering how unsafe the structure really was. Were all the warning signs just a ruse to deter squatters?

The grand front door stood bold and firm in place, solid and seemingly impenetrable. She walked around to the side where the wall barely reached to first floor height. Here there was a breach, in the form of tumbled stone in place of a flank wall, revealing a floor covered in earth, trampled papers and fallen beech leaves.

She stepped across the rubble and into a long large room, which would have been at the rear of the original house. It stretched way out in front of her to a winding staircase at the far end. She dismissed climbing the staircase. That was inviting trouble.

Instead, she wandered into the centre of the room and looked about her. On the back wall, two alcoves stood either side of what would have been at some point in the house's history a fireplace. Now it was boarded up, against which were two metal shelf units and a grey rusting filing cabinet, its top drawer half open. She walked over to peer inside. Empty. Had she honestly thought there'd be something inside? She smiled. That would have been a treasure worth discovering. At her feet lay muddied papers pressed into the soil and she bent down to pick one up. It was a manilla folder which had once held a file but the label on the front was too blackened to read what was typed on it. She dropped it back on to the ground.

In the corner on the far wall was a panelled door, lying partially open. She picked her way across the room and gave the door a tentative push. It swung open silently with surprising ease to reveal a set of stone steps, leading down to what she assumed must be a cellar. The smell of must and damp rising from the cavernous blackness below was overpowering. Her thoughts turned to the house's role as an SOE training centre. Perhaps, somewhere within these walls, the operative learned the skills which might keep them alive when they were parachuted into enemy held territory – transmitting coded messages, vital to communication back to London, bomb making for sabotage and the ability to kill in silence. The image of the tine dagger fashioned from a pitchfork lying in Mel's display cabinet came into her head. *Primitive but effective*, Mel had said.

Esme shuddered, backing away and retreating into the larger room. As she turned, she heard a clatter from somewhere else deep inside the house. She spun round, trying to work out the direction of the sound. But the house fell silent. An animal, perhaps. A bird caught up in the upper floor, flown in from a broken window.

She made her way back the way she'd come, and when she reached the bottom of the stairs, another sound descended from above. Footsteps? She turned to peer up the stairs, her heart pounding in her chest. Instinctively she put her foot on the lower tread and began to climb.

But half way up the flight she heard another noise, this time from outside. Through the window on the half-landing, opaque with grime, she saw a flash of jade green.

She hurried back down the stairs, and stumbling out of the

building, ran round to the front, scanning the grounds as she went. As she rounded the corner, she saw a woman wearing a green coat standing on the edge of the laurel hedge, staring up at the facade.

'Hello there?' Esme said, walking towards her.

The woman started. Clearly she'd been too absorbed to notice Esme was there until she's spoken. Immediately she began to back away.

'No, don't go,' Esme called out, hurrying over.

But the woman turned away and, in a few moments, had disappeared into the undergrowth.

21

The encounter with the woman left Esme strangely unsettled as she drove home. She told herself she was reading more into it than she should, influenced, perhaps, by Dunsford House's history and everything she and Max had discussed over lunch about the secrets surrounding Gallimore. The woman may, like Esme, have merely been curious about the ruined building and, having assumed Esme to be the owner or developer, had made a hasty retreat for fear of being accused of trespassing.

The following morning after breakfast, Esme donned her jacket and walking boots and headed out on to the cliff path, determined to make the most of her coastal residence while she had the chance. Her workload was light – other than the potential job Max had lined up for her – and she wanted to keep it that way for a week or two at least. Why move to such a stunning location and not take full advantage?

By the time she'd reached the last step up to the headland, her heart was pumping and she was out of breath. She stopped at the top and looked down at the cottage below, nestled in the valley, the track and footpaths splaying out away from it in all directions. Beyond it, in the distance, she could see the tower of Stoke church peeping out from the trees. She breathed in the salty air which buffeted around her head and lost herself in the sound of the waves pushing across the strange regimented rock formations of the beach below. Had Bea spent time on the coast when she was growing up during the war or was she confined to the farm? A teacher friend had once told her how shocked she'd been that some children in her primary school class had never seen the sea, even though they'd lived less than fifteen miles from the coast, because their parents were always too busy on the farm to take them. Esme had gaped at the story. She'd grown up in a town almost a hundred miles from the Welsh coast but she'd visited it many times, sometimes just for a day trip. It seemed inconceivable to live so close and never experience the wonder of the sea.

Thoughts of Bea pushed questions back into her head concerning decisions she needed to make. One, about working for Max, and two, what, if anything, should she tell Ruth about Gallimore? And if she decided to accept Max's offer and research Gallimore's family history, was that the time to tell him about Vivienne? Instinctively she felt it was more prudent to keep the two investigations apart. If she let Max know that she had her own reasons for finding out more about Gallimore, it would be harder to detach herself if she discovered that Max's motives were less than reputable. If she told Ruth what she knew about Gallimore, Ruth might change her mind about digging around in the past, worrying at the implications. Given Bea's apparent hostility to the idea, it wouldn't take much for her to get cold feet and decide to let sleeping dogs lie.

And would that be so bad, Esme asked herself? Wasn't the whole point of coming here to turn the page on a new chapter? Perhaps she should practice curbing her insatiable appetite for the truth, take on board Maddy's philosophy of the other day and accept that it didn't necessarily turn out with best outcome.

She snorted. Much use she'd be as a historical researcher if she lost her interest in searching out the truth. So what did that mean? That she'd decided to accept the job Max had asked her to do, dig into Gerald Gallimore's past?

She took one last long gaze out to the horizon and turned back for home. Seemed like it did. She'd better inform Max and make a start. As to what she'd tell him about Vivienne, she'd leave that decision for another time. It would resolve itself eventually.

22

Gerald Arthur Nathanial Gallimore, born in 1921, had been an only child and his parents had died young, both in the same year. Esme wondered at the cause. An accident? Illness? She wondered if little Gerald had been brought up by his grandparents who, conversely, had lived to a good age. She planned to order copies of the relevant birth, marriage and death certificates marking the key points in Gallimore's family history to hand over to Max for their meeting in a few days' time.

The last item on the list was Gallimore's own death certificate and she wondered idly if it would yield anything significant in the question of his murder. Though that seemed unlikely or newspaper reports would have made something of it already or it would have surfaced during any subsequent inquest.

She entered all his details on the screen when the telephone rang. She hit the SEARCH button and grabbed the phone. It was Ruth.

'Just wondering how you were getting on, that's all,' Ruth said. 'I hope Mum and her little jaunt hasn't bothered you at all. I'd hate for you to have second thoughts about moving down here.'

'No of course not,' Esme said, laughing. 'How is Bea, anyway?'

'A bit withdrawn. But she's talking to me. That's got to be a plus.'

'Actually, I was going to give you a call later,' Esme said, getting up and wandering to the window. The gorse bushes lining the path to the cliff quivered in the onshore wind. 'I met a friend yesterday – and old colleague of Tim's, as it happens – whose doing some research for a book. We may have a mutual interest.'

'Oh? How?'

Esme hesitated. She'd been thinking how to approach the subject without things becoming too complicated. 'Well, strangely enough, he's been researching World War Two and it the name of Vivienne's CO came up.'

'The one who wrote the letter?'

'Yes that's right. I mean, it's a bit of a long shot but he'll put a few feelers out. He's got researchers nipping in and out of the Imperial War Museum and National Archives every five minutes. Anyway, I thought, if you like, I could ask him to keep a look out for Vivienne's name?'

Esme realised she was holding her breath.

'Well, yes, I suppose so,' Ruth said. 'D'you think he'd mind? It's very good of him.'

'Oh, he won't mind in the slightest,' Esme said, feeling a little uncomfortable at being less than candid. 'As it happens, I've offered to do something for him, which might actually give us some leads of our own. I won't bore you with the details. I'll fill you in if I come across anything.'

'Right, OK.' Ruth's tone sounded strained. Did she sense Esme was holding back on something? Or perhaps Bea had walked in and caught Ruth unawares.

'Well, I'd better get on,' Esme said, before she succumbed to telling Ruth more than she planned. 'I'll catch up with you later.'

She disconnected and dropped the receiver down, hoping she'd not just opened a can of worms. But if she did discover anything untoward connecting Gallimore and Vivienne, she would have no option but to inform Ruth. So it was good to have mentioned him. If she did have to confess all, it wouldn't come as a complete shock.

She returned to her desk. The computer had slipped into hibernation mode and she tapped a key to wake it up. When the screen refreshed, she peered at the results thrown up from the information she'd entered before Ruth's call.

As expected, Gallimore's death appeared on the index for 1981, the year of the murder. But as she stared at the screen she saw the search engine had found another match. A different Gerald Arthur Nathanial Gallimore had died fifty-eight years earlier, aged two. And even more of a coincidence, it was in the same year and in the same quarter that she'd recorded for the deaths of Gallimore's parents. Surely there couldn't be two Gerald Arthur Nathanial Gallimores born on the same day?

The more she processed the information in front of her, the more her mind became convinced of the obvious, and disturbing, explanation. Lt Colonel Gerald Gallimore had stolen the identity of a dead child.

23

The pub adjacent to the Quay Hotel was quiet, the wet weather no doubt dampening the midweek lunchtime trade even more than usual. Max was waiting at the bar when she arrived, passing the time of day with the barman. They took their pints of the local brew to the table beside the window.

'How's the research going?' Esme said as they sat down. 'Did your man in the archives find out anything more about Gallimore's SOE involvement?' She was still trying to decide whether to mention Vivienne.

Max took a long draught of beer and studied her carefully. He reached inside his jacket and pulled out a piece of A4 paper, folded longways, which he dropped on to the table and pushed it towards her.

'What's this?'

'What you just asked about. A list of F section missions from Gallimore's early days in France when he was under cover. Anyone sent out to his particular circuit is highlighted.'

'F section? Circuit?' Esme said with a wry grin. 'You'll have to fill me in with the jargon, Max, or I won't have a clue what you're on about.'

'F section means France. Circuit's the term they used for a group of agents in the field, one of whom would be a radio operator who communicated with HQ back in London.'

Esme picked up the folded sheets and opened them out, eagerly scanning the names picked out by highlighter pen for Vivienne's name, but she didn't appear on any of the pages. She told herself she was being overly optimistic to believe she'd simply stumble across Vivienne's name on a random list. And even if she did, other than confirm that Vivienne was indeed an SOE, it didn't answer the key question of what happened to her.

She realised that Max had asked her a question.

'Sorry, what did you say?'

'Turned up anything in Tim's notes, yet?'

She shoved the papers back at him across the table. 'Oh, give it a rest, Max. How many more times do I have to tell you? There are no notes.' A cold uncomfortable feeling seeped somewhere deep inside. She forced herself to ask the obvious question, her voice little more than a whisper. 'Why are you so convinced this has got something to do with Tim?'

Max shook his head. 'Convinced is too strong a word. Suspicious, that's all. But only because Gallimore's case intrigued him.'

Esme felt herself relax a little. So that was all. No revelations to throw her out of kilter. 'I thought we'd agreed it didn't go any further because no one was that interested and other stuff was going on?'

'You're not holding out on me, are you, Ez?'

'Of course not,' Esme said, flushing. 'Why would I?'

Max shrugged. 'Just a hunch. A sense that you're keeping your powder dry. But I suppose I couldn't blame you if you are blanking me. It can't be easy putting yourself back there, after what happened to Tim, not to mention what you went through.'

She flashed him a scowl. 'Don't give me the sympathy act, Max. You're the one who searched me out to stir it all up, remember? And as I told you then, I've moved on and I've no reason to go back there again.' Was that completely true? The image of Tim's box burning a hole under the spare bed in the cottage floated into her mind.

'Fair point,' Max conceded with a nod. 'I get that. Sorry.'

She wrapped her hands around her drink and sighed.

'Look. I'm sure that if he *had* turned up anything interesting, he would have told you.'

'You don't think we were capable of a little journalistic rivalry?'

'Well…then he would have told *me*, wouldn't he? As his researcher, I'm the obvious one he'd discuss it with. And ask me to do some digging. But he didn't. OK?'

'Sure. If you say so.'

She stared into her drink. 'Look. Perhaps your hunch was right, in a way.' She flashed him a warning look. 'But it's got nothing to do with Tim.'

He cocked his head. 'With what then?'

She took a gulp of beer and lowered the glass on to the beer mat. Was she sure about this? Once she said it, she was committed. There was no way back. And she may learn nothing anyway. She shuffled in her seat.

'Anytime this month would be good, Ez.'

She flicked him a glance. 'Sorry,' she said, with a half-laugh. 'Just getting my thoughts in order. Tell me, in your digging around for Gallimore, have you come across the name Vivienne Lancaster?'

'Who's she?'

'A client's aunt. Died in the war.'

'SOE?'

'According to the family, she was a nurse. I've got a photo of her in a FANY uniform.'

Max nodded, clearly understanding the significance. 'And you think there's a connection with Gallimore?'

'All I know is that his name was on the letter of condolence to her parents.'

'That's why you asked about a desk job.'

Esme nodded. 'That's right. Starts and ends there, though, as far as I know.'

Max scratched the side of his nose with an index finger. 'Gallimore did return to England at some point and became part of the training team.'

'Yes, so you said before. At Dunsford House?'

'Apparently.' Max leaned forward. 'What else do you know about her?'

'Nothing more than what I've already told you.'

'So why the big secret?'

Esme shrugged, trying to play it down. 'No big secret. Information's got a bit muddled over the years, that's all. Like I said, the family doesn't know a lot about it. Look, forget Vivienne for the moment. Let me bring you up to date with what I've got on Gallimore, which is infinitely more intriguing.' She dragged her bag towards her.

Max sat back into the settle. 'Fire away, then. What've you got?'

'It's quite a story, actually,' Esme said, unable to dampen the bubble of excitement of what she'd uncovered. 'Except it's not exactly Gallimore's family we're talking about.'

Max raised an eyebrow. 'Sounds interesting.'

Esme pulled out four documents which she laid down on the table. 'Whatever the Gallimore family history might throw up becomes completely irrelevant, because I suspect our friend is not Gerald Gallimore at all.'

'Now that *is* interesting.'

Esme tapped the documents. 'That's *our* Gerald Gallimore's death certificate, dated 1981. Cause of death, as we know, due to gunshot wounds.'

'And the rest?' said Max, picking up the papers.

'Death certificates for two-year-old Gerald Gallimore and his parents. All killed outright in a car accident in 1923.'

'Ah. He took on the kid's identity?'

'The birth date and names match exactly. And even if there *was* another person with the same profile, there'd be another birth record. Which there isn't. I checked.'

Esme picked up her drink and sat back in her seat. 'So who's Gallimore really? When did he take the name? How come he was never found out? Surely, SOE did checks on things like that?'

Max pulled a face. 'SOE recruiting procedure was pretty unorthodox, particularly in the early days. If your face fitted. Who you knew...' He shrugged.

'Obviously we don't know how long ago he'd been playing the part. His wife's family – he married early in 1946 – were pretty well-heeled, from what I gather and might have unwittingly helped in establishing his legitimacy, especially if the two were already a couple before the war. But what about his military history? Surely he couldn't invent that?'

'Who said he had one? He was probably given his rank while with SOE. They were a mixed bunch. Everything from bankers to business men. Chosen for a completely different set of skills than your average army officer. Gallimore's was languages, as I think I mentioned before. He tutored in a private school before he joined up.'

'I'm still amazed he got away with it.' Esme took a sip of beer. 'Do you think his family knows who he really is? God, what a shock. This is going to put the kibosh on his son's political career, isn't it?' She paused as the realisation seeped through into her consciousness. She slumped back in her seat and glowered at Max. 'Hang on, this is just the sort of thing you were looking for, isn't it? Oh, great. After everything I said to you about not wanting to help you dig the dirt, and now look at me. I've just handed it to you on a plate. Priceless.' She turned and stared out of the window.

'Don't be so bloody stupid, Ez,' Max said, folding his arms. 'This has got much more potential than a seedy headline.' He leaned forward and lowered his voice. 'Look. Tell you what. I'll make you an offer. I'm interviewing an old boy next week, ex-military and former SOE. Worked with Gallimore, briefly. Why don't you come along? You might pick up something useful about your girl.'

She shot Max a guarded look and contemplated the idea while fiddling with her glass. It certainly was tempting.

'You've got to admit,' Max added, 'that Gallimore's story

takes on an even more interesting twist now, with what you've brought to the party.'

Esme sat up in alarm. 'Oh, no, Max, no. It's highly unlikely that Vivienne's story is in any way connected with what happened to Gallimore.'

'You can't possibly know that.'

'Well, I...'

'Come on, Ez. I'm offering you a way in. If you're serious about learning more about this woman, you should be biting my hand off. I don't usually share my sources so easily. And we'd make a good team.'

She peered at him warily. 'You saying we should work together?'

'Makes sense to me.'

Esme rubbed her finger along the edge the beer mat. There was no doubt that Max's sources could be valuable. And as the man said, if she really wanted to find out about Vivienne, she'd be a fool to turn him down. Besides, what else did she have to go on? Having drawn a blank with Frank Crombie on the mystery legacy, she'd reached an impasse.

She sighed. 'OK, Max. You may have a point. It could be useful. Thanks.' She picked up the certificates she'd brought with her on Gallimore. 'D'you want to take these?'

Max reached out and took them, then stopped, his hand in mid-air and a glazed expression in his eyes.

'You all right, Max?' Esme said.

He nodded towards the papers in his hand. 'Something you said earlier,' he said, a shadow falling across his face, 'about being amazed that Gallimore got away with re-inventing himself.'

'I still am.'

'Ah, but did he?'

'Did he what?'

'Get away with it. Maybe someone found out.'

Esme stared at him. 'What are you saying? That his false identity is tied up with his murder?'

Max drained his glass. 'Worth a punt, I reckon.' He wiped his mouth with the back of his hand and looked at Esme, frowning. 'D'you think Tim might have come to the same conclusion?'

24

Max had arranged to meet Joe Paxton, the former SOE, at Joe's daughter's home in Wanstead, North London. Esme would go up by rail from Devon and Max would join her at Reading.

An encounter with a flock of sheep on the road and getting stuck behind a painfully slow tractor meant Esme almost missed her train. She drove down the North Devon link road faster than she knew she should and by the time she arrived at Tiverton Parkway and found a parking space, the 9.06 to Paddington was pulling into the station.

She found her reservation at a table and dropped thankfully into her seat by the window as the ricocheted clatter of slamming doors heralded the train's departure. It would be ironic, having initially resisted Max's invitation to attend the interview, only to mess up the timing and miss the train. She pulled out her phone to text Max and let him know the train was on time before settling back in her seat to watch the West Country farmland speed past.

She'd not yet completely forgiven Max for questioning whether Tim had inadvertently stumbled across the truth of Gallimore's identity. Despite Max's apology and insistence, he hadn't meant to imply it was connected with Tim's death, the conversation had left her unsettled. She'd done her best to quash the idea, pointing out that if Gallimore's false identity was significant, he was more likely to be the perpetrator not the victim. He'd have reason to silence someone for threatening to expose him, not the other way around.

At Reading, Esme saw Max immediately amongst the grey crowd waiting gloomily on the platform, carrying briefcases. He disappeared temporarily, reappearing moments later, rocking down the aisle towards her. He lobbed his document bag on to the luggage rack and threw himself in the seat beside Esme, allowing the trail of fellow passengers to file past.

Esme slid a carton of coffee towards him. 'Thought you might be in need.'

Max nodded. 'Cheers. Bloody cold on that platform.'

While Max drank his coffee, Esme gazed out of the window, watching the people left behind, some milling around, others striding purposefully to the exit, wheeling cases behind them.

Max threw his head back against the seat rest and let out a long sigh. 'This could be interesting, don't you think.'

'Hopefully,' Esme said, looking round. 'What have you told him about me?'

'That you're looking for information on a potential female SOE. It's not a secret, is it?'

'No, of course not.' Esme turned back to the window as large, bland buildings of commerce flashed by. A flutter stirred in the pit of her stomach, partly anticipation, partly anxiety. Was it being in league with Max which made her anxious? Or because of what they might find out?

*

Joe Paxton's daughter's house was a tall terraced property a short walk from the Tube. It stood on a quiet street regimentally adorned with cherry trees, currently skeletal but doubtless frilly with blossom in spring.

His daughter showed them into a clutter-free room with a wide bay window, beside which Joe Paxton was sitting in a high winged chair. When they entered, he pushed himself shakily to his feet and introductions were made. As Esme shook Joe's hand, she was surprised at the firmness of his grip, despite his apparent frailty. He was clearly a man who, despite his age, took care in his appearance. His thinning grey hair was combed and neatly parted. He wore a suit which she suspected had been part of his wardrobe for a good many years.

'It's good of you to see us, Mr Paxton,' said Esme, as Joe lowered himself back into his chair.

'It's Joe, my dear. And you are very welcome.'

'Oh, don't you worry,' laughed his daughter. 'He's loving all this attention. The BBC are coming next week, aren't they Dad? He's quite the celebrity.' She invited them to take a seat before offering them coffee and withdrawing from the room. Esme sat down on the large sofa against one wall and Max took the adjacent armchair.

'So you want to know about Gallimore, eh?'

'That's right,' Max said. 'I understand you were in France together.'

'Briefly, yes. Our operations crossed, you might say. He was called back to Blighty shortly after I was parachuted in. To debrief HQ, one assumes.' He looked wistful for a moment. 'Damned lucky anyone survived to make the report. Could have been a lot worse.'

'What happened?' Esme said.

'When I arrived, a female agent had been betrayed to the Gestapo and just been arrested. Word had it Kruger was involved.' He shook his head. 'She wouldn't have stood a chance.'

'Kruger?' Max asked.

'Viktor Kruger. Commandant of Jurgensbrück, one of the most brutal prison camps in Germany.' Joe folded his hands together in his lap and addressed Max. 'The torture and execution of many British SOEs can be laid at Kruger's door. The worst of it didn't come to light until after the war but agents all over occupied Europe had heard enough to know what an evil and sadistic bastard he was.'

Joe inclined his head towards Esme. 'Apologies for my language, my dear.'

Esme gave him a weak smile and shook her head.

'So, only a few days after being dropped into France, we had to close down operations and move on before the Germans had time to act on any intelligence they'd beaten out of her.'

Esme winced and thought of the photo of FANYs she'd seen on Mel's wall. How had those women coped with such atrocities being inflicted on them? Weren't agents issued with cyanide pills for when they found themselves in such a situation? But it almost took as much courage in making the decision to use it. Though, if you were taken by surprise, you may not have had the option. And the enemy would want to keep you alive for whatever information they could prise out of you. They'd not sanction an easy way out. Certainly not someone like Viktor Kruger.

She heard Max saying her name and she realised Joe had asked her a question about who she was looking for.

She sat up straight and concentrated. 'Vivienne Lancaster. Gallimore knew her, apparently. He wrote to her parents after she went missing.'

'And you want to know if she was part of Gallimore's circuit or whether they were romantically involved?'

'Oh.' Esme glanced at Max, momentarily thrown off course. Why had that not occurred to her before? 'Well, we did hear he was a bit of womaniser but...'

'Such liaisons weren't uncommon, of course. These were intense times. Passions run high. Men and women pushed together in perilous situations. And Gallimore was a charismatic individual.' Joe chuckled. 'He certainly seemed to attract more attention than most.'

'So Vivienne could have been one of his admirers?'

'There was certainly one young woman who took a particular shine to him but I don't know if it's the girl you're talking about.'

'Do you remember her name?'

Joe frowned, causing his face to crease into deep folds. 'Yvette. But that would be her code name, of course. I wouldn't know her real identity. It was safer that way, you see.' His expression grew dark and his eyes lost their shine for a moment. 'The less you knew, the less they could thrash out of you if you fell into enemy hands.'

*

'So, what do you think?' asked Esme as they walked back to the Tube station later. 'Could Yvette be Vivienne?' The mystery of the unknown benefactor stirred in her head. Could it have been Gallimore?

'Worth a try,' said Max. 'Easy enough to check out the name.'

At Paddington station, they bought coffee and found a table on the concourse. Max took out his laptop and connected up to the station Wi-Fi. Esme sipped her latte and watched the ebb and flow of train passengers while mulling over Joe's information. The visit hadn't moved her investigation on any further, unless they were able to confirm that Yvette and Vivienne were the same person. And even supposing they did, where did it take her? If the pair had been lovers and it *was* Gallimore who'd remembered Vivienne in his will, that would confirm her suspicion that Gallimore had lied in the letter to Bea's parents. But it didn't explain why.

'There *is* an Yvette on the list of SOEs,' Max said.

Esme swivelled round in her seat and peered round the edge of Max's laptop. 'Really?'

'Don't get too excited. Real name's Celia Bradshaw not your Vivienne.'

Esme sighed and slumped against the back of her chair. 'Oh well. Would have been too much to hope for, I suppose.' She sat forward again. 'So if Vivienne's not on the list, perhaps she wasn't an SOE after all?'

'Can't be sure about that. It's based on files which actually exist. Figures differ as to how many SOEs there were and even taking the most conservative estimate, there aren't files for all of them. Vivienne's may be one of those missing.'

Esme nodded. Mel had said the same.

'There's one avenue you could follow, though.' Max said. 'Now we know Vivienne wasn't Gallimore's bit of skirt, you wouldn't be trampling on sensitive ground by speaking to Gallimore's wife.'

'She's still alive?'

'And kicking. Actually that's not strictly true She's wheelchair bound. But don't be fooled. She's no feeble geriatric, despite her advancing years.'

'You've met her?'

'Fleetingly. Before she booted me out. Seems to have taken a dislike to journalists over the years.'

'What makes you think I'd fare any better?'

'You're a genealogist. Different angle. If Gallimore spilled out his experiences on the conjugal pillow, she might have something to tell you.'

Esme picked up her coffee and sipped it thoughtfully. It was worth considering. Her enquiry was genuine – a member of a family searching for information on a lost relative. The story's appeal might find a sympathetic ear.

She heard Max inhale noisily through his teeth and she turned to see him shaking his head, his eyes fixed on the laptop screen and his mouth turned down. 'Joe Paxton certainly didn't exaggerate Kruger's ruthlessness,' he said. 'Kruger's fingerprints are all over a number of SOE executions, some from Gallimore's circuit. Brutal interrogation, authorising medical experiments on women and sickening punishment regimes are amongst Kruger's specialties. Here.' He swivelled the machine around but Esme turned away and shook her head.

'No thanks. I'll take your word for it.' How was it that war brought out the worst in the human species? Yet conversely, it brought out the best in others.

'Nah, don't blame you,' Max said, turning the laptop back round to face him. 'It's not pretty reading. Says here the callous bugger seem to have some sort of warped sense of pride for what he did – saw it as his duty to his enemy.'

Esme shuddered. 'He went on trial for war crimes, I assume.'

'Died in custody just after the war while waiting for his case to come up. '

Esme's head shot round. 'Someone got to him, you mean?' She leaned across the table and peered at Max. 'What if it was Gallimore, taking revenge for executing his fellow agents? Then say someone found out years later and gave him a taste of his own medicine?'

Max laughed. 'Nice theory, Ez. But Kruger died of pneumonia.'

A station announcement echoed around the concourse and Esme glanced up at the departure board. 'Come on,' she said, standing up. 'Our train's in.'

They gathered up their belongings and made their way to the barrier. As they hurried along the platform to their carriage, Esme's phone buzzed. She slowed down to take the phone out of her bag and checked the screen. There was a text from Frank Crombie. *I've remembered something*, it said. *Call me.*

25

'I should've thought of it sooner,' Crombie said, when Esme eventually got hold of him the following day. There was a breathlessness to his voice, suggesting he was walking along as he spoke. 'Thing is, it was all a bit embarrassing. You'd work it out soon enough for yourself, if you get hold of his will, so I'm not telling tales out of school. Anyhow, there was a dispute. He'd left everything to this woman, not his wife and daughter. Wife tracks me down. Begs me to pretend I couldn't find this woman so that the estate would revert to her and her daughter, rightfully in her eyes. I told her it wasn't up to me. Suggested she took it to court. She'd have grounds.'

'So, I might track it down through court records?'

'If she went down that route. But I wouldn't hold your breath. I got the impression she'd shy away from anything so public, if you know what I mean.'

'She'd rather let it drop?'

'Wouldn't surprise me in the slightest.'

'I don't suppose you remember the family's name?' Esme said.

'Something like Cope or Cox is my best effort but I can't be sure. But what I can tell you is that I do remember he was a doctor from south Devon. That might help narrow things down a bit.'

Esme thanked him and cut the call. If Dr Cope or Cox had died in the 1960s rather than the 1990s, there would have been sufficient information on the National Probate Calendar database. Back then the main beneficiary, as well

119

as the value of the estate, was invariably named so finding mention of Vivienne would have been straight forward. But in more recent years the information was more restrained. She could hardly send for a copy of every will left by someone with a surname beginning with a C in and around 1990. And it was no advantage knowing he was a doctor, as the database didn't use titles.

But perhaps the little Crombie had mentioned might jog Ruth's memory. She needed to speak to her anyway, to tell her about her visit to London. She picked up the phone and dialled the farm.

'Doesn't mean anything to me, Esme,' Ruth said, when Esme had relayed her conversation with Frank Crombie. 'But I'm not even sure Mum told me a name. Sorry, I can't be more help.'

'No, that's OK. Worth passing it by you.'

'Was he a medical doctor or was he some sort of professor?'

'That's a good question, Ruth. I shall have to check with Frank. While you're on, though, I must tell you that I came away empty handed from the old soldier I went to see yesterday. He doesn't remember Vivienne, I'm afraid.'

'Oh, that's a shame.'

'Don't despair, though. I've got someone else on my list. She may know something. We're not beat yet.'

As Esme put down the phone, she felt a dent in her optimism. Every avenue they explored seemed to go nowhere. Would a visit to Faye Gallimore go the same way? That's even assuming she was prepared to talk. She went to her bag and dug out the telephone number Max had given her, along with an address and a rough map of the location on the edge of Taunton. *About half a mile past the Health Centre*, he'd written.

Esme frowned. Health Centre. Assuming Dr Cope or Cox or whatever he was called, was a medical man, perhaps he'd been a GP? And if he'd been well known in his local community, might there have been an obituary in the local paper? Crombie had mentioned south Devon. It should be fairly easy to check.

Esme hurried into the sitting room and booted her laptop. Once active, she signed into the database of the British Newspaper Archives which, while still far from complete, covered provisional as well as national titles. But a quick check of the dates showed that the archive for newspapers of the South West only covered up to 1957.

She sat back, drumming her fingers on the desk. What other organisation would publish an obituary on a doctor? Of course. The British Medical Journal.

A few clicks of the mouse later and she'd found him on the journal's website. Dr Donald Cole. A GP in the Sidmouth area who'd died in October 1990. It had to be him, didn't it? Surely the chances of there being two doctors, surname beginning with C, both dying in the south Devon area in 1990 seemed highly unlikely.

She scanned the obituary.

Dr Cole seemed to have been well regarded amongst his patients as well as other medical professionals. There was mention of his work with penicillin and research in developing a method for manufacturing large quantities for use in army field hospitals during the Second World War. Esme was surprised that his career had not continued in that vein, that he'd not specialised and become a consultant in his field, rather than a GP.

She peered at the screen, frowning. According to the account, Cole had come over to Britain from Germany just before the war. She paused to consider. So Cole was German. So what? Was that relevant? Only that the connection with Vivienne was harder to establish. Esme had imagined that for Cole to leave Vivienne all his worldly goods, he'd have been an old family friend, someone she'd known for years. If he'd only arrived in the UK as war broke out and Vivienne had died before its end, the timing didn't work out.

Then again, they still had no conclusive proof that Vivienne had died in the war. Was the fact that she'd known Cole another indicator that she survived?

As she read through the rest of the page, her eye fell on the closing sentence. She grabbed the mouse and clicked it to bring up the website of the General Register Office. She had to get a copy of Cole's death certificate. She needed to know exactly what the obituary had meant by his "tragic death."

26

Esme was pleased to have the visit to Faye Gallimore to occupy her mind until Cole's death certificate arrived. The meeting had been surprisingly easy to set up. Her telephone enquiry had been received with enthusiasm by a woman with a sing-song eastern European voice, who introduced herself as Magda, Mrs Gallimore's carer and companion.

'And you're sure she'd be happy to talk to me?' Esme said, having explained the reason for her visit.

'Oh yes, be sure!' sang Magda. 'Is good for talking of past, no? Good for memory. She will be most happy.'

Esme parked her car in accordance with Magda's instructions, in a leafy car park on the outskirts of Taunton, hoping that Magda's comments didn't imply Faye's memory was fading. But Max had referred to Mrs Gallimore as "no feeble geriatric" so she decided her fears were unfounded.

She walked back along the street to Bridgeland Lodge, a large Georgian property hidden behind a high stone wall and a number of mature trees. She took an iron pedestrian gate and followed the path to the front porch. The door was answered by a tall, skinny woman of around forty years old – Magda, Esme presumed – dressed in black trousers and a pale green V-necked sweater. Her hair was pulled tightly off her face in a ponytail, emphasising her narrow sharp nose and high cheekbones.

Magda smiled and clapped her hands together when Esme introduced herself.

'Ah, good! You time well. Please, come in.'

Esme stepped into a hall of tall proportions, dominated by an elegant cantilevered winding staircase. She followed Magda down the hall and into a spacious, bright room with an alabaster fireplace, in which a large vase of dried grasses sat between two highly polished brass fire dogs. Two winged chairs stood either side.

'Please sit,' said Magda. 'I fetch Mrs Gallimore.'

Esme took one of the armchairs and looked around. A door at the back of the room matched the panelled style of the one to the hall, and four side tables, adorned with vases of similar content to that of the fireplace, stood against the walls. A pair of French doors looked out on to a stone flagged terrace set with lead containers and, beyond, an ornate conservatory flanked an adjacent wall.

The hall door opened and Magda returned, pushing a wheelchair in which sat an elderly lady, white hair forming a soft halo around her head. She was dressed formally, in a navy-blue skirt and cream blouse.

Esme stood up.

'Who's this?' said Faye, her tone sharp.

Esme's hopes plummeted. This didn't sound promising. She smiled and held out her hand.

'Good morning, Mrs Gallimore,' she said. 'It's very kind of you to agree to see me.'

'I wasn't aware that I had.' Faye looked across at Magda. 'Well?' she said, with authority. 'Explain yourself.'

'This Mrs Quentin,' said Magda, with a broad smile, coming around to the front of the wheelchair and leaning towards the old lady. 'She want talk you bout past times.'

'Does she indeed.' Faye's eyes bored into Esme.

Esme shot a glance at Magda. 'I do apologise. Magda led me to believe that she'd arranged this with you.'

'Is nice for you,' said Magda. 'Talk of old times.'

'That's as maybe, Magda. But Mrs Quentin and I are not acquainted and therefore have nothing to talk about.' She turned to Esme. 'I'm sorry that you've been inconvenienced.'

'You wrong,' said Magda, with a determined expression. 'I tell you often. You keep all cooped up in here.' She patted her chest. 'You need to talk. Mrs Quentin want to ask you about war.'

'What?'

Esme lowered herself on to the edge of the armchair so she could address Faye at the correct level. 'I'm doing some family history research,' she explained hastily. 'I'm trying to find out about my client's sister, Vivienne Lancaster...'

'No, I'm sorry. This will not do. Magda, show Mrs Quentin out, please.'

'But is interesting story,' protested Magda. 'She tell me. You help her.'

'NOW, Magda.'

Esme picked up her bag from beside her chair. 'I'm sorry to have disturbed you, Mrs Gallimore,' she said, standing up. She hesitated, feeling she wanted to say more, but couldn't think what. Either Vivienne's name hadn't meant anything to her or – and instinctively Esme sensed it as the more likely – it had triggered alarm. So why would that be?

As she made to leave, a door opened behind her. She glanced round as a stocky man, wearing an open necked checked shirt and corduroy trousers, marched into the room. There was something familiar about his high forehead and thick, dark eyebrows. Esme realised immediately it must be Gerald Gallimore's son, Lloyd, the subject of Max's interest.

'Who's this, Mother?' he said, striding towards the fireplace.

'No one. She's just leaving.'

'She want to talk about war,' said Magda, seeking an ally. 'Is good for your mother, yes?'

Lloyd Gallimore turned his head to regard Esme. 'You're this Cole woman, aren't you? Well, let me tell you, this has gone far enough –'

'Lloyd,' snapped Faye. 'I have just explained. *Mrs Quentin* is just leaving.'

Esme inclined her head towards Faye, colouring under the scrutiny. She gave Lloyd Gallimore one last glance, before marching towards the door and out into the hall, the name Cole reverberating around her head. Magda scurried after her, closing the door behind them.

'Oh, is so cross for me,' whined Magda, her fists clenched at her sides. She tipped her head to one side and regarded Esme. 'Sorry for you also, that you not able to talk what you want. Please forgive.'

Esme smiled. 'I'm sorry, too, Magda, but there's nothing to forgive. It's not your fault. Thank you for trying.'

Magda threw her hands up in the air. 'She seem strong to you, yes? But she no. Much worry.' She tapped her forefinger against the side of her head.

'Worry about what?' said Esme.

Magda shrugged. 'Who say?' She patted her chest, as before. 'I feel. In here.'

'She's never confided in you, then?'

Magda's answer was to roll her eyes to the ceiling. She stepped in front of Esme and pulled open the front door. 'Thank you to come.'

Esme smiled. 'I only hope my visit won't cause you any problems.'

Magda shook her head. 'Is OK. You see.'

As Esme stepped across the threshold, she hesitated. 'Who did Mr Gallimore mean by the Cole woman?' she said, turning back to Magda.

Magda wrinkled her nose. 'Ah. Him got – what you say? Fly in bonnet?'

'Bee,' said Esme, smiling to herself. She wondered how Magda had come by the position at the Gallimores. From what she'd seen, she couldn't imagine either of the Gallimores fully appreciating Magda's delightful idiosyncrasies. She hoped today's episode wouldn't result in losing her job, particularly as she sensed Magda's concern for her employer's anxieties was genuine.

'Yes, bee in bonnet. Lady phone. Want to visit but Mr Gallimore, he say no when he hear name.'

'And that was Cole?'

Magda nodded.

'But you don't know what she wanted?'

Magda cast a look over her shoulder before moving closer to Esme and pulling the door half closed. 'She not say to me,' she said, in a stage whisper. 'But it caused big arguing. Not since I come her, I hear shouting like this.'

They said their goodbyes and Esme heard the front door close as she walked away down the path. Cole. It couldn't be a coincidence. There had to be a connection. But how could she establish one?

She turned right into the street, back in the direction of her car. As she did so, something caught her eye from across the road. When she looked over, she saw someone standing on the opposite pavement, staring towards the house. She slowed down.

The woman saw Esme watching her. She held her gaze for barely a second before turning on her heel and hurrying away.

As Esme stared after her, she registered the woman's bright green coat. Could it be the same woman she'd seen at Dunsford House?

27

Esme sat on a washed-up log on the beach by the cottage, lobbing pebbles into the encroaching tide. She let the gentle rhythm of the sea soothe her as she mulled over her visit to Faye Gallimore. If it had been only that the old lady preferred not to discuss the past, she could have understood. From what Joe Paxton had told them, Gallimore could have experienced many horrors during his time in occupied France. Perhaps his wife was aware of his traumas. Why would she want to share what she knew with a stranger?

But Esme sensed it wasn't as simple as that. Lloyd Gallimore's intervention, his mistaking her for "that Cole woman" and his subsequent hostility were enough to cause her unease even before she'd seen the woman in the green coat watching the house. How did these things tie up? Was Faye Gallimore's reticence to do with Vivienne Lancaster in particular? And the "Cole woman" – Cole's wife? Sister? Daughter? – what was her connection with the Gallimores?

Esme took a deep breath, filling her lungs with the salty air blowing in on the incoming tide. She'd learned little more about Vivienne than she'd known at the start of this journey. She knew that Bea was wary of discussing her elder sister, that the family's knowledge of Vivienne's role in wartime was flawed and that Gerald Gallimore was somehow involved. She now knew that a doctor called Donald Cole left his estate to Vivienne. But that didn't add up to much, not in providing answers, anyway. Neither did it offer any new direction to look for those answers. There was still

Cole's death certificate to come. It should have arrived by now. She'd ordered a fast track and had been expecting it in that morning's post. But even supposing his death had been suspicious, as they'd speculated, it only added another piece of unrelated information to the meagre scraps they already had.

Esme focused on the foam of the waves engulfing the rocks as the tide crept its way closer towards the log. So, what did the woman want with Faye Gallimore? Or perhaps her interest was with Lloyd? And did it have anything to do with Vivienne? She felt a moment of irritation that she'd not gone after the green-coated woman. That was twice now. She'd be ready if she came across her a third time.

She stood up. If she didn't move soon, she'd get wet feet. She climbed the stone steps from the beach and turned back to the cottage, as a battered Volvo bumped down the track. It did a three-point turn in the pull-in beside the cottage and parked up next to Esme's car.

Esme strode over to meet the driver as he climbed out of the vehicle. He held an envelope in his hand. He acknowledged Esme with a brief nod. 'Mrs Quentin?' he said.

'That's right. How can I help?'

The man handed her the envelope. 'Yours, I think. Got delivered to us by mistake.' He cocked his head back the way he'd come. 'We're up yonder. On the corner.'

'That's very good of you to bring it,' Esme said. Thank you.'

'Not a problem. Thought it might be important.' He smiled, got back into his car and drove off.

Esme looked down at the envelope and recognised the distinctive style of the General Register Office. There was only one thing it could be. Cole's death certificate.

She hurried inside the cottage to find her reading glasses and tore open the envelope. She discarded the application form and scanned the death certificate itself.

Date of death, 12th October 1990. Donald Eric Cole.

General Practitioner. Cause of death –

She flinched. Cole had killed himself with a lethal drug overdose.

28

Esme sat down, dropping the document on to the table. So what did it mean? Could it be related to the dispute over Cole's will that Crombie had told her about? Was the dispute, in fact, not to do with the will at all? Perhaps his wife had disputed that his death was suicide? She may have even suggested that it was suspicious?

According to Crombie, Mrs Cole had found it difficult to cope with the shame of the situation. Perhaps she'd not wanted to accept that he'd taken his own life and was desperate to find an alternative explanation.

But, even if that was true, the situation with the will still stood. Mrs Cole had come looking for Crombie, to beg him to say he couldn't find Vivienne, in the hope that the estate would revert to her. Esme wasn't sure if that's what would have happened automatically, without Mrs Cole having to contest the will in court which Crombie suspected she'c never do. Why not?

Presumably there would have been an inquest, so had there been a suicide note? But if Crombie's assessment of Cole's wife was correct, if there had been a note and she didn't like the contents coming out in the open, she may not have owned up to finding one.

Esme picked up the death certificate and looked at it again. Had Cole's reasons died with him?

She got up and wandered over to the kitchen window. She stared out at the hill beyond, the yellow gorse flanking the steep steps climbing out of the valley to the headland and thought of Lloyd Gallimore's words. *That Cole woman.*

She returned to her previous list of possibilities. So, which was it? Wife, sister or daughter? If it was his wife, she'd be in her late eighties or early nineties and Esme thought she would have noticed by her gait if she'd been elderly. Any sister would be of a similar age, unless there was a huge age gap between siblings.

She gasped and spun away from the window. Stupid. What was the matter with her? The answer could be there, right in front of her. She'd been so distracted by how Cole had died, she'd not thought to look who'd registered the death.

She snatched up the certificate and checked the informant. Yes. Mrs Ingrid Favell. Daughter.

She took the paper into the sitting room and sat down at her laptop, shaking with anticipation. If she could track down Ingrid Favell, nee Cole, she may have found a way to prise open a closed door, behind which there may be answers waiting to be discovered.

It didn't take long. Finding her marriage, confirming her maiden name and some cross referencing with the electoral roll and Esme had an address in Exeter. There was no entry in The Phone Book, suggesting the Favells were ex-directory.

Esme sat back in her chair and rubbed a finger down her scar. Despite the frustration that a telephone call may have produced a quicker result, it was probably better that contact be made by letter. It was a difficult area, even more so when she had no idea of the woman's connection and interest in the Gallimores.

How should she pitch it? Perhaps a vague reference to family history research would be best, inviting her to get in touch.

She pulled up her chair and began typing. She kept the letter vague, mentioning only that Dr Cole's name had come up during some family history research. That, at least, was true. She tried to give her query a sense of urgency, suggesting she was working to a tight deadline, and hoped it was enough to get a response.

She printed out the letter, signed and sealed it, and walked up to the village to catch the last post.

*

Esme walked down Exeter high street, encumbered by carrier bags and close to her shopping threshold. She'd had a fairly successful morning buying some new clothes. She should quit while she was ahead. She knew it had only really been a distraction exercise.

It had been a week now and she'd heard nothing from Ingrid Favell. No email, no telephone call and no note returned in the stamped address envelope she'd enclosed with her letter.

She stood outside John Lewis's department store and considered her options. Perhaps she should follow up her letter with a visit? What had she got to lose? She was in the area and it was Saturday. It could be a good day to find Dr Cole's daughter at home.

She hurried back to her car and threw her purchases in the boot. She checked the address location on her phone and headed off to the St Thomas area of the city. Traffic was heavy and she almost changed her mind. But she knew she'd be annoyed with herself once she got home, if she'd not tried.

Ash Road was a neat street, lined with modest Victorian terraces on either side. She found a parking space at the top of the street and walked down the hill to number 77. The front garden was an uninspiring patch of grass, bordered by a concrete path to the front door. Unlike many of its neighbours, there was no new plastic porch glued around the front door, only a simple canopy to protect visitor and owner alike from the rain. But there was no rain today, only dull clouds, though already it grew darker and more threatening.

Esme pressed the doorbell and heard its chimes echo inside before the front door opened and she found herself face to face with Ingrid Favell. No green coat, of course. She was dressed in jeans, a baggy blue T-shirt and an unzipped grey fleece, her thinning grey hair sticking out behind her ears.

'Mrs Favell?' said Esme.

'Yes?' Ingrid eyed her warily.

Esme held out her business card. 'My name's Esme Quentin. I'm sorry to bother you but I wrote to you a few of days ago about –'

'I know who you are,' said the woman.

'Who is it, Ingrid?' called a voice from inside.

The woman looked anxiously over her shoulder before turning back to Esme, her face pale. 'I can't help you,' she said in a low voice. 'I don't know anything about what happened to your husband.'

And she slammed the door in Esme's face.

29

Esme stumbled back to her car and sat in the driver's seat, staring out into a vision of nothingness through the windscreen, Ingrid Favell's words repeating over and over in her head. *I don't know anything about what happened to your husband. What happened to your husband...what happened to your husband...*

At some point, she must have fired the ignition and driven home, though she had little recollection of the journey. She pulled into the parking bay in front of the cottage and turned off the engine, allowing the sound of rain drumming on the roof to envelop her.

After a few moments she climbed out of the car and pulling her coat around her, stumbled down to the cove to lose herself in the roar of the breaking waves. She stood on the pebbles letting the rain pepper her face. The wind picked up her hood and flung it repeatedly at the back of her head. *What happened to your husband. Happened to your husband. Your husband.*

She closed her eyes and swallowed down the lump of panic in her throat. She mustn't get over agitated. She needed to take a slow, calm look at matters and not let her emotions fuel her fear. She must focus on the key questions. Had Ingrid Favell known Tim personally? If so, in what circumstances had she met him? Why had she made a specific point of denying any knowledge of what happened to him? Did it have anything to do with her urgent need to see the Gallimores? And finally, given her father's untimely death and acrimonious legacy, did it have any connection with Vivienne?

Esme picked her way across the stones towards the shoreline, wondering how to begin finding out any answers, particularly if Ingrid wouldn't speak to her. She stopped at the point where the pebble beach merged into the rock strata running from the beach and stared out to the horizon across grey swirling waters. *What happened to your husband. Your husband. Husband.*

A wave rushed up the shore, threatening to engulf Esme's ankles in icy water. She shrieked and staggered backwards, stumbling to catch her balance. With a sob born of anger and frustration, she turned and staggered back towards the cottage, cursing Ingrid Favell for picking at a wound she'd thought was healed.

*

A hot shower warmed her and allowed her to gain some perspective. She knew now what she had to do. There was only one way to deal with this and that was to hit it head on. Some part of her psyche had perhaps known that this day would come, when she would be forced to pick up the mantle of the dark corner of her past and this time, follow it through to its conclusion, however difficult that may be. Wasn't that what she and Ruth expected of Bea? *Truth doesn't always heal a wounded soul*, Maddy had said. Esme shuddered. Maybe not always. But she had to remain hopeful that this was occasion when it could.

She gave her damp hair one last rub of the towel, before running her fingers through it and giving it a shake. She bent down in front of the wood-burner and threw another log on the fire, watching the amber sparks fly and die as they hit the side of the stove. They gave a warm flickering glow to the semi-darkened room and offered her some succour. The wind outside would ensure a good draw of the fire tonight, unlike cold still evenings when the room would fill with smoke.

She took a deep breath and went back into the kitchen,

draping the wet towel over the rail of the Rayburn, before going upstairs. In the spare bedroom she knelt down on the floor and flicked up the old-fashioned counterpane to reveal the space under the bed where she'd hidden Tim's box of belongings. She slid out the box and, making her way carefully down the steep staircase, took it into the sitting room and put it down in front of the fire.

She knelt down beside it and opened the flap. Last time she'd convinced herself that a brief glance in his notebooks was sufficient to conclude that Tim had not uncovered anything connected with Gallimore's murder. This time she must look deeper.

Systematically, she unpacked the box's contents on to the floor in neat piles. Childhood mementos – swimming certificates, crayoned drawings, a tarnished school's league football medal, a photo album of his parents' and a threadbare teddy – were mixed in with bundles of photographs, newspaper cuttings of copy from the early days of his journalist career when his byline first appeared in print, business cards of contacts, bulging envelopes of scribbled memos. When the box was empty, she was amazed at what had been inside and not a little guilty that the contents were so unfamiliar.

She sat back on her heels and planned a strategy. This wasn't going to be a five-minute browse. How many years of journalistic detritus were here? Tim had been reasonably methodical and would have regular purges. She had to be confident that most of what lay before her he'd kept for good reason. She got to her feet and retreated to the kitchen for some sustenance. She had better be prepared for a long haul.

*

An hour later, she stood up to stretch her calf muscles and put another log on the fire. Barely a quarter of the bundles had yet given up their secrets. She went into the kitchen to recharge her glass. She looked longingly at the unopened bottle of wine on the worktop but decided that was a bad move. If she found something she may allow herself a celebratory tipple, or, perhaps more appropriately, a dram or two of comfort. She turned on the tap and filled her glass with water before returning to the task in hand.

She dragged the small table closer to one of the fireside armchairs and put her drink on it, gathering up a bundle of manilla envelopes and collapsing into the chair. Infinitely more comfortable than kneeling on the carpet. She chided herself with a wry grin. What was the point in having comfortable furniture and then shunning it in favour of the floor? She must be nuts.

She tipped out the contents on to her knee and began sifting through them. They seemed to be a disparate mix of oddities, with no obvious connection in date or subject. She glanced at each item – photos mainly – and then dropped them back into the envelope.

It was as her concentration was dwindling and she was considering crawling off to bed when she found the photograph. If it hadn't almost slipped from her fingers and jolted her back to attention, she may have missed it completely.

As she stared at it she noticed that something was attached to the back with a paper clip. She also realised that the building in the picture was familiar. She took it over to the table lamp for a closer look and felt a stab of shock as she recognised the building. Dunsford House.

She flipped it over to see what was clipped to the back. There was a small square head and shoulders photograph of a woman in Edwardian dress. Underneath was a small sheet of paper with something written on it. She unclipped it and looked, her mouth going dry as she recognised Tim's handwriting. But she had no idea what it said. It was in shorthand.

As she stared at Tim's scribbles, her eyes fell to another pencil note in Tim's handwriting, on the back of the photograph itself. This time, though, she could read it easily. *18th Sept. 3.30 Dr Donald Cole.*

30

The fire died and Esme found herself staring into the fading embers. She shivered. She had no idea how long she'd been sitting there. She glanced up at the clock. It was close to midnight. She should go and find her bed. Yet still she sat, examining the significance of her discovery. At least she now knew there was a connection with Ingrid Cole, as her name would have been then. But what else was there to know?

She picked up the photograph again and stared at it. There was no question it was Dunsford House. The name was printed clearly in neat white writing on the bottom. The date was 1887 – the year it was built, perhaps.

She turned it over and looked at the date Tim had scrawled on the back, her stomach lurching at the proximity of another date forever etched on her mind. It was exactly one month before Tim's death. And two months before Cole's suicide.

The photograph of the Edwardian woman looked vaguely familiar but she couldn't place her. Was she the owner of the hall, perhaps? If so, what was her connection with Cole? And what was Tim meeting Cole about?

The remaining small sheet of paper written in short-hand was no use to her at all. As she'd confessed to Max, she'd never mastered it. But Max would be able to translate it.

She didn't have the energy to deal with it now. It was time to rest her weary brain. She dropped the photograph on to the table and with one final glance, she climbed the steep stairs to her bedroom.

*

Unsurprisingly, the information and misinformation churning around in Esme's head resulted in a restless night. She awoke before it was light and tuned in her ear to the rhythmic ebb and flow of the sea, in an effort to soothe her fraught brain.

She'd showered, dressed and had breakfast but it was still too early to phone Max, especially on a Sunday. A walk on the headland could have passed the time purposefully but that was out of the question. With rain lashing at the windows and the wind whipping itself into a frenzy, she decided venturing out was unwise. Besides, she didn't need another soaking.

Instead she sat down and studied the scrap of paper with Tim's shorthand notes. It looked like a list. She scoffed. Ironic if it turned out to be a note of things he needed from the supermarket. Perhaps the list was hers. Maybe she'd called him and asked him to drop by to pick up a few things on the way home.

Unlikely. Why would he attach it to the photograph of Dunsford House? It had to be something to do with his meeting with Cole – either prompts for questions to ask, or notes about what Cole had told him. But told him about what? Gallimore? In connection with what? Dunsford House being an SOE training centre? She tried but failed to get out of her head that this was the house name wrongly given to the emergency services when Gallimore was murdered.

She scanned the list and emailed it to Max as an attachment. She couldn't face writing a long-worded explanation so she didn't mention the photograph, saying only that she'd come across the list when she'd been sorting through some old papers. Besides, she wanted to know what it said first before committing herself to telling him the latest developments.

As she pressed SEND, the questions began bombarding her again. Cole. Vivienne's benefactor. Would Bea recognise the name? Would it help if she did? The question was academic, given that without going behind Ruth's back, which she wasn't prepared to do at this stage, Bea was out of bounds. So who else might know more?

Jimmy Beer's name slipped into her head unbidden. Bea had said that it was Jimmy who was convinced something about the circumstances of Vivienne's death was covered up. But why? Was it merely as a result of being in denial, as Bea had suggested? Or did he have evidence? Perhaps no one had ever taken him seriously. Maybe that explained his hostility.

Esme switched off the computer and went into the kitchen for her coat and car keys. If she couldn't talk to Bea, she'd talk to Jimmy.

*

She pulled up in the yard of Crossways Farm and cut the engine. If only she could cut the speed of her heartbeat so readily. The barns around her seem to ooze menace, an image of Jimmy holding a shotgun aimed in her direction hidden behind every one. She told herself to stop prevaricating. Things imagined were always worse than they eventually turned out to be. She unclipped her seatbelt and climbed out of her car.

There was no answer from her knock on the back door of the farmhouse and she hesitated whether to walk in calling Jimmy's name or begin a search of the outbuildings. She decided to go inside.

After another sharp rap she held her breath, turned the knob and pushed open the door. The kitchen was empty. She exhaled noisily and wandered inside. Now what? Sit and wait? Run for the hills? She stepped over to the sink and peered out of the window. No sign of anyone outside. Perhaps Jimmy wasn't on the farm at all. Perhaps she'd wasted her time.

There was a sound behind her and she spun around to see Jimmy standing in the doorway. His hands hung empty at his side. No firearm this time.

She forced a smile. 'Hello, Jimmy,' she said, her voice slightly croaky. 'I need to talk to you about Vivienne.'

31

Jimmy scowled. 'I got nothing to say to you.' He looked around as if expecting to see someone else.

'Bea doesn't know I'm here,' Esme said. 'If that's who you're looking for.' Did Jimmy think she'd come because of something Bea had revealed? 'Look,' she added hastily. 'All Bea has told me is that you've always been convinced there was a cover up about what happened to Vivienne. Ruth thinks it would help Bea to understand –'

Jimmy snorted. He strode over to the Rayburn and turned his back on her.

Esme yearned to sit down. Her knees felt shaky. Had her decision to come to see him been the right one?

'You don't think knowing the truth would help?' she said.

Jimmy turned round to face her and rested his rump against the towel rail. 'And you reckon I know it, do you – the truth?' he said, folding his arms.

'You know more than I do.' She watched his unshaven face for signs he might be prepared to give it up. 'Is that more than Bea does?'

He glared at her. 'What truth I knows bain't what you're after. It bain't no happy ending.'

'That's no reason to keep it secret.'

He shrugged. 'You reckon? Best for Bea, though.'

She gripped the back of the chair in front of her. 'Who says you're allowed to decide what's best for Bea?'

Jimmy threw her a glare which would sear meat. ''Tis kinder that she thinks her sister died for king and country than turn her back on her family?'

Esme let the information sink in. 'She came back, didn't she?' It was a statement as much as a question.

A flick of a nod, his eyes fixed down at the floor. 'Her trusted me. Her knew I could keep a secret. And I have.' He lifted his head, proud to say the words.

'How come Bea never saw her?'

'Gone back to London by then. War was over.'

'But why didn't Vivienne want anyone to know she'd survived?'

'Her had her reasons.' His face was grey, his mouth turned down in an expression of bitterness and despair. Esme waited. Maybe that was all he was prepared to say – that Vivienne had asked for his loyalty and he'd given it.

He wiped his nose with the back of his hand. 'In a state, she was, when I saw her,' he said. 'Thin, scrawny-like. Her lovely thick hair...' he swallowed. 'It wore like rat's entrails. "Hell on earth, Jimmy," her said. "That's where I've been."'

'What did she mean?'

Jimmy shook his head. 'Her wouldn't say. Didn't have the words, she told me. Reckon the place they locked her up was the sort you wouldn't put a dog in.'

'A prison camp?' Esme said. She recalled Joe Paxton talking about a female agent being taken by the Gestapo the day he'd arrived in France.

'Reckon. But her escaped, didn't her? Made her way back here to see me.'

'Why didn't she get in touch with her family?'

Jimmy straightened up. 'Like I said, her had her reasons. And her had unfinished business.'

'What sort of unfinished business?'

He hesitated. For a moment Esme thought he wasn't going to say any more. He sniffed and raised his chin. 'Betrayed, she was.' He wagged a finger in the air. 'And she woren't going to let him get away with it.'

'Betrayed? By who?'

'By him as was supposed to look out for her. Her commanding officer.'

'Gerald Gallimore?' said Esme. 'He betrayed her?'

'You know what her said?' He leaned towards her, spittle forming on his lips. '"I thought I'd left the Devil behind me, Jimmy. But seems I was wrong."'

'What did she mean?'

'They were in it together.' Jimmy spat on the floor. 'Bastard.'

'They?'

Jimmy clenched his fist. 'Standing as close together as I am to you now, like butter wouldn't melt. That's what her said. Her knew him the minute her clapped eyes on him.' He peered at Esme. 'I never wanted her to go but she wore adamant.'

'Go where?'

Jimmy frowned at her as though she was a child asking a stupid question. 'To challenge him, of course.'

'Challenge Gallimore? About what she'd seen?'

'I wore worried for her, see. And I wore right, weren't I?'

'Why?' Esme felt a jab of fear. 'What happened?'

Jimmy shook his head and stumbled across the kitchen.

'Jimmy?' she said, taking a step towards him. 'What happened to Vivienne?'

He pushed past her and out into the yard, the rattle of the slammed back door reverberating around the empty room.

Esme allowed the unanswered questions to form neat rows in her head. Who did she mean by *the Devil*? Gallimore? Or the other man she'd seen with him? Who was it – Cole? But he was Vivienne's benefactor – why would he betray her? And what had she meant by betrayal, anyway?

Esme shook her head. She didn't understand. She needed more. She followed Jimmy outside.

Sounds echoing across the farmyard suggested Jimmy was in the barn at the far end. She made her way across the yard and peered in over the half open stable door. She blinked to allow her eyes to adjust to the gloom, almost crying out as Jimmy brought down a long-handled axe on to a block on the floor, smashing a log in two. He picked up the split pieces and threw them unceremoniously on to a pile in the corner of the stall. Whatever Bea's assessment of Jimmy's mental state, there was no doubt to fitness, despite his age. Old farmers never die, the old saying went, they go out to pasture. Clearly this one hadn't. Not yet anyway.

Esme rested her arms on the lower half of the stable door. 'Jimmy?'

He looked up and glowered at her. 'You still here?'

'Just one more thing. That man Vivienne saw with Gallimore?'

He grunted and took another large log, setting it down on the chopping base in front of him.

Esme pressed on. 'What was his name?'

'Dunno.' Another smash with the axe.

'Was it Donald Cole?'

'No.'

'You know who I mean, though? Bea must have told you. He left everything in his will to Vivienne. She never mentioned him?'

'No.'

'Does Dunsford House mean anything to you?'

He seemed to falter as the axe came down. For a second she thought he was going to miss. 'Never heard of it,' he said, hurling the split logs aside.

'Are you sure she knew the person with Gallimore?'

He stopped to glare at her. 'You calling me a liar?'

'No, of course not.'

Jimmy shook his head. 'Not a face she'd forget, I'd reckon. Not after what he'd done.' He dragged the back of his hand across his eyes and glared at her. 'I dunno what you think you're doing,' he said. 'It's too late. He can't hurt her now. He's long gone. Won't help Bea, neither, digging it all up.'

'It might. Perhaps it's better to know the truth and come to terms with it, than never knowing.'

'Bea dun't need to hear what her sister suffered. And I bain't about to tell her, neither. So you better not be thinking of it or I'll –'

'I understand you'd want to protect Bea, Jimmy. But isn't it right that we try and find out what happened?'

He scowled and grabbed another log from the pile.

'What did Gallimore say when Vivienne challenged him?'

'How would I know?' Jimmy lifted the axe and let it fall again. The log bounced into two and rolled on to the straw covered floor. He rested the chopper on the base and stared at her, his eyes glinting out from his grubby face. 'Her never come back.'

32

Jimmy's information whirled around Esme's head as she drove back to the cottage. She'd expected more resistance from him about what he knew and had been surprised after his initial reluctance to talk to her that he'd told her what he had. But something deep down made her suspicious that it had been too easy and that he'd been selective about what he'd shared. Had he set her up, fed her with his own version of events? Had the story been growing in his head since that last day he'd seen Vivienne?

But at least he had shared something useful, in that she now knew for certain that Vivienne had survived the war and returned to England. The question was, should she tell Bea? Or did Bea already know? Was that why she was so nervous about Vivienne's past being investigated? And if so, was she party to what Jimmy meant by Vivienne having "her reasons" for not getting in touch with her family?

While she understood Jimmy's desire to protect Bea from the horrors her sister endured, it was still perfectly possible to avoid the details of what sounded like her incarceration in a prison camp. The most important fact in everything, surely, was that Vivienne was alive. In 1946, anyway. What happened to her after that remained a mystery. One not too late to solve, Esme hoped.

She bumped down the track to the cottage and parked up outside, before climbing out of the car and wandering over towards the sea. She stood on the grass above the cove and stared out across the beach. Weak sunshine spilled from a line of cloud above the horizon, making the water appear like silver mercury running in amongst fingers of black rocks.

Had Jimmy really not known Cole? Could Cole have been the man Vivienne had seen with Gallimore? But if it was Cole, Vivienne must have been mistaken to refer to him with such hostility, given he would become her benefactor years later. And what had happened when Vivienne had confronted Gallimore, an assignment from which she'd never returned? Had she already suspected Gallimore of betrayal before she'd come home? Had he been a collaborator in France? Had he been the cause of her arrest and imprisonment? If Gallimore's murder had been in 1946 rather than 1981, Esme might have suspected Vivienne as the perpetrator.

She recalled Jimmy's reaction to her question about Dunsford House. Did he really flinch or did she imagine it? If he knew the name and was trying to hide it, why? What did he know about it? Had Vivienne told him she'd trained there? So what if she had – what reason could he have for pretending he knew nothing about it?

Her mind drifted to the photograph of the building she'd found and to Tim's scribbled note on the back. Perhaps she should see what else she could find out about Dunsford House. Maybe she was missing something.

She turned away from the shore and walked back to the cottage, heading straight for the sitting room where she'd left her laptop. As it booted, she picked up the photo again and studied it. What was Tim investigating, she asked herself for the thousandth time? Why hadn't she known about it? Why hadn't she come across the photograph before? Perhaps she had but with her mind in turmoil she'd packed it away without registering it, along with everything else to do with Tim's journalistic life. When a career proves to be the cause of an untimely death, the instinct is to have nothing more to do with it. It was no surprise, therefore, that the fact of facing it again was so terrifying. But now she'd begun, she had to see it through.

A few moments on the Internet and she'd established a few new facts about Dunsford House. It had been built as a mental hospital in the late nineteenth century by a philanthropist called William Dunsford, whose wife had campaigned for a more understanding treatment of the mentally ill. She guessed the photograph of the woman must have been Dunsford's wife. It had reverted to being a mental institution again after the Second World War, presumably after the MOD no longer required it to train their SOE agents.

She sat back and considered the new information but she could see nothing which threw any further light on the unanswered questions thrown up by her visit to Jimmy.

Her phone rang and she reached over to pick it up, her eyes still on her laptop screen.

'Esme Quentin.'

'It's Ingrid Favell,' said a hushed voice. 'I'm sorry. I was very rude when you came. You wanted to talk to me. Do you want to meet?'

33

Esme arranged to meet Ingrid Favell, nee Cole, on her break at the charity office where Ingrid was a part-time volunteer. The office was one of several similar units in a bland, box of a building beside the Exeter canal, at the back of the industrial estate.

Esme'd hoped that Ingrid would be wearing the distinctive green coat she'd worn before, verifying her identity as the woman at Dunsford House and outside the Gallimores' home. But instead she was dressed in baggy jeans and a shapeless red fleece, emblazoned with the charity's logo. Her short grey hair was cut in no discernible style and her long, broad nose seemed to drag her cheeks downward, as though it was too heavy for her face, giving her a melancholic expression.

Ingrid pulled out a packet of cigarettes from her fleece pocket and took one out. She lit up and took a long drag. 'This better not take long,' she said. 'I've only got ten minutes.' She seemed nervous, and Esme wondered if she was regretting her decision to make contact. 'So, what do you want?' she added, flicking ash on to the floor.

Esme hesitated. Her priority from the moment Ingrid had telephoned was to discover what Ingrid had meant by her pronouncement about Tim. Now that the time had come, she found herself shying away.

'I thought perhaps you wanted something too,' Esme said. 'Given that you got in touch.'

Ingrid shrugged. 'I want to find out why you came knocking on my door. That's what I want.'

'Then why not talk to me when I called at your house?'

A shadow flickered across her eyes. 'I couldn't.'

'Because you were worried I was going to ask something you didn't want someone else to overhear, perhaps? Your husband, maybe?'

Ingrid glanced at her watch. 'Look, can we get to the point?'

Esme lifted a hand. 'OK, OK. I did contact you first, I suppose.' She cleared her throat. 'As I said in my letter, I'm doing some research on behalf of a client. I'm hoping you may be able to help me.' The side door opened and two young women came out, giggling. They glanced at Ingrid and exchanged glances before hurrying away, arm in arm. Ingrid ignored them. Esme waited until they'd disappeared around the side of the building before continuing. 'The thing is, it's a bit delicate. I wouldn't normally…'

'Delicate? How?'

'It concerns Vivienne Lancaster. Your father remembered her in his will.'

Ingrid glowered at her. 'And that's your client?' she said, her voice mocking. 'Vivienne Lancaster? My father's tart?'

'What?' Esme blinked. 'No. Vivienne isn't my client.'

'So who, then?'

'Hang on. You're telling me that your father and Vivienne had an affair?'

Ingrid snorted. 'Pretty obvious, wouldn't you say? Why else would he leave all his money to her instead of his wife and daughter?' She slumped her back against the building and took another drag. 'So why do you need to know about her? Because I can tell you now, I know nothing, other than she ruined my parents' marriage.'

'Her family is trying to find out what happened to her. You must know that the probate researchers came looking for her and never found her because, as far as the family knew at that time, she died during the war. Perhaps you know different?'

'No, I don't. And I don't care much, either.' Ingrid threw

down her stub end and crushed it under her shoe. 'So, if that's all, it seems you've had a wasted journey and I ought to get back inside.' She straightened up.

'So if it's not Vivienne Lancaster you're interested in, who is it?' Esme said.

Ingrid threw her a sharp look. 'Sorry?'

'You were hoping for something else from me, weren't you? You thought I might know something useful to you.'

'I don't know what...?'

'Why were you trying to see Faye Gallimore?'

'What?'

'Well, I had a go myself, so I know how difficult it can be. She wouldn't talk to me either, by the way.'

Ingrid narrowed her eyes. 'Why would you want to talk to her?'

'Faye's husband worked with Vivienne during the war. I went to ask her if she could throw any light on to Vivienne's whereabouts in the years afterwards. But I didn't get the chance. She obviously didn't want me there. Then Lloyd Gallimore came in and accused me of being "that Cole woman". I was shown the door.'

Esme waited while Ingrid processed the information. After a few moments, Ingrid folded her arms with a half-laugh. 'Congratulations. At least you got inside. I never got across the bloody threshold.'

'So what's your reason for wanting to see them? What are they hiding? D'you know?'

Ingrid threw an anxious glance across her shoulder. 'I can't talk now.'

'You must have a lunch break?'

Ingrid chewed her lip and stared at the floor while Esme waited for her answer. If Ingrid couldn't speak to her husband about whatever it was which forced her into stalking someone outside their house, the chance to share it with a person in a similar position must surely be too tempting to turn down.

'I finish here at one,' Ingrid said, eventually, turning towards the glazed door. 'I'll see you at the Double Locks, the pub further down the canal, at a quarter past.'

'Thanks,' said Esme.

Ingrid hesitated, looking back at Esme, as though she was about to add something. But instead she merely nodded before pulling open the door and disappearing inside.

Esme watched her go, hoping she wouldn't have changed her mind by one o'clock. If she didn't show, the opportunity to find out what Ingrid knew about Tim may have just evaporated.

34

They opted for a picnic table on the canal-side terrace outside, as Ingrid wanted to smoke. Esme was glad she was wearing a thick coat. The air was damp, cloud hovering over the water and reducing visibility to the opposite bank. The ghostly outline of a cyclist travelled down the tow path, as though floating several inches above the ground.

'Have you ever had that feeling,' said Ingrid, as Esme arrived with their drinks, 'that everything you'd ever known was made of sand and if you dare give it a prod, it would disintegrate?'

Esme thought back to the moment she stumbled upon her sister's secrets. 'I'm sure it happens more than we know. Most people don't say.'

'Or don't prod,' said Ingrid, reaching for her cigarette packet from a bottle green snakeskin handbag.

'And you did?'

'I didn't get the choice. Vivienne Lancaster had already reduced my certainties to dust.' She lit her cigarette and dropped her lighter back into her bag.

'You seem very certain about her.'

'I had some inkling of it a few years before Papa died.' Esme detected a hint of accent in Ingrid's use of the familial term and was reminded of Cole's German heritage. 'He and my mother had an almighty row about something. I wasn't party to what. By the time I arrived they'd reached the stage of hurled accusations. I heard my mother say he carried a burden of guilt, that he'd betrayed everything he stood for.'

'Meaning the affair.'

'Obviously. Of course, at the time I didn't know that, especially as he talked about doing it for her.'

'What could he have meant by that?'

'I don't know. Perhaps I didn't hear it right. It was after he died that it all came out, of course. Mother was devastated. It all but destroyed her. Our solicitor advised challenging the will, but she was too proud. She didn't want the world to know. Well, why would you want the grubby little goings on your husband had got up to announced in public? She wouldn't do it.'

'Pity she didn't. Vivienne wasn't tracked down so I guess the estate languished somewhere before being absorbed into the treasury. Isn't that what normally happens if the beneficiary isn't found?'

'How do you know she wasn't found?'

'Not according to the agent who looked for her, anyway.'

'Doesn't mean she's not still out there.'

'No, it doesn't,' Esme said, thinking of everything Jimmy had told her. 'So where does Faye Gallimore fit in? Do you know her?'

'No, but Papa did. And she came to see him, shortly before he died. I wanted to know why. But, as you know, she wouldn't see me.'

'You think her visit was linked to his death?'

'Why he killed himself, you mean? You don't have to tread on eggshells, you know.' Ingrid blew cigarette smoke into the air and shrugged. 'Who knows? And if she won't speak to me, I'm never likely to find out, now.'

'But it's still important to you that you do find out?'

Ingrid transferred the cigarette to her left hand and rested her right elbow on the table. 'My husband says if I don't let it go, that it will *consume* me.' She spoke the word theatrically, drawing it out, as though she was trying to ridicule its meaning.

'If you fail to find any answers?'

'Whether I fail or succeed, he believes the outcome will

be the same, that in the end it will destroy me.'

'What do you think?'

'Perhaps it would be easier not to bother, to pretend I didn't care.' Ingrid took one last drag of her cigarette before stubbing it out on the upturned terracotta pot in the middle of the table. 'But when you discover someone's lied, you begin to wonder what else they lied about don't you? And it's too late by then. It's already taken hold of you – you have to know.'

'And you think Faye holds the key to finding out.'

Ingrid nodded.

'How did your father know her?'

'Through Gerald Gallimore.' Esme's stomach flipped at hearing the name. 'He helped my parents with the bureaucracy side of my adoption after the war.'

'You were adopted?'

'Yes. And before you put two and two together and make five, I'm not my father's love child with Vivienne Lancaster. My real mother was called Jean Barber and she died of typhoid in 1943, shortly after I was born. My father's family – my adoptive father, that is – looked after me until I was four years old, when I came over to England.'

'From Germany? I understand your adoptive father was German.'

'Yes, he escaped when he saw the writing on the wall.'

'Just before war broke out, according to his obituary.'

Ingrid nodded. 'The rise of the Nazis terrified him. Fortunately, with his medical know-how, he had plenty to offer this country.'

'His work with penicillin.'

'He was one of the early pioneers. It was from work done by the team that he was part of, that the Americans were able to develop a way of producing penicillin in enough quantity to save the lives, firstly of soldiers in the field, and then in the civilian population.'

Esme recalled reading how Cole had been well respected by his medical colleagues. 'You're clearly very proud of him.'

'As a doctor, yes, I was. Which is why his affair –' She shook her head.

Esme dwelt on the poignant irony of Ingrid's mother dying from a disease which not only would be curable a few short years later, but that it would be her daughter's adoptive father who had made it possible.

'Do you know anything about your real father?' asked Esme.

Ingrid gave Esme a pitying look. 'What do you think?'

'I'm guessing not.'

'It was hardly a problem for me,' said Ingrid, resting her forearms on the table. 'So many fathers were absent, away at war, their children sent to the countryside to avoid the city bombings. Had I been older, I might have made up something. But I was only interested in keeping warm and having enough to eat.'

'I guess life was hard in Germany during the war.'

Ingrid gave a humourless laugh. 'You have no idea. The bitter cold, living in a wooden hut, the sound of rats in the cellar. Everything we had was slowly given away in exchange for food, even my toys. And furniture, too, if it wasn't chopped up for firewood. The piano for a bag of potatoes.' She hugged herself and looked out across the canal. 'Sometimes trains came and people would throw food from the windows. Word would go round that one was on its way. Everyone would rush to the tracks and grab what they could – apples, maybe. Or coal. One time we took home a bag of rusks, so I'm told, and the Gestapo got wind of what was going on. They came and searched the huts. My grandmother hid them under the floor and they never found them.'

'And if they had?' Esme asked.

Ingrid's face darkened. 'She'd have been shot.'

The noisy jibes of two men arriving at the next table seemed to disturb Ingrid. She grabbed the handles of her bag and pulled it towards her. 'I should go.' Had she said more than she'd intended? Or more than she thought she should.

157

'What will you do about Faye?' Esme said.

Ingrid shook her head. 'I'm not sure. Perhaps my husband's right. Would it change anything? Knowing, I mean?'

Esme thought of Bea, and what Ruth had said about closure. About her own situation. 'Perhaps that answer's different for each one of us.'

'And you?' said Ingrid, looking at Esme intently.

'Me? This is what I do. It's my job.'

'But if you had my problem. I sense you'd want to keep searching.'

Esme held her gaze. 'It has been said before. Which is why I need to ask you something.'

Ingrid stared back. She seemed nervous, suddenly. 'What?'

Esme swallowed. 'You haven't given me an explanation for what you said about my husband.'

A shadow crossed Ingrid's face. 'I was telling the truth when I said I don't know anything about what happened to him.'

'But why say it? In fact, why mention him at all?'

Ingrid looked uncomfortable. 'It was your letter. I recognised the name.'

'You knew Tim?'

The shake of her head was barely more than a twitch. 'Never met him.'

'Not even the day he came to see your father in September 1990?'

Colour drained from her face. She sat rigid on the bench. Her mouth opened but no words came out.

'I found the appointment scribbled on the back of a photograph of Dunsford House,' Esme said, watching Ingrid closely. 'Did his visit have something to do with why you were there the other day?'

Ingrid stood up again and clambered off the bench. 'I really have to go. I can't help you.'

'It *was* you, wasn't it? I tried to talk to you but you disappeared.'

Ingrid glanced at the men on the next table before thrusting her face close to Esme's. Her voice was low and clipped. 'You made out you had something which could help me,' she said, her jaw clenched. 'But you had nothing and all you've done is waste my time. Now leave me alone.'

And she turned and marched away, leaving Esme wondering what she'd said to earn such a reaction.

35

Esme sank back into the cavernous armchair in Maddy's sitting room and allowed two of Maddy's cats to climb over her. She'd called in to Maddy's house in Bideford to relate the events of her Exeter visit.

'So what's your best guess?' Maddy asked. 'Guilty of something? Or just embarrassed at spilling out everything she had bottled up inside for years?'

'Could be either or both,' Esme said, wriggling into a more comfortable position and guiding the youngest of the cats away from her face so his fur didn't go up her nose. 'I don't think she knows what she wants. I felt a bit bad that I'd not been more help.'

'How could you when you don't know what she's looking for? If she'd have been more forthcoming –'

'I think she'd argue she was more than forthcoming and got nothing in return.'

Maddy sat on the arm of the opposite chair. 'Sounds to me like the both of you were banging your heads against brick walls.'

'Well at least we found out why Cole left Vivienne his money.'

'Doesn't move us on much, though, does it? Will you speak to Ruth?'

Esme gathered up the tabby kitten in her arms and held it to her.

'Esme? I said, are you going to tell Ruth?'

'I know. I heard.' She put the cat back down on her lap and

stroked the delicate velvety fur between its ears. 'I went to see Jimmy the other day to ask him about Vivienne.'

'You what? After what happened last time? Are you mad?'

Esme shook her head. 'It was fine. He didn't know me last time. No shotgun this time around.'

Maddy rolled her eyes. 'Well, hallelujah for that.' She came over and sat down on the footstool next to Esme's chair. 'So,' she said, cocking her head to one side. 'What did he say?'

'Not a huge amount more than Bea already told me, to be fair. He embellished his conspiracy theory with a few unsavoury facts about what Vivienne suffered while serving overseas which, perhaps understandably, he said he didn't want to distress Bea about.'

Maddy's eyes narrowed. 'And he knew about this, because?'

Esme gave her a weak smile. 'You've joined the dots, I see. Yes. Vivienne came back to see him.'

Maddy raised an eyebrow. 'So we were right. What happened then?'

'Then, she promptly disappeared,' Esme said, 'after she went to confront Gallimore about something.'

Maddy exhaled noisily. 'Bloody hell.' Voices from the footpath outside of two people chatting as they walked past Maddy's house filtered into the room. 'Confront Gallimore about what?' Maddy said as the voices faded. Esme relayed Vivienne's accusation as Maddy listened, her face troubled.

Esme stood up, returning the kitten to the seat of the chair and wandered over to the window. 'So,' she said, gazing out at the church tower opposite which loomed upwards into the sky. 'What do I do now? Jimmy's keen that Bea doesn't hear anything to distress her.'

'I'll bet. Including that he lied to her by never letting on that he'd seen Vivienne after the war had ended.'

Esme watched a puppy bounding around on the grass bank in front of the church. 'It would be easy enough to put Bea in the picture, but perhaps the best thing would be to encourage

Jimmy to confess that bit to Bea himself.'

'Is he likely to do that?'

'He might. Now that he's told me. He doesn't have to reveal all the nasty details.'

'And will you prepare the ground? Suggest to Bea that Jimmy knows more than he's said?'

Esme folded her arms and sighed. 'I don't know. The thing is, even if I did tell Bea, I'm no wiser as to what happened to Vivienne after she saw Jimmy. The Gallimore connection still looms large.' She shuddered. Why did Ingrid have to go and say what she had? It would be so much easier if there weren't complications.

Maddy came and stood next to her. 'You're thinking about Tim and where he fits in?'

Esme nodded.

'What about the list you found? Have you heard back from Max?'

'Not yet.'

'Well, when you do, it might prove the breakthrough. Better still, prove he wasn't involved at all and it's a complete coincidence.'

Esme sighed. 'I admit it does seem unlikely that the two things are connected. Tim had been digging around potential dodgy international trade deals, despite Max's wild idea that it was Gallimore's murder he was looking into.'

'What sort of dodgy international trade deals?'

'Drugs. Prescription, though, rather than Class A.'

'Not drugs as in penicillin, then?'

Esme's head shot round and she stared at Maddy. 'You think that could be the link to Cole? I'd never thought of that.'

'Well you wouldn't. We've only just found out about Cole and his association with penicillin. So, d'you think it's possible Tim was on to something in that line?'

'Who knows? I never did find out the details. There were inter-government trade talks going on at the time, you see.

162

So no one was interested in poking a stick in and stirring. All I ever got when I tried to find out afterwards were doors slammed in my face.'

'So you weren't researching for him on this one before he was killed?'

Esme shook her head. 'No. By the time he'd found out whatever it was, I wasn't there. I'd gone away for a few days on some fact finding mission up north. Came back to an empty flat and a note saying he was meeting a contact.'

'So what happened? Did you guess something was wrong – is that when you went after him?'

Esme felt a chill grip her. She clamped her jaw tightly shut and took a deep breath in through her nose. 'I haven't talked about it in a long time,' she said.

Maddy held up her hand. 'Hey, look, pretend I never said anything. You don't have to tell me if you don't want to Let's forget all about it for a while, eh? At least until Max gets back to you.' She squeezed Esme's arm. 'Though, if ever you do want to talk. I'm here. Anytime. But it doesn't need to be now.'

Esme took a deep breath. 'Then again, perhaps it does.' Maybe fate was trying to tell her the time had come. Max may have started it by turning up out of the blue, asking about Tim's notes, and Ingrid had played her part by blowing a hole in her defences with her shocking statement. But who was it who'd emptied Tim's box and discovered the photograph of Dunsford House with the date scribbled on it? Clearly, part of her needed to address it, whether the other half of her wanted to or not.

'*Truth doesn't always heal a wounded soul*, you said the other day.'

Maddy threw her head back. 'Oh God, did I? Trying to be too bloody clever for my own good, that's my problem. Look, it's only a point of view. One to take, perhaps, if you want out.'

Esme turned away. 'Not one Tim would have adhered to.' She thought of Bea and her wanting to avoid talking about

Vivienne. But it didn't solve the problem. It didn't shine light on the dark places. 'Besides,' she added after a while. 'If it turns out he is connected, I don't have much of a choice, do I?'

'You don't know he is yet, though.'

Esme hugged herself. 'No. But maybe it doesn't matter one way or the other. Perhaps I'd take the pressure off myself if I accepted the possibility.' She rubbed her hand across her eyes. 'What should I do, Maddy?'

'Not like you to be indecisive.'

'No. That's what's so scary.' Esme looked round at Maddy, perched on the arm of the sofa. 'Can we go for a walk? I think I need some air.'

36

They headed down past the church and towards the river. There was a large ship moored up against the quay wall, cordoned off while aggregate was loaded into its hold from a lorry. They walked around the end of the cordon and along the quay, the new Bideford bridge ahead of them straddling the estuary in the distance.

'You were right about me sensing there was something wrong,' Esme said. 'I wouldn't have gone looking for him, otherwise.'

'What made you think there was a problem?'

'I'd arrived home to find a note from Tim saying he'd gone out to meet someone. Then the phone rang and the bloke I assumed Tim was meeting was on the other end asking to speak to him. And no, he hadn't arranged to see him and was nowhere near the pub. What was I talking about.'

'He was set up?'

'Looked that way, yes. Maybe they followed him, established where his local was, saw him meet people there – I don't know.'

'So when you realised this guy hadn't arranged the meeting, you high tailed it to the pub.'

Esme nodded. 'Only to find no sign of Tim. Landlord said he wasn't far away. That he'd gone off out the back in a hurry. There was a pint stood up on the bar.' She paused to clamp down on a renewed sense of alarm which had prompted her actions all those years ago. 'I went out the back. Asked a young kid coming out of the Gents if there was anyone in there. No.

Carried on past the Ladies and into the back yard. There was a gate out to an alleyway. It was half open. I looked out. Nothing. But the alley ran down behind some old buildings. I don't know why but it was as though I could see something beyond, even though there was no one there. I couldn't go back inside without checking. There were trees in the garden on the opposite side with overhanging branches, making it dark and shadowy. I was about to head down towards the corner, when I heard voices in the direction of the road. It sounded like an argument. I turned that way instead.'

She paused. There was little point in saying it again. It didn't change anything. She'd managed to prevent herself from making that small, toxic phrase into a mantra of self-deprecation these past few years. Like a recovering alcoholic, she mustn't falter or she may not be able to stop. She moistened her dry lips, swallowed and continued. 'I crept towards the voices, my back against the fence and peered out of the entrance to the alleyway. A young couple was having a slanging match on the pavement. They didn't even notice me. I retreated back into the alley and retraced my steps.' In her mind she was hurrying again, consumed by panic that she'd made the wrong call. She reached the critical place in the alley, maybe two yards from the end, where it happened. 'He came at me round the corner,' she continued. 'Slim, he was. Not very tall. Hooded, of course. I couldn't see his face. I didn't have anywhere to run.' She'd shrank back against the fence, hardly feeling him go past. Maybe a breath of moving air as he went by.

'And Tim?' Maddy said.

'Found him slumped on the ground. I ran back to the pub for help, apparently, though I don't remember. I didn't feel the slash to my face, either. Someone else noticed I was bleeding.'

They walked in silence until Maddy spoke. 'No one saw the attacker?'

'No. Vanished. Nobody noticed anyone suspicious in the pub. No one who looked handy with a stiletto, anyway.'

They paused at the railings beyond the shallow steps where the rowing club accessed the river. Esme rested on the top rail and stared across the water to the tall buildings of Ethelwynne Brown Close on the opposite bank.

'So what did the police say?'

'They seemed to think it was a random attack. Next thing I heard, they were looking for a gang. There'd been a disturbance in the next street. Somehow the two incidents got morphed into one.'

'Did you say anything?'

'I tried but it was like pushing at a locked door. I suppose they put it down to a widow in denial or something.' She pushed away from the rail, feeling drained. But at the same time, relieved.

Maddy put her arm round Esme's shoulders. 'Thanks for telling me. I know it wasn't easy.'

Esme shook her head. 'No, you were right. Tim is tied into this. We don't know how, but he is. I have to accept that.' She took a deep breath. 'Which means that this isn't just about Bea and Ruth any longer. It affects me too.'

'Of course it does. It also means you have to talk to them. Let them know you have a stake in this.'

Esme nodded. 'I intend to.'

'You might be surprised, too.'

'By what?'

'By what Bea can tell you.' Maddy's face was grim. 'I keep remembering what you said that time that Bea went AWOL.'

'What did I say?'

'That you thought there was more to it than simply the painful subject of Bea losing her sister.'

Esme thought back to the half-truths Bea had already told to deflect attention – that Crossways Farm had been sold and implying that she saw little of Jimmy when Pete confirmed she was a regular visitor. What other secrets did she keep?

37

Esme was awake before first light. Early morning was the best time to call on Bea. Having never thrown off the routine of the farming day, Bea would be up and about at a time when no one else was likely to call to disturb them.

She forced herself to eat a light breakfast while considering how best to approach the subject to cause Bea as little distress as possible – if that wasn't asking too much. The visit would be uncomfortable, there was no avoiding it, but the stakes were too high now. She had to press on. She had to know.

When she was ready to leave, she picked up the photograph of Dunsford House and tucked it inside her coat. Slipping on her gloves against the chill of the early hour, she closed the door behind her and set off to walk to Bea's bungalow.

The sky was shot through with streaks of candy pink and the air held a freshness which belied nature's warning of forthcoming rain. Esme climbed up on to the headland and followed the coastal path as far as Warren's Quay before diverting across the fields towards Ravens Farm. At the point where the hedge met a bend in the lane, she scrambled over the gate and walked along the rutted, metalled road until she came to the entrance to Bea's bungalow.

From the side path which led to the back door, she saw Bea's face through the window. Having rehearsed every possible way of approaching the subject, these fell away to nothing when Bea answered the door.

'Hello, Esme. You took your time.'

'My time?'

Bea gave her a rueful smile. 'You forget, dear. I've known you a long time. I knew you'd come eventually.'

Esme gave her a sad smile. 'Did you? I'm not sure I would have. Until a couple of days ago I might have let it go. But I can't, I'm afraid. Not now.'

Bea frowned. 'I don't understand.'

'Perhaps you don't. But that's why I'm here. To tell you why we're both caught up in this together.'

Bea stared for a moment before pulling open the door. 'You'd better come in and explain yourself.'

Esme stepped inside. The kitchen table was covered in pieces of fabric and a sewing machine stood on one end Bea swept the fabric to one side and gestured for Esme to sit down.

'So,' Esme said, pulling off her gloves. 'If you were expecting me, I assume you have your speech ready?'

'Not exactly.' Bea sat down and laid her hands palms downward on the table. 'Though, I suppose I should give you a ticking off about poking your nose in where it isn't wanted.'

Esme gave a half-laugh. 'Like the old days and your fears for Ruth.' She unbuttoned her coat and sat down.

'Ruth was never adventurous. You know that. Yet when you were here she would push herself further than she'd ever do herself. In one way, it did her good. You, on the other hand, didn't always know when to stop.'

'I never forced her to do anything.'

'Perhaps. But the desire to follow in your wake was sometimes stronger than her ability to cope with where that took her.'

'You make me sound like the school bully.'

Bea shook her head and smiled. 'No. Ruth had to learn to be who she was. She had to make mistakes along the way. As we all do.'

Esme watched Bea's face. 'Mistakes?'

Bea sat back in her chair. 'Caught up in this together, you said. What do you mean by that?'

Esme took the photograph from inside her coat and put it on the table. 'I came across this. The time and date scribbled on the back is an appointment to see a Dr Cole. The same Dr Cole who left his fortune to your sister.'

Bea leaned over and peered at the photograph, holding it out and tilting her head to focus on it through her glasses. 'Am I supposed to know where this is?'

'Well, do you?'

Bea pointed to the caption at the bottom of the photograph. 'Dunsford House, it says here, as I'm sure you've seen yourself. So what's its significance?'

'All I know for certain at the moment is that it was a training base for Special Operation Executives. It's possible Vivienne was an SOE and may have trained there.' Esme paused. When Bea didn't question her analysis, Esme took that as confirmation that she already knew Vivienne's wartime role. So why hadn't she admitted it at the outset?

Bea shrugged. 'Is that it?' She laid down the photograph and shoved it towards Esme. 'I don't see why you think I should know something.'

Esme turned over the photograph and pointed to the name scribbled on the back. 'Donald Cole. *Doctor* Donald Cole. I believe Vivienne and he were lovers –'

'What?'

'It was Cole who left her all his money. I've spoken to his daughter. She knew nothing about Vivienne until her father's death.'

Bea sat in silence for a few moments, then she got up and went over to the window. She stood with her back to Esme, staring out over the boundary hedge which ran down the lane. A tractor drove past, its trailer banging along behind as it bounced in and out of the potholes.

'There's something you should know, Bea,' Esme said, when the noise had faded. 'That scribbled note on the photograph. It's in Tim's handwriting.'

Bea turned round. 'Tim's?'

Esme nodded.

Bea came across the kitchen and grasped the back of the chair opposite Esme. 'But how was Tim involved?'

'I don't know. The only connection I know about is that Tim looked into the murder of Vivienne's commanding officer, Gerald Gallimore.'

'Tim did?'

Bea's comment threw Esme for a moment. She would have expected Bea to have picked up on the word *murder* not Tim's involvement. She pressed on. 'Not seriously, though.' Esme swallowed and looked down at her hands. 'At least, I didn't think so. Neither did his work colleague at the time, Max Rainsford. But for some reason, Max thought Tim might have looked into it a good deal more than we thought And the evidence so far suggests he was right.' She looked up at Bea. 'Not only that, it seems to be inextricably tied in with Vivienne. The links are too strong. Where does Vivienne fit in? I need to know what you know, Bea.'

Bea's face looked grey under the fluorescent light of the kitchen.

When she said nothing, Esme continued. 'I went to see Jimmy.'

'Jimmy?' Bea recoiled. Esme could see fear in her eyes. 'Did he talk to you? What did he say?'

Esme side-stepped the question. 'You wanted me to believe you'd not seen much of Jimmy over the years. Why would you do that, if you'd nothing to hide?'

Bea lowered herself back into the chair, her gaze focused on nothing in particular.

Esme reached out across the table. 'Help me, Bea. You see, now, don't you, what I meant about us both being caught up in this together? I need to know what Tim uncovered and if –' The words caught in her throat.

Bea's head snapped up and she stared wide-eyed at Esme. 'If it's tied in with why he died.'

Esme squeezed her eyes shut and bowed her head. When she opened them again, Bea was still staring at her.

'You think that if you find out who killed Gallimore,' Bea whispered, 'you'll know the truth about your husband's death too, don't you?'

Esme clamped her jaw tight and nodded.

Bea stared at the table and spoke quietly, her voice barely audible. 'I know who killed Gallimore, Esme. And I desperately wish I didn't. Because, God help me, it means that had I spoken out –'

'Who?' Esme didn't want to hear Bea's regret. It might break her. 'Who killed Gallimore?'

Bea closed her eyes. 'Jimmy.'

Esme took a moment to process this. 'Jimmy did?' she said. 'But how do you know?'

Bea opened her eyes and looked directly at Esme. 'Because I was there.'

38

Bea pushed back her chair. 'Can we walk while we talk?' she said, standing up. 'I need some fresh air.'

Esme scrambled to her feet. 'Yes, of course. Whatever you like.'

Bea took her old brown coat off its hook in the kitchen and put it on, pulling a headscarf from one of the pockets to wrap around her head. They went outside, Bea leading the way to the field gate across the lane, where a public footpath sign pointed boldly seaward. Bea opened the gate and they went through into the field.

'I've already told you how Jimmy became obsessed with what had happened to Vivienne,' began Bea, thrusting her hands deep into the pockets of her coat. 'Of course, I wasn't fully aware of this in the early years. The war ended and I went back to my home. The letter to my parents about Vivienne arrived and, in our own ways, we mourned our loss. It was only later, when I came back to Devon, that I visited the farm again. Jimmy's mother was still alive then, and little had changed. She and Jimmy ran the farm between them and Mrs Beer, at least, imagined that Jimmy would marry and the next generation would continue in the usual way.'

The track veered to the right and they followed it along the hedge line. 'But that never happened,' said Esme. 'Because Jimmy couldn't forget Vivienne.'

Bea nodded. 'And worse, he wouldn't accept her death.'

'His conspiracy theory?'

Bea nodded. 'Perhaps if he'd spoken any sense I might have

been ready to listen but all he'd say was that he couldn't betray a confidence. I just thought that was his way of perpetuating the myth so I didn't believe a word of it. Not then, anyway.'

'So when did you change your mind?'

'Oh, not for years.' They reached the end of the field and slipped through a walkers' gate in the corner, leading on to a fenced-off pathway which fell away in the distance, revealing a stunning view of the sea breaking on to rocks in the bay. 'Things carried on much as normal,' Bea continued. 'Jimmy became more and more sullen, Mrs Beer passed away and the farm became run down. I'd almost stopped calling in. At least, I did drop in now and again but I wasn't sure I was doing any good. I'd convinced myself I only reminded him of Vivienne which wasn't what he needed.'

'But you didn't stop.'

'No. One day I went over there and he was really agitated. He said he'd found out where Gallimore was and he was going to demand answers. He said Gallimore had betrayed her.'

'Did he say how?' So far nothing Bea had said suggested she'd known that Jimmy had seen Vivienne after the war. Did Bea really not know? Or was this another of her half-truths? Esme decided to say nothing of what Jimmy had said until she'd established what Bea already knew.

'Oh, he didn't do me the courtesy of giving me chapter and verse,' Bea said. 'I was supposed to take his word for it. Of course, I just thought he'd finally lost his mind. I was so busy working out who to tell and what I was going to do about it, I almost missed what he was saying.'

'Which was?'

'He wanted me to come with him so that Gallimore would take it seriously. He'd worked it all out. As Vivienne's sister, he thought I'd have more luck getting Gallimore to confess.'

Bea pulled away and walked across to the small gateway out on to the coastal path. She stopped and rested her arms on the top bar, staring ahead. Esme came over and stood next to her. The thud of the breakers in the bay below echoed around their ears.

'So what happened?' Esme said, after a while. 'Did you go?'

'Yes, God forgive me. I thought this was the best opportunity for Jimmy to get it through his thick skull that Vivienne wasn't coming back, that the whole thing had been his fantasy. Of course, I was worried that he wouldn't believe what Gallimore said but it seemed to me the best chance there was ever going to be.'

'Did he say how he'd found Gallimore?'

'No. But he used to scour the newspapers avidly. He told me that the truth was beginning to come out. That journalists were starting to write about things that had previously been kept secret.'

'Perhaps files were being released from the archives.'

'Not then, I don't think. But former SOEs were writing memoirs, bits and pieces were slowly seeping out. He used that, I think.'

'So he'd tracked down Gallimore and you went to see him.'

Bea looked round at Esme. 'I didn't want to go. I thought Jimmy was making a big mistake. I almost said no.'

'So why did you?'

Bea shrugged. 'Oh, I don't know. I wanted to know the truth more than I feared going, I suppose. But if I'd ever thought...' She shook her head.

'So what happened?'

'The whole thing was surreal. Even though we talked about what we'd say when we got there – that was assuming Gallimore was at home – by the time he answered the door, Jimmy was so pent up, he just ranted, making very little sense. I could see Gallimore was about to slam the door, and probably ring the police. But I managed to calm Jimmy down and I think Gallimore had put two and two together by then. Certainly, when I said who I was, that Vivienne was my sister, his manner changed.'

'In what way?'

'He softened.'

'Softened? Not defensive, then? As though he had something to hide?'

'No. Not at first. He spoke of her in terms of loss, not as in dead, but lost to him. He'd obviously not grasped anything Jimmy had been saying, about betrayal and cover up.'

'He must have thought it odd to be confronted so many years afterwards.'

'I'm sure he did and I tried to explain that Jimmy had spent years looking for him, to find out what happened to Vivienne. Gallimore was adamant he'd not seen Vivienne. That's when I asked him about the letter.'

'The one he'd written passing on his condolences?'

Bea nodded. 'I wish to God I'd not mentioned it. For some reason it seemed to fire Jimmy all over again and this time I couldn't do anything to stop him. When he pulled out the gun –' She faltered and put her hand over her mouth. 'I should have guessed,' she continued when she'd composed herself. 'I was so stupid. I should have realised what he'd been carrying in his pocket.'

'That's when he shot him.'

Bea turned her back on the seascape and leant against the gate. 'No, not then. A woman – his wife, I assume – came into the hall, followed by a young man. There may have been someone else too, I can't be sure. I was too busy trying to usher Jimmy out of the house. I grabbed his arm and tried to pull him away. I thought with the other people arriving on the scene he'd see sense and come away.'

'But he didn't.'

Bea wiped her eyes with the back of her hand and fumbled in her pocket. Esme dug into her own and handed Bea a tissue. She waited while Bea blew her nose, the sound of the waves behind them filling the space between them.

'I was halfway across the lawn, running back to the Land

Rover, when I heard the scream,' said Bea. 'I knew then what he'd done. I was terrified. I didn't stop running until I saw the phone box.'

Esme blinked. 'So it was you who called the emergency services?'

'I had to. I suppose I was trying to distance myself from it. As though I was a passer-by and just concerned by what I'd heard.'

'Why did you give the wrong house name?'

'Dunsford House was a name Jimmy had gone on about. It was the first name that came into my head.'

'What did you do then?'

'I ran back to the Land Rover. I was pretty sure Jimmy would have left the keys in the ignition, as he always did on the farm. My only thought was to get away as quickly as possible. But as I got there, Jimmy arrived at the same time. He saw me but we didn't speak, just got in and Jimmy drove off. I don't remember the journey back. I wondered later if I'd blacked out and when I got home, whether I'd imagined the whole thing. A throw-back nightmare from the time when we'd first heard that Vivienne wasn't coming home.'

'Until it was reported in the press.'

She nodded. 'I expected the police to arrive at any time, then. I was a nervous wreck, Esme. You can't imagine. I didn't go anywhere near Crossways Farm for weeks.'

'And yet no one came.'

'No.'

'But the Land Rover must have been spotted?'

'Oh, I'm sure of it. And there was the gun, of course.'

'What about it?'

'Jimmy left it behind.'

Esme processed this information in silence. They had the gun, the chances of a sighting of the Land Rover must have been high and yet no one had come to arrest Jimmy.

Something Max had told her came to mind the time she'd

asked about Gallimore's SOE file. Max had said his file was still classified. *Which might suggest he got transferred to something else in intelligence*, had been Max's assessment. Had the intelligence services wanted to cover it up? Is that why they never came for Jimmy? But even so, surely they wouldn't let Jimmy get away with it completely? She shuddered. Wouldn't they have their own ways of dealing with Jimmy?

'Come on,' Bea said, turning away from the sea. She nodded towards the sky, heavy with metal-grey clouds. 'Rain's not far away.'

They turned and walked back towards the bungalow, neither speaking. Esme turned everything Bea had told her over in her mind. Uneasiness grew within her at every step. If Jimmy was Gallimore's killer, was this what Tim had uncovered? And had Jimmy found out that Tim knew? She glanced at Bea. Would Bea have known that? But she dismissed it. Bea had been shocked when Esme had mentioned Tim. Besides, Bea had just told her she'd not gone anywhere near Crossways Farm for weeks. But there was something stewing in her head about Bea's account. Something which didn't ring true. Frustratingly, she couldn't work out what it was.

'Have you ever talked to Jimmy about what happened?' asked Esme as they made their way across the wet grass.

'He won't discuss it. Never has. Well, you know how stubborn he is.'

'So you've no idea on his theory as to why they never came looking for him?'

'No, though he was cock-sure they wouldn't. I thought at first that his confidence was misplaced, but history's proved he was right, hasn't it?'

Esme held open the field gate to let Bea through. As she pulled the gate closed and secure the bolt, her back to the lane, she heard Ruth's voice. She turned round to see Ruth march towards Bea and grab her by the arm.

'Where the hell have you been?' she said. 'I was worried sick.'

Esme reached over and put her arm around Bea's shoulder. 'Bea was rather upset –'

'*She's* upset? That's rich. What about me? I thought she'd done it again. Gone off without a word to anyone, least of all, me. And then I find that you, Esme, you, of all people, are party to her thoughtlessness.'

'That's enough, Ruth,' Bea said. 'Esme had every right.' She flicked a look at Esme as though to ask for her approval before facing her daughter.

Ruth hesitated. 'What's going on?' she said, anxiety clear in her voice.

'It's about Vivienne,' Esme said. 'There's something you need to know.'

Bea put her head in her hands and quietly began sobbing.

39

They returned to Ravens Farm in silence. Ruth's expression suggested that, having demanded to know what was going on, she was now frightened by what she might hear. Esme sympathised. The conversation wasn't going to be easy.

'I'm sorry it's come to this, Ruth,' Esme said, as they arrived back at the farmhouse. 'Things have escalated. I've hardly had time to take it in myself, let alone find you to fill you in.'

Ruth looked alarmed. 'What do you mean, escalated?'

'Let Bea tell you what she needs to, first. Then I'll explain.'

They sat down at the kitchen table, Ruth beside her mother, clutching her hand while Bea spilled out everything in a low monotone. Ruth said nothing during Bea's explanation, other than utter an occasional gasp or groan.

Bea finished her account and slumped against the back of the chair, drained by the effort of relaying for a second time the horror of what she'd kept imprisoned inside her for so many years. Ruth gave Bea's hand an affectionate pat and stood up. She wandered over to the Rayburn where she leaned back against the towel rail and folded her arms. Her expression was grim.

'What the hell was Jimmy Beer thinking of, dragging you into something like that?' she said. 'How dare he.' When Bea bowed her head, Ruth added, 'For goodness sake, it's not your fault, Mum.'

Bea lifted her head, and stared at Ruth, her face red and blotchy. 'Whose fault is it then? I could have refused to go, couldn't I?'

Esme leaned over the table. 'But you said yourself, Bea. You didn't know about the gun. Why would you?'

Bea looked round at Esme, regarding her with red-rimmed eyes. 'But I knew the reason he was going there. To confront Gallimore. I should have guessed what might happen, knowing how volatile he could be.'

Esme shook her head. 'Even so.' Silence fell for a moment, the images Bea had conjured up were playing over in Esme's mind.

'Bea' Esme said, after a while, 'tell me again what happened after you heard the scream.'

'Oh, for goodness sake, Esme,' said Ruth. 'Haven t we heard enough?'

'This is important, Ruth,' Esme said. 'There's something wrong here.'

'You can say that again,' Ruth said.

'No, I don't mean that. Something about the timing.

Ruth frowned. 'What about the timing?'

Esme leaned her elbow on the table and looked across at Ruth. 'Bea heard the scream and ran to the phone box to make the call. Isn't that right, Bea?'

Bea nodded. 'Yes. I don't think it was a conscious plan. I was too distraught. I saw the call box and ran to it instinctively. I dialled 999 and called for an ambulance.'

'What did you tell them?'

'That I'd heard a shot coming from the big house. I called it Dunsford House which of course was the wrong name. But I also gave them the location of the phone box.'

'It's a wonder they took it seriously,' said Ruth. 'You hadn't witnessed anything. They get hoax calls all the time.'

Bea sighed. 'That's true. I was in quite a state so I must have sounded desperate.'

'Convincing, anyway,' Esme said. 'So then what did you do?'

'Went back to the Land Rover.'

'And that's my problem,' said Esme, turning to Ruth. 'Stopping to make the call must have taken some time. Ringing 999, getting put through, explaining what she'd heard.'

Ruth's face was grey. 'Go on,' she said.

'But when Bea got back to the Land Rover, Jimmy arrived almost immediately after.'

'Yes, you're right,' Bea said, eyes wide.

'Right about what?' Ruth said, impatiently. 'What are you talking about?'

'Don't you see?' Esme said. 'After firing the gun, Jimmy would've just run for it. He'd have got to the Land Rover before Bea. He might have even driven off to get away as quickly as possible. But he didn't. What was he doing in the in-between time between shooting Gallimore and getting to the Land Rover?'

They fell silent.

'So what are you saying, Esme?' Ruth asked, her voice low and anxious.

'I don't know. But Bea said Jimmy was never concerned that anyone would come after him. And they never did. So why didn't they?' She stood up. 'I'm going to ask him about it.'

'Esme, no,' Bea said, reaching out to try and grab her hand. 'You mustn't.'

'But we need answers, Bea. You've tried, and failed, to get Jimmy to tell you everything. Now it's my turn. I have to know – 'She swallowed, but it was impossible to find the words to explain her need to discover to what extent Tim's involvement was significant. She looked at Ruth. 'And I think Jimmy owes Bea an explanation, don't you?'

'I'll come with you,' Bea said, pushing back her chair.

'No, you won't,' said Ruth, grabbing Bea's arm. 'You're going nowhere.'

'But Esme's right, Ruth,' said Bea. 'Do you have any idea what it's been like all these years? It's been exhausting, suppressing everything. If Jimmy's been lying to me, then it's time he told the truth.' She reached out and squeezed her daughter's hand. 'It's like lancing a boil, Ruth. It can't fester any longer.'

'OK,' said Ruth, holding up her hand. 'I understand you need to know what Jimmy's got to say for himself. And I accept your reasons for needing to find out. He's not been straight with you and you want to know what he's been hiding all these years. I'd like to give Jimmy Beer a piece of my mind, myself. But I draw the line at you confronting him.'

'Ruth's right, Bea,' said Esme. 'You're too upset. You stay here. I'll go on my own. '

'You can't,' said Ruth. 'You haven't got your car.'

Esme closed her eyes and swore under her breath. Of course, she'd walked to Bea's via the cliff path.

The sound of a tractor coming into the yard broke the heavy silence. 'That'll be Pete,' said Ruth, marching across the kitchen and snatching a set of keys from the hook by the back door. 'He can stay with Mum.' She held the keys aloft. 'Jimmy's less likely to burst a gasket if he sees our Land Rover.'

'Oh, that's really good of you, Ruth.' Esme said. 'Thank you.' She held out her hand.

'No, you don't,' Ruth said, clutching the keys to her chest. 'I'll drive. I'm coming with you.'

40

'I'm not sure this is a good idea, Ruth,' Esme said, as Ruth pulled the Land Rover out on to the main road. Bea's earlier accusation reverberated around her head that Esme dragged Ruth into situations where she couldn't cope.

'There was no point in wasting time fetching your car. It's best we get this over and done with.'

'That wasn't exactly what I meant. I shouldn't have let you badger me into you coming along.'

'Too bad, you're stuck with me now. Anyway, I'd have only driven over on my own.'

'That would have been asking for trouble. We've got to handle Jimmy carefully, Ruth. Things have changed since I last spoke to him. We don't know how he'll react when he finds out Bea's told us everything.'

Ruth stared out of the windscreen at the road ahead, her jaw fixed. 'Don't worry about Jimmy Beer,' she said. 'I can handle him.'

Esme pressed herself back into the passenger seat and hoped Ruth's assertion wasn't an idle boast.

Ruth slowed down and took the turn off the Atlantic Highway towards Crossways Farm.

'It makes my blood boil to think what he's made my mother go through all these years,' said Ruth. 'She couldn't even confide in me, she had to cope with it all on her own –' Her voice cracked and it was a moment before she could continue. 'I knew there was something but I could never have imagined…anything like this.'

'Ruth, pull over for a moment, will you?' Esme said, laying a hand gently on Ruth's arm. 'We need to think this through.'

Ruth pulled into a gateway and stopped. She turned off the engine and pressed her head back into the seat. 'You're not going to talk me out of this, Esme, if that's what you think.'

'No, I realise that.'

'I couldn't let Mum come, could I? And she deserves better than the way Jimmy's treated her. All that loyalty. And where has it got her? No. I've got plenty to say to that lying scheming...' She swallowed and closed her eyes.

Esme rubbed her scar with her forefinger. 'In the past you'd have tried to convince me that this was a police matter.'

'Huh?' Ruth threw her head back against the neck rest. 'And how's that going to happen? Phone 101 and log it with some administrator in a call centre somewhere? Oh, yes, they'll soon come running. No, Esme, I'm older and wiser these days. Besides, how could I expose Mum to all that? She's been through enough.' She turned her head away and looked out of the driver's window.

'You may have to yet, Ruth,' Esme said, gently. 'Once we know all the facts, we may have no choice.' And Ruth wouldn't be the only one having to face difficult issues, she reminded herself.

'Mum said something about you having your own reasons for getting involved in all this, Esme. What did she mean by that?'

Esme closed her eyes and took a deep breath. 'I didn't know at the start, Ruth, I promise.' She turned to look at her friend, the image of her as a young girl from holidays years ago still clear to see in her older face. 'It seems there's a connection – though I don't quite understand how, yet – with something Tim was investigating.'

Ruth blinked. 'Tim? But how –?'

Esme shook her head. 'I don't know. I only wish I did. I'm –' She turned away and stared out at the irregular dry stone walling of the Devon bank beside the gatepost, partly hidden by sprouting grass long since dead. 'I'm struggling with it at the moment, if I'm honest.'

'You surely don't think Jimmy had any part to play –'

'I don't know what to think.' Esme turned back to Ruth. 'And there's something else you should know, which I don't think Bea is aware of.'

'What's that?'

'I don't think Jimmy's ever told Bea that he saw Vivienne after the war.'

'He what?'

'His grand conspiracy theory seems to have been hatched after that point. What he told me suggests it was Vivienne's own evidence which let him to come to that conclusion. That's why he was so furious at Gallimore – he seems to be at the centre of it. Jimmy said Vivienne went to see Gallimore and never returned. According to Bea, it took him years to track Gallimore down. Not that I think he really knew how to go about it properly, or he'd have probably found him a long time before.'

'Mrs Beer was still around in the early days, don't forget.'

'Yes, that's true. She was probably a calming influence. But once she died, then the isolation and bitterness would have taken their toll.' It was all very well speculating over the deterioration of Jimmy's state of mind but it didn't identify where the two parts of this mystery merged. Did Jimmy even know where Ingrid and Cole fitted in? He'd claimed not to know the name Cole. Perhaps she was looking for links where there were none. It was a port of comfort in a wild storm of doubt.

Ruth exhaled noisily and started up the Land Rover. 'Well then, there's no point hanging about here torturing ourselves. Let's get this over with and see what Jimmy's got to say for himself.'

'Let's just say that Bea's explained that the two of them

went to see Gallimore but she didn't say more as she got upset,' Esme said, as Ruth thrust the Land Rover into gear. 'Our best chance is to appeal to his concern for Bea.'

'You think that'll work? If we say that much, he might guess that Mum's confessed what happened.'

'He might. But she's kept his secret for this long, he might take it at face value that she couldn't bring herself to say any more.'

Ruth guided the vehicle back on to the lane and they drove the rest of the way in silence.

As they turned into Jimmy's, Ruth slowed. A gleaming white Range Rover was parked in the yard. 'Looks like Jimmy's got a visitor,' Esme said, glancing over to Ruth. 'Anyone you know?'

Ruth shook her head. 'Too clean for around here,' she said. She parked up beside the vehicle and they both got out.

Ruth shouted Jimmy's name. They waited for a response but none came.

'Let's try the house,' suggested Esme. 'If he's entertaining, they'll probably be in the kitchen.'

They tramped across the yard to the farmhouse, Ruth leading the way. She banged on the door to the outer porch before pushing it open, calling Jimmy's name as she went, carrying on through to the kitchen. Esme came up behind her and looked over her shoulder. The room was empty.

'I suppose he or she could be important enough to take into the front room,' Ruth said, making her way across the kitchen. 'Though I doubt he's used that room since his mother died.'

As they reached the hall door, there was the sound of an engine revving outside. Esme sprinted back the way they'd come and reached the yard as the Range Rover roared pass her, its wheels squealing as it sped out of the farm and on to the lane. She ran after it, coming to a stop when she realised it was hopeless.

187

She bent over to catch her breath and heard Ruth come up beside her, panting. 'Did you get the number?'

'No! Too busy trying to see the driver. You?'

Ruth shook her head. 'I didn't think about it until it was too late.' She spun round. 'Where did he come from?'

'The barn, I expect,' Esme said, standing up straight. She began walking across the yard. 'Let's go and see what Jimmy says.'

She'd gone two strides when Ruth grabbed her arm. 'Esme, look.' She turned her head to where Ruth was pointing to the ground. The partial print of a boot was clear to see. 'Is that –?' began Ruth.

'Blood?' Esme said. 'I don't know. Don't jump to conclusions, Ruth. It could be anything.' Esme wondered who she was trying to convince – herself or Ruth.

They hurried across the yard. 'Jimmy?' she shouted. 'Are you in there? It's Esme and Ruth.'

Esme reached the barn ahead of Ruth and grabbed hold of the door. She yanked it open and blinked into the darkness.

'Oh my God,' said Ruth, rushing ahead of her.

As Esme's eyes adjusted she registered a man's body, prostrate on the floor. Beside it lay Jimmy's long-handled axe.

41

'I'll call an ambulance,' Esme said, pulling out her mobile phone. 'Oh shit, there's no signal here, is there?'

Ruth dropped to her knees. 'There's a phone in the house. Kitchen wall.'

'Yes, I remember,' Esme said, heading to the door.

Ruth began pulling off her coat. 'I'll see what I can do until they get here. Assuming he's still alive, anyway.'

Esme turned and ran across to the farm house, throwing open the door so it banged against the wall behind. Her eyes surveyed the chaos of the kitchen, before pouncing on the telephone. She stabbed in three nines, cursing as she heard the slow ticker-ticker-ticker of the old technology locating the number.

Once she'd conveyed all the relevant information, she went in search of a blanket and found one draped across the sofa in the front room. She paused briefly in the kitchen, casting around for anything else useful. Everything was so dirty they'd make the situation worse by adding infection to whatever injury Jimmy had suffered. That's if he wasn't already dead. Who had done this? Who wanted to silence Jimmy?

She ran outside and back to the barn, a sense of helplessness overwhelming her, wondering what she'd find when she went inside. She yanked open the barn door and rolled a brick against it to stop it closing. They'd need the light.

Ruth looked up from her kneeling position. She was applying pressure to a wound on Jimmy's leg.

'They're on their way,' said Esme, shaking out the blanket

and regretting she'd not done it outside. Dust and bits of straw flew everywhere. 'This isn't the cleanest in the world but it will keep him warm. How's he doing?' Was he still alive or had they arrived too late?

She stood over Jimmy, holding up the blanket, ready to place it over him and peered over the top into the gloom. Ruth was looking up at her with anguish in her eyes.

'Esme?'

'Yes? What? Is it bad?'

'Esme, it isn't Jimmy.'

42

Esme threw some more coal into the Rayburn's firebox and slammed the door shut. It was burning nicely now and the half bucketful of fuel she'd found in Jimmy's kitchen should generate enough heat for a saucepan of hot water so Ruth could wash her blooded hands. If not she supposed she could get some logs from the barn, though whether the police would allow her anywhere near there was another matter.

The back door clattered open and Ruth emerged, her face pale.

'What's happening out there?' Esme said, picking up the saucepan and taking it over to the sink. 'Here, use this. I've taken the chill off it. It'll be a while before the boiler gets going.' She poured the contents into the bowl and stood back to let Ruth plunge her hands into the water.

'They're mumbling between themselves at the moment. Probably deciding if it warrants bringing anyone else in. I told the sergeant that if he didn't let me go and wash my hands I'd wipe them on his uniform.'

Esme stood beside Ruth watching crimson clouds form in the water as Ruth rubbed her fingers clean.

'You saved his life, Ruth.'

'Don't make it sound dramatic. I merely put pressure on the gash. It'll be for the surgeons to save his leg.'

'You think it's that bad?'

'Difficult to tell. It was so dark in there and –' she stopped and leant her elbows on the edge of the sink and dropped her head.

Esme snatched up a towel and thrust it towards her. 'Dry your hands and come and sit down. You need the sweet tea treatment.' She jerked her head towards the Rayburn. 'Kettle's on. I assume there's not an electric one?'

'No, I don't think so.' Ruth took the towel and wandered over to the table. 'What do you think happened?' she said, sitting down amongst the habitual debris in which Jimmy lived. 'Who is he? D'you think he's someone Jimmy knows?'

'From what Bea said, I got the impression she was his only friend.' Esme recalled her first visit to the farm. 'At least he didn't use his shot gun.'

'Oh, don't.' Ruth said, shaking her head. 'What was he thinking?'

'Ruth,' Esme said. 'We don't know it was Jimmy who attacked him.'

'How can you say that when we know what else he's done?' Ruth stared at Esme with anxious eyes. 'Should we say something, d'you think?'

'About what? We've already told them as much as we know.'

Ruth scowled. 'You know what I mean. About what Jimmy's done.'

'What we *think* he's done. Until we speak to Jimmy and iron out those anomalies, we don't even know whether your mum's got it right.'

Ruth stared down at the table. 'No, I suppose not.'

'But it's up to you, Ruth,' Esme said. 'If the only reason for not calling the police earlier really was because you thought you'd be fobbed off at a call centre, then here's your chance. You can speak to them in person and voice your concerns.'

'No. I'd be going behind Mum's back. I can't. I'm not subjecting her to an interrogation until I've spoken to her first, at the very least.' She put her hand across her eyes. 'God, what a mess.'

Esme grabbed the kettle and slid it back and forth across

the hob. 'Hurry up, you. Ruth needs a cuppa.'

'My gran used to do that,' said Ruth, with a sigh. 'I don't know why. I can't imagine it makes it heat up any quicker.'

Esme jumped at the sound of the latch. The sergeant they'd spoken to earlier, a tall, burly man with tight curly hair and a weathered face, stepped inside. He had to duck his head to get through the doorway.

'How is he?' Esme asked.

'We won't know that for a while, Mrs Quentin. He's still unconscious. They're just taking him off in the ambulance now.' He glanced between them. 'Either of you know the gentleman?'

'No,' said Ruth. 'He's certainly not local. At least, I don't know him and I've lived around here all my life.'

The sergeant glanced at Esme. 'Mrs Quentin.'

'Esme's been here barely a month,' Ruth said. 'She hardly knows anyone.'

'And you don't have any idea of the whereabouts of Mr Beer?'

'No, we don't, as we've already told you,' Ruth said, an irritated tone creeping into her voice. 'As far as I'm aware, he never leaves the farm.'

'We'll need you both to make a statement so –' The sergeant's radio crackled. 'Excuse me a moment, will you?' He retreated back out into the yard.

'Kettle's almost boiling,' Esme said. 'Let me make that drink. I think I could do with one myself, too.'

Ruth picked up a couple of mugs from the detritus on the table and peered inside. 'Dare we risk it, d'you think? Goodness knows what we might catch.' She selected two and took them over to the sink. 'I guess these might clean up well enough.' She emptied the bowl of now brown water down the sink, swilling it out from the tap before putting down the mugs. 'How does Jimmy live like this? It's awful.'

'Here,' Esme said, bringing over the kettle and pouring some boiling water in the mugs.

'What am I supposed to clean them with? Everything is filthy.'

'Leave them to stand for a minute or two, perhaps.' She cast around. 'There must be something we can use.'

Ruth sniffed. 'Can you smell burning?'

'It's probably the Rayburn,' said Esme. 'It doesn't look like it's been lit in a while.'

Ruth shook her head. 'God, what's the matter with him? I didn't realise it had got this bad. Mum never said.'

The back door opened and the sergeant came back into the kitchen, his notebook in his hand. 'They've found the Range Rover you reported seeing. Abandoned in a gateway about half a mile away. You're sure it wasn't Mr Beer driving it?'

Ruth sighed. 'As we said before, neither of us saw who was driving it. It was out of the yard before we got the chance.'

The sergeant glanced down at his notebook. 'The vehicle is registered to a Lloyd Gallimore.' He looked up. 'Mean anything to either of you?'

'Oh my God,' said Esme. She grabbed a cloth and leaped towards the Rayburn. 'He's left something in the oven.' She yanked open the oven door, flapping away the acrid smoke which billowed out. A box sat on the middle shelf, smoldering. She pulled out the shelf as far as it would come, placing her hand over her mouth and nose to protect herself from the fumes.

'Careful there,' said the policeman.

'It's OK.' She snatched up the poker from beside the stove and dragged the box off the shelf. It landed upside down on the flagstone floor.

'For goodness sake,' said Ruth. 'What on earth has he got in there?'

'Life savings, probably,' said the policeman. 'You'd be surprised where people keep their cash around here.' He slipped his notebook back into his pocket as his radio burst into life once more. 'Apologies again, ladies,' he said, slipping back outside.

As soon as the door closed behind him, Esme turned to Ruth who was looking back at her with wide eyes. 'Gallimore? Isn't that –?'

'Yes,' Esme hissed, glancing back to the door. 'But what was he doing here?'

Ruth's wordless shrug said everything.

'If only we'd got here earlier,' Esme said. 'We could have talked to Jimmy before he turned up. We might be a little wiser, then.'

Ruth wrapped her arms around herself. 'I think I'd rather be in ignorance than have been around when Jimmy Beer lost it with an axe, thank you very much.' She glanced at Esme, guiltily. 'If it was him, I mean.'

Esme raised an eyebrow before stooping down to appraise the blackened upturned box on the floor. She tested it gingerly with her fingertips before flipping it over to reveal the contents underneath. 'Oh, no, what have I done?'

'What?' Ruth crouched down beside her. 'Not cash then,' she said, as they stared down at the pile of photographs, now tinged black at the edges.

Esme prodded the pile with the poker, separating them. She picked up one of the photographs with a finger and thumb and studied the face in the semi-charred image. She looked up at Ruth and sighed. 'Looks like I've wrecked Jimmy's personal memento collection of your Auntie Vivienne.'

The back door opened and Ruth stood up as the sergeant reappeared. He nodded at the blackened mess on the floor. 'Fire out, then?'

'Yes, thanks,' Esme said, straightening up. 'Quite safe.'

'Good,' the sergeant said, glancing round the room. Well, I'll leave you to it, then. Make sure that Rayburn's extinguished before you leave.'

'You're going?' Ruth said. 'I thought you wanted to take our statements.'

The policeman flushed. 'Er, someone will be in touch.'

195

With a brief nod, he dipped his head and went out of the back door, allowing the sound of engines starting up in the yard to filter into the kitchen.

With a puzzled glance at Esme, Ruth went over to the window by the sink and strained to see into the yard. 'Looks like they're off,' she said.

'All of them?' Esme said, coming over to join her. 'Are you sure?'

'Positive. That's the last one now.'

They stared out of the window until silence fell again at the farm.

'So what now?' Ruth said, turning away from the window. 'Do you think we should stay and wait for Jimmy to turn up?'

'No,' Esme said, a thought coming into her head. 'We should get out of here before the media get wind of what happened. We don't want to get caught up in that.'

She went over to the Rayburn and crouched down beside the singed shoebox, scanning around for something to put it in. 'We should take this back with us,' she said, spying a carrier bag on the table. She took out the stale loaf inside and shook out the crumbs over the sink. 'Perhaps Maddy can do her magic on these and salvage them.' She rubbed the tips of her fingers. 'They're a right mess.'

Ruth wrinkled her nose. 'Stink of smoke, too.'

They left the farmhouse, closing the back door behind them, and strode over to the Land Rover. As Esme climbed inside, she cast one last look around the yard, wondering if Jimmy was hiding somewhere in one of the outbuildings, watching events unfold. Had the police searched the farm? She'd been too busy to notice.

Ruth started up the Land Rover. 'The police will ask him what he was doing here the minute he comes round, won't they?' she said.

'Yes,' Esme said, reaching for her seat belt. 'I wonder what he'll tell them.'

43

Back at Ravens Farm Pete leant against the Rayburn, his arms folded and his face sour as he watched the women at the kitchen table. Esme glanced up at him occasionally, wondering whether his surly expression was anything to do with the exchange she'd witnessed between him and Ruth on their return to the farm.

'So are the police looking for Jimmy as a suspect or what?' Maddy said, her gaze flitting between Ruth and Esme. Jimmy's singed photograph collection lay on the table in front of them.

'They didn't exactly confide in us,' Esme said. 'They asked all the usual questions, you know – whose place was it, who we were, what were we doing there – and then they seemed to lose interest once the casualty – which we assume is Lloyd Gallimore, though they didn't confirm that – was on his way to hospital. It was all a bit odd really.'

'Whole thing's bloody odd, if you ask me,' Pete said. 'I've always said Jimmy Beer was a strange one. I trust you'll think twice before helping him out any more, Bea.'

'You mustn't jump to conclusions, Pete,' Ruth said, flicking a glance at Esme. 'We should wait until we know more.'

'I think I know everything I need to, thank you. And I don't like what I'm –'

Esme cleared her throat. 'So, what d'you think, Maddy?' she said, sifting through the damaged photographs. 'Can you save them?' She almost said *and my skin* but stopped herself in time. Pete wouldn't thank her for joking about Jimmy's anger for what she'd done to his mementos.

'Oh, I should think so,' Maddy said. 'Only some are badly damaged. Most are salvageable.'

'I still can't believe he kept them in the oven,' Ruth said.

Maddy rubbed the smut residue off her fingers. 'He may not have. There's some evidence of mould which suggests they've been kept somewhere damp. So maybe Jimmy had only recently put them in the oven.'

'Could be. The Rayburn wasn't lit, remember,' Esme reminded them.

Ruth sat back in her chair and folded her arms. 'Well I still think it was a stupid place to put them. Lit or no.' She turned to Bea. 'Don't you think, Mum?'

Bea gave her daughter a brief nod. She'd been subdued since they'd returned. Listening to the account of events seemed to have sapped all her energy. She was also coming to terms with discovering that Jimmy had kept the truth from her about Vivienne's return to England after the war.

Esme felt sure that keeping the police away from Bea had been a wise move. Bea had already revisited enough of her painful past for the moment. She needed a time for recovery before any other horrors surfaced. Esme tried not to dwell on Maddy's quote about the truth and a wounded soul. Would she ever be able to put it out of her mind?

'Perhaps Jimmy shoved them in the oven when his visitor arrived?' Esme said, thinking of Lloyd Gallimore driving up in his flashy Range Rover.

Ruth frowned. 'To hide them.'

Esme nodded. 'Which begs the question, is there something in here which might give us a clue as to what this is all about?'

Maddy pulled the photographs towards her. 'Well, let's have a look, shall we? Bea can help, can't you Bea?' She picked up a photo and slid it across the table. 'This your sister, Bea?'

Esme came over and stood behind Bea and looked over her shoulder. A group of land-girls working in the fields posed for the camera with broad smiles on their faces and arms around one another's shoulders. 'Yes, that's her,' Bea said. 'Before she decided she wanted to "do more than pick cabbages" as she put it, for the war effort.'

Esme guessed that all of them were thinking that if only she'd stayed working on the land, the outcome of her story would have been very different.

'This has survived pretty well,' Maddy said, picking up a small book and flicking through the pages. Esme could see the words *The Countryman's Diary* clearly printed on the front cover. 'Shame there's nothing written in it, though.'

She dipped into the box again. 'Here's Jimmy's mother's ID card from during the war.'

'I've got one like that somewhere,' Esme said. 'It was my Mum's. They moved house during the war and it's got a gummed sticker with the change of address stuck over the top of the old one.' She took the card from Maddy and looked at the familiar cover, its border framing the royal crest in the centre. Inside she read the name Edith Beer, and the address of the farm written in a neat sloping hand at the bottom of the page. What would old Mrs Beer make of current events? She must have been aware of her son's feeling towards Vivienne. Had she approved? Or had she been protective, sensing that the age gap condemned Jimmy to disappointment. But, as they'd surmised, it was likely Jimmy's infatuation had grown out of control only after his mother's death.

'Is this Jimmy?' Maddy said, holding up a photograph of two men, both in uniform. One was a young man, lanky and boyish, the other much older.

'Yes, that's him. In his Home Guard uniform.' Bea seemed to have recovered a little now. 'He was too young to enlist, of course, so he did what a good number of boys his age did – joined the local volunteers.'

Esme studied young Jimmy, pride glowing in his face. How much of that was due to how he viewed himself in Vivienne's eyes? Would he have felt that she might see him as a credible suitor, now that he had his part to play?

Pete stood upright and approached the table. 'Who's the older man?'

'Jimmy's father,' said Bea. 'He was too old to serve in the regulars.'

'A World War One veteran?'

Bea nodded. 'I believe he was, yes.'

Pete nodded. 'Same as my granddad. Previous soldiering expertise came in useful to the local defence force. And before you start making jokes about *Dad's Army* and a bunch of bungling geriatrics,' he added, though no one's expression suggested levity was on their minds, 'I can tell you it was no sitcom, even though they did use broomsticks and pitchforks for arms while they learned their drills.'

Esme flinched as the image of the tine dagger Mel had showed them, made from the prong of a pitchfork, slipped unbidden into her head. *Primitive but effective.*

'Well, I suppose they liked to think they were doing their bit,' Ruth said.

'There was a lot more to it than that,' Pete continued. He still seemed rattled. 'There was a darker, more serious side. Some of them were well trained and ready to go under cover should Germany invade.'

'To do what?' asked Esme.

'Similar sort of thing to what the SOE were doing in occupied France. Sabotage and surveillance. A thorn in the side of the enemy. There were hundreds of arms dumps hidden all across the country, including here in the South West, as well as hideouts for the auxiliaries to hold up if the worst happened. My granddad had some pretty hair-raising stories about the stuff they were taught, I can tell you.'

A sombre silence fell over the room. Pete turned away and walked over to the dresser where he picked up the post left on the top and began flicking through it.

Ruth stood up. 'You'll need something better than that

bag to put all this lot in, Maddy,' she said. 'I've got a shoebox upstairs. It'll be just the thing.' She headed towards the hall door, saying something under her breath to Pete as she went by. He replied in kind. Ruth tossed her head and disappeared out of the kitchen.

Esme watched their exchange with a spasm of guilt, conscious of her part in the situation. She slipped off her chair, leaving Maddy and Bea browsing through the rest of the items in Jimmy's collection and went over to the dresser.

'I'm sorry, Pete. If I'd known where this was going –' She didn't know how to end the sentence. She was pragmatic enough to know the outcome was out of her hands before she'd started.

Pete looked round and forced a smile. 'It's not you, Esme. Ruth just doesn't seem to be taking this seriously. When she hared off earlier, I'd no idea what was going on until Bea owned up. And then I was stuck here like a lemon, babysitting, while she went off to confront Jimmy Beer.'

'Which never happened, as you know.'

'By luck than judgment, though.' Pete jerked his head towards the table. Bea and Maddy were sitting head to head, peering at a photograph. He lowered his voice. 'What I just said back then, about the auxiliaries, just sums it up. Jimmy was no Private Pike with his scarf and his teddy bear, Esme. Auxiliaries were trained killers. And you don't lose that skill. Especially someone like Jimmy.'

*

Maddy rested the box of damaged mementos on her hip as she and Esme walked across the farm yard towards Maddy's van. Pete had offered to run Esme home but she felt the three of them needed time on their own to talk things over, so Maddy had stepped in as chauffeur.

Esme's head still buzzed with Pete's words but she decided he was probably over reacting because of his concern for

Ruth's safety. Esme thrust her jangling thoughts to one side and focused on what Maddy was saying.

'...keeping his head down.'

Esme frowned. 'Sorry, Maddy. Who are we talking about?'

'Jimmy, of course,' Maddy said, throwing Esme a perplexed glance. 'Are you OK?'

'Yes, fine. Just thinking of something. What were you saying about Jimmy?'

'That perhaps he's feeling guilty at giving Bea the runa-round all these years and is why he's gone to ground.'

'The longer he leaves it, the deeper the hole he's digging for himself. Bea wants some answers and so do I.' Pete's words about Jimmy's auxiliary experience and his violent attitude echoed in her head as they reached the van. She stopped and looked across at Maddy. 'Do you think if you're trained as a silent killer that it's a skill which stays with you?'

Maddy stared back, blinking. 'What the hell's put that in your head?'

Esme wrinkled her nose. 'Something that Pete said, about Jimmy. And he has a point, doesn't he? It's not something you're likely to forget.'

Maddy considered for a moment. 'I suppose not, in theory. Then again, Jimmy may have been trained to kill but there's no saying he ever had to do it. Not like SOEs out in the field. That's where you'd most likely find yourself in a life or death situation. You or him.'

'Or her,' Esme said, automatically, thinking of the photo-graph on Mel's wall.

Maddy nodded. 'True.' She opened the van and they climbed inside.

'It's funny,' Maddy said, clicking her seatbelt into its hous-ing. 'I find it difficult to visualise these old war veterans as actual soldiers, and as killers.'

Esme gave a humourless laugh. 'You might change your mind, if you'd been there that day I first met Jimmy and his shotgun.'

'Oh, sorry, Esme. I didn't mean to belittle how terrifying that was.'

Esme shook her head. 'No, it's OK. And you do have a point.' She was reminded of Joe Paxton talking about his experiences. 'However much we listen to their stories about what they did for king and country, they just don't fit our image as trained assassins.'

'Which means we can be fooled into thinking they're harmless.'

Esme frowned and looked round at Maddy. 'Are you just reiterating what Pete said or are you hinting at something else?'

'Not sure, really. No, forget it. It doesn't matter. She turned on the engine.

'Maddy. What?'

Maddy exhaled and turned to meet Esme's eyes. 'It was something you said the other day when you were telling me about what happened the day Tim was killed.'

Esme's stomach flipped over. 'Which was what?'

Maddy pressed her lips together as though debating how to phrase her words. 'You said no one had seen anyone suspicious in the pub. *No one who looked handy with a stiletto, anyway*, you added. But perhaps everyone was thinking stereotype. Maybe he *was* there in the pub, but he was disregarded because he didn't fit anyone's criteria as a credible killer '

44

Esme found herself dwelling on Maddy's words more than she cared. Had Tim's killer been in the pub earlier and fooled everyone because they didn't fit the imagined profile? She should stop torturing herself. It was far too late to go back to all those potential witnesses and ask them to consider the same question from a new perspective, even if she had access to anyone with the authority to do it.

When she got home she switched on local radio for news of Lloyd Gallimore and busied herself with practical chores. None of the bulletins mentioned him. She turned on the television for the evening regional news programme. When nothing was reported there either, she flicked around the other channels but drew a blank.

Her phone rang out. She sighed and picked it up.

'Max. Hi. Did you get my list?'

'Yeah, sorry Ez. Meant to get back to you on that.'

'Anything?' She held her breath.

'Not so far. Looks like a list of names to me but nothing that jumps out. Leave it with me.'

'OK, thanks.' She hadn't realised how much store she'd put on it providing some answers. 'Oh, while you're on, I've got something that might interest you.' She relayed the incident at Crossways Farm.

'Ouch!' Max said. 'OK, I'll put out some feelers. But Gallimore won't want the world and his wife to get hold of this and he's not without influence. Happening in such an isolated location will have given him the edge on keeping it quiet.'

'I'm assuming he survived or we'd have heard otherwise,' Esme said. 'And that'll be down to Ruth. As for what's happened to Jimmy – who knows? He may have returned to the farm after we left but none of us are keen on going over to find out. So we're in limbo for the time being.'

'Well, keep me in the loop. Er – are you busy at the moment?'

'That depends.' She remembered it was him who'd phoned her. 'Why?'

'I'm staying at Warren Quay. How about we meet up? I'll buy you a drink.'

'That's nice of you, Max, but as you've heard, I've had one hell of a day and –'

'It's just that we've found some pretty damning intel on Gallimore. And I think you'll want to see it.'

*

Max was standing at the bar, already half way down his pint when Esme arrived. He had a large buff envelope in his hand which she eyed with interest. What had he discovered? Did it reveal anything about Vivienne? She hoped it was worth her turning out.

The tables in the main bar were full so they took their drinks into the other room which housed the snooker table and took a seat in the corner.

Esme took off her coat and slid into the bench with its back against the wall. Max dropped the envelope on the table and sat down on a chair opposite. Esme felt like she was about to be interviewed under caution for a crime she didn't commit.

Max leaned his elbows on the table. 'If you recall, the reason I put you on to researching Gallimore's family history –'

'Which turned out to be a complete fabrication.'

Max nodded. 'Was because we knew virtually zilch about what he'd done before the war.'

'Hadn't he been a language tutor at some posh school?'

205

'The school bit's right but not languages. He was a tennis coach.'

'Oh, yes. You did say at some point that he played tennis.' She looked at Max and frowned. 'Should I read something into that?'

Max pushed his pint to one side and picked up the envelope. He pulled out a photograph and slid it across the table to Esme. 'National Youth Tennis Championships 1938,' he said. 'You might recognise the champion.'

Esme picked up the picture. It showed a young man dressed in white trousers and shirt, standing on a tennis court, holding a large silver cup – a young man with a striking resemblance to the actor Dirk Bogarde. 'Gerald Gallimore?' she said, looking up at Max.

Max nodded.

'You're sure?'

'Remember the eyes, Ez. Look for yourself.'

She looked down at the face. The telltale difference in shade between the left eye and the right was as clear in this photograph as the one Max had shown her before.

She tapped the image. 'But this isn't Wimbledon, is it?'

'No. Hamburg.'

'Hamburg? Gallimore played tennis in Germany?'

'But not under the name Gallimore.'

Esme's mouth fell open. 'You've found out who he is.'

Max nodded again.

'So what's his real name?'

'Take a look,' Max said. 'It's on the back.'

She flipped over the photograph. On the reverse, in thick black ink, was written *Heinrick Kruger*.

'Ring any bells?' Max asked.

A disturbing realisation stirred in the pit of Esme's stomach. 'Joe Paxton mentioned a prison camp. I can't recall the camp's name but wasn't the commandant called Kruger? Nasty piece of work, you said.' She recalled telling Max she didn't want to hear the details.

'That's him. Jurgensbrück was the camp and Viktor Kruger was its notorious commandant. He and Heinrick, here, were cousins.'

'Wow. Gallimore was related to the evil Viktor Kruger?' Esme swallowed, grappling with the information. 'He was the one arrested for war crimes but died in jail before they could get him in the dock, wasn't he?'

'Except he didn't.'

'Didn't what?'

Max's expression became stern. 'Viktor Kruger's family was told he'd died of pneumonia. But the bastard hadn't died at all. He was taken on by British Intelligence and given a new identity. And it seems Gallimore was his handler.'

45

The implications of Max's information hit Esme like a boulder tossed from a raging sea. She recalled Jimmy talking about the state Vivienne had been in, without the words to describe the horrors she'd suffered. Had Vivienne been the SOE who'd been picked up by the Gestapo the day Joe Paxton had arrived in France? Had Jurgensbrück been the camp where she'd been taken? It had to be. It all added up. *The Devil* Vivienne had said. She'd seen Kruger.

Little wonder that she'd spoken of betrayal. She'd have judged seeing Gallimore with Kruger – the commandant responsible for the atrocities she'd endured – as nothing less than treason.

Esme realised Max was speaking to her. 'Sorry,' she said. 'Pieces dropping into place.' She recounted everything Jimmy had told her, including Vivienne's determination to bring Gallimore to justice. She was sure Vivienne would have told Jimmy the identity of who she'd seen with Gallimore. Why had Jimmy chosen to leave it out of his account?

'According to Jimmy,' she said, 'Vivienne went to confront Gallimore but never came back.'

Max frowned and rubbed his chin. 'Signing up Kruger was top secret, of course. He was a hated war criminal with the blood of British agents on his hands. The great British public wouldn't have been happy to know he'd been let off the hook.'

'So Vivienne recognising him would be a potential PR disaster, to put it mildly.'

'If she'd let on to anyone, yes. Which she may have threatened to do. So, was she warned off? Or eliminated.'

Esme shuddered. Could Gallimore have arranged for Vivienne's disappearance, then callously written a letter of condolence to her parents? If he was protecting his own position, he'd have done whatever he considered necessary.

'Did the British authorities know about Gallimore's German ancestry?' she asked Max. 'Is that why he was Kruger's handler?'

'That, I can't tell you,' Max said, scratching his cheek. 'But it wasn't unheard of for German nationals to serve as agents. And Gallimore's false ID was pretty robust – as it would have to be for someone in such a precarious position.'

Esme didn't want to think too much about the fate of someone exposed as a double agent. Had that been on Gallimore's mind when he arranged for Vivienne to disappear? But he was back in the UK by then, and the war was over. It didn't make any sense.

'Alternatively,' Max said. 'It's possible Kruger could have blackmailed Gallimore into somehow engineering his release. Nothing I've seen so far suggests Kruger was much of an asset worth cultivating, so it could be a plausible scenario.'

Esme thought of Ingrid's explanation of Cole escaping from Nazi Germany when he realised how things were panning out. Had Gallimore done the same, only to get exploited by a villainous member of his own family?

'So, what it looks like,' Esme said, 'is that Jimmy, knowing all this and believing that Gallimore was responsible for Vivienne's disappearance, not to mention spending forty years brooding about it, finally tracks Gallimore down and kills him in revenge.'

'Except you don't buy that.'

'No. The timing's all wrong but I can't get my head round what it means. And until Jimmy shows up to ask –'

'Assuming he'll co-operate.'

'That too, of course. Which I'm beginning to doubt. He's kept it quiet all these years, he's not going to give it up lightly.'

Max leaned across the table. 'If Gallimore was in intelligence after the war, it would explain why they hushed up his death, especially given the history with Kruger.'

She nodded. 'But would Kruger have still been an asset by then? Surely not.'

'Doubtful, I agree. Though given some wartime files have only very recently seen the light of day there would be plenty the authorities would want to remain hidden twenty-odd years ago.'

'But not now. It's ancient history.'

Max spread his hands. '*We* might think so but some former SOEs consider it a breach of honour that ex-colleagues even told their stories.'

'Enough to kill to keep it quiet?' Esme shook her head. 'No. I'm not swayed by that argument. There's something deeper here, I'm sure of it. We've barely scratched the surface.'

*

Esme made herself some supper. She hadn't the patience to cook anything complicated – she wasn't that hungry but knew she should eat – so she threw a jacket potato in the microwave and had it with some leftover coleslaw she found at the back of the fridge.

As she ate, she chewed over Max's revelations about Gallimore's German connections. Max said it wasn't unusual to use foreign nationals as agents; they invariably had the necessary language skills, as Gallimore had. Perhaps it explained the friendship with Cole – was Cole aware of Gallimore's ancestry?

She realised she hadn't asked Max what he made of Lloyd Gallimore's reason to visit Jimmy. She wondered if Lloyd had regained consciousness yet and what he'd told the police.

And where was Jimmy hiding himself all this time? Why had he kept Bea in the dark all these years? Was there any credit to his claim that it was to protect Bea from discovering the horrors of Vivienne's war? Or was he still hiding something?

Maddy's words about credible killers reverberated around her head, along with Pete's about Jimmy as a threat. Did Tim also visit Jimmy? What did Jimmy know about what happened to Tim? She still had no idea why Tim had visited Cole. If Ingrid genuinely didn't know, she was at a loss as to how to find out.

By the time she dragged herself off to bed, her eyes were red and her brain pickled. She tumbled underneath the duvet with a desperate need for sleep but the certain knowledge that she wasn't going to get any. She was right, but not in the way she anticipated.

Having spent a restless few hours barely dropping below the surface of unconsciousness, she was woken by the phone beside the bed buzzing angrily. She rolled over and grabbed it, peering with swollen eyes to read the time – 4:35am. She sat up, held the phone away from her and peered at the number but it was too blurred to read. She swiped the screen and lolled back against the bed head. 'Yes?'

A hushed voice said something down the line.

'Bea?' said Esme, sitting upright. 'What on earth –?'

'Jimmy,' Bea hissed. 'He's here in my kitchen. What do I do?'

Esme wriggled to the edge of the bed and threw back the duvet. 'Keep him talking, Bea. I'll be right over.'

46

Esme pulled up into a gateway a short distance from Bea's bungalow and cut the engine, opting to go the rest of the way on foot. She didn't want Jimmy to hear the car and panic. She hurried down the lane, the beam of her torch bouncing around in front of her. Nearing Bea's drive, she slowed down and got her breath back before cautiously making her way around the back. As she turned the corner, she saw that Bea had put on the outside light, enabling her to turn off her torch. She continued noiselessly along the side path, pausing at the back door to listen to the murmur of voices.

She strained to pick out what was being said but it was too muted. She stood for a moment wondering what to do next. Did Jimmy know she was coming?

She considered walking in unannounced, but decided it was too abrupt. Instead she tapped lightly on the door and waited.

The pitch of the voices rose, suggesting that Bea hadn't prepared Jimmy for Esme's arrival. Now she could hear the words, Bea appealing for Jimmy to calm down, that she was only trying to help him get out of the mess he was in. Esme lifted her hand, hesitating as she reached for the door handle. She heard the scraping of a chair. Either it was Bea getting up to open the door for her or Jimmy on his way out. She depressed the handle and pushed open the door.

Both Bea and Jimmy were on their feet, their eyes trained on Esme. Jimmy stood on the right at the head of the table, a plate of food in front of him, knife and fork lying across it, abandoned. Bea was on the opposite side, her hands resting on the table top. She was wearing her outside coat over her nightdress. Her hair was unkempt, her face colourless.

Esme stepped inside and closed the door behind her. 'Hello, Jimmy,' she said, taking a step into the room. 'Don't worry. There's only me here.' She turned to Bea. 'Are you OK?'

Bea nodded and resumed her seat. 'Sit down, Jimmy. And finish your meal, you'll be hungry, else.' She looked up at Esme. 'I've had it out with him. About not telling me about Vivienne coming back.'

Jimmy grunted and sat down. 'And I told you why I said nothin.' He jabbed his fork in Esme's direction. 'And I told 'er, too.'

'Oh, very honourable, I'm sure,' Bea said. 'But I don't like being lied to, Jimmy Beer.' She tapped the table in front of him with her forefinger and glared at him. 'Even when you persuaded me to go on that fool's errand to Gallimore's house you never said anything.'

Esme watched Jimmy, waited for a reaction that the story was out but he merely shovelled another forkful of food into his mouth and ignored her. Bea looked round at Esme with an expression which said, *you see what I'm up against.*

Jimmy swallowed his mouthful and scowled at Bea. 'What you bought her here for?'

'I asked Esme to help.'

Jimmy snorted. 'I dun't need her help.'

'Well, I do,' said Bea, jutting her chin at him. 'And I think you do too. You can't go on like this. You can't spend the rest of your life ducking and diving, hoping it'll all go away.'

'You'm talking in riddles woman. What'll go away?'

'The police, for a start. You can't go around attacking people with axes and get away with it.'

Jimmy scoffed. 'Don't see no police,' he said, scraping his fork around the plate and setting Esme's teeth on edge. 'Reckon you got hold of the wrong end of the stick.'

Esme and Bea exchanged glances. Esme thought of the lack of news coverage. He had a point.

'Well, police or no police, Jimmy,' she said, pulling out a chair and sitting down. 'We want some answers from you. Don't we, Bea?'

Jimmy raised an accusing finger pointed at Esme. 'This is your fault, all this. It were all settled till you came along, stirring everything up.'

'Jimmy,' said Bea, catching his hand and pushing it aside. 'You don't understand. Esme needs these questions answered as much as I do. Her husband was the journalist.'

Jimmy snatched his hand out of Bea's grip and glowered at her. 'Journalist? What you on about, maid? I know nothing about no journalist. What's she been saying?'

'Bea's right, Jimmy. You don't need to keep it all bottled up any more. Please tell me what you know. I need to understand the whole story. Did Tim come to see you? He'd been to see Donald Cole, hadn't he? Was it something to do with that?'

'I dun't know what you'm talking about.'

'Don't you?' Esme said. 'Are you sure? What was Lloyd Gallimore doing at your place? You must know.'

Jimmy shoved his plate away and stood up. 'You don't understand,' he said, banging the table with his fist. 'I had to do it. To protect her, don't you see? That was the deal.'

'The deal?' said Esme, getting to her feet. 'What deal?' Then it struck her. The oddity in the timing of Bea's account of events, why it had taken him so long to get back to the Land Rover after the shooting. They'd done a deal. But about what? 'What happened that day, Jimmy? What was this deal about? Vivienne?'

Jimmy backed away from the table. 'This bain't got nothing to do with you.'

'What was the deal, Jimmy?' Esme said again, shadowing him. 'It was with Lloyd Gallimore, wasn't it? Is that why he came to see you the other day? Did you argue over something?'

But Jimmy was shaking his head. He'd said everything he was going to say. He stumbled across the kitchen and out through the back door.

47

Esme took her morning mug of coffee and sat down on the window seat in the cottage's sitting room, looking out across the garden to the stream. The vivid yellow of the gorse cut through the grey of the day and the bleached tones of the surrounding vegetation. Her eyes still felt gritty from her disturbed night. After talking over events with Bea in her kitchen after Jimmy left, Bea had shooed Esme away, insisting she get off home and back to her bed. With everything going round in her head, Esme didn't expect to sleep and was surprised when she woke suddenly, realising it was gone 9 o'clock. She showered and dressed, even finding the appetite for a modest bowl of breakfast cereal.

She heard the sound of a car's engine and peered out, recognising Max's Qashqai as it pulled in the parking bay. Had he got any new information on Vivienne? She downed the last of her coffee and went to greet him.

'Not too early for you, I hope?' Max said, as Esme opened the door.

'No,' she said, thankful he hadn't arrived an hour before. She stood back to let him in. 'So what brings you here? Got something for me?'

Max pulled a piece of paper out of his pocket and handed it to her. 'Your list of names.'

'Oh, right, thanks,' she said, disappointed. 'But you could have emailed it.'

Max shoved his hands in his pockets and shrugged. 'Well, I was passing, you know and –'

She gave him a wry smile. 'You're just being nosy.'

He grinned. 'Why not? Wanted to see what's lured you out here.'

'Be my guest,' she said, waving her arm around. She looked down at the list. 'So, anything useful?'

'Nothing that jumped out at me. A list of women's names from a bygone era. No obvious connection that I can see.'

'Female SOE agents?' she said, grasping at possibilities.

'My first thought too but cross checks with my researcher's list drew a blank.'

'Oh well, thanks anyway.' Perhaps she shouldn't be disappointed but relieved. If the list had included names they'd recognised it would have made the link with Tim stronger. So maybe finding no connection suggested Tim hadn't been digging around in the Gallimore murder after all and she wasn't about to stumble upon – and have to confront – some new and terrifying evidence. But perhaps she was grasping at straws.

She dropped the list on the table. 'Coffee?'

'Thanks. Black. No sugar.'

'Great little place,' Max said, wandering around. 'So long as you're vertically challenged, that is,' he added, ducking his head to avoid cracking it on a ceiling beam.

Esme laughed. 'Not a problem for me.' She filled the kettle and slid it on to the Rayburn hob, grabbing two mugs from the draining board while Max strolled into the sitting room. She spooned coffee into the pot and followed him.

'Cosy,' he said, nodding. He bent down and peered through the window. 'Bit wild, though, isn't it?'

Esme folded her arms and smiled. 'Suits me fine. Blows the cobwebs away whenever I'm in need.' She extended a hand. 'Take a seat.'

Max dropped down on to the armchair to the side of the fireplace. 'So how's things?' he said. 'Anything new on your girl?'

'Nothing you can get your teeth into. I feel I'm going nowhere fast. Unless you count what happened last night.' She gave him a quick summary of the night's events.

'Deal?' Max said, cocking his head to one side. 'What sort of deal?'

'My words exactly. At which point he scarpered.'

'So was he bricking it or just pissed off?'

'Both, probably.'

'And you've still no idea why Gallimore paid him a call?'

Esme shook her head. 'He didn't come right out and say it, but reading between the lines, I'm sure it's Lloyd Gallimore who's the deal maker.'

'Which puts a big hole in any theory that he'd tracked down Jimmy as the old man's killer.'

'He did say,' Esme said, suddenly recalling Jimmy's words, 'that the deal had to do with protecting Vivienne and because of that he'd had no choice but to go along with it. I think it's to do with Jimmy keeping quiet about something.'

Max rubbed his chin. 'Could be that Gallimore thinks it's gone sour?'

'What – that Jimmy's welched on the deal?'

Max made a pragmatic gesture with his hand. 'Or was about to.'

'So he went to the farm to remind Jimmy not to say anything?'

'Or to make sure he couldn't.'

Esme's eyes widened. 'You think he'd go that far?'

'Depends how much is at stake. Would account for him being so jumpy about the police swarming all over it. And he wouldn't want Jimmy picked up in case he blew the whole keg sky high.'

'But Jimmy's kept his part of the bargain for years. Why sell out now? What's changed?'

Max looked at her. 'Not what, but who. You, for starters. You went to see Faye Gallimore to ask about Vivienne

Lancaster. And you weren't the only one stirring the hornet's nest.'

Esme put her hand to her mouth. 'Ingrid Cole. Yes, of course. Lloyd Gallimore was already rattled even before I arrived.' She stood up at the shrill whistling of the kettle. 'I'll get that coffee.'

As she filled the cafetière her mind drifted back to Ingrid. Had it really been their respective visits to Faye Gallimore which had prompted Lloyd's confrontation with Jimmy? But if Lloyd had attacked Jimmy and accused him of breaking whatever arrangement they'd had, how come Jimmy was so willing to remain loyal and not disclose everything to herself and Bea? It could only be because of Vivienne. But where exactly did she fit into the puzzle?

She put the mugs, milk and cafetière on to a tray and carried it into the sitting room. Max was engrossed in something over by the printer. She put the tray down on the low table by the sofa and looked over at Max. He had the photo of Dunsford House in one hand and the photograph of William Dunsford's wife in the other.

'Dunsford House, as I'm sure you recognise,' she said, going round the other side of the table.

'What's the significance of Typhoid Mary?' Max said

'Who?'

'This woman with the immaculate hairdo and a bow on her head.'

Esme stood next to him and looked over his shoulder.

'You know who I mean, don't you?' Max said, tapping the photo with his finger. 'Mary Mallon. The woman was a typhoid carrier in the States in the 1930s.'

'The cook? Wouldn't accept she was a health risk and infected dozens of people before the authorities caught up with her.'

'That's the one. Got locked up, eventually. Spent the last twenty-five years of her life in quarantine.'

'Oh, for goodness sake,' Esme said, flushing. 'What's the matter with me? I suppose it's because it wasn't the photo you usually see, of that large woman in glasses wearing a white coat. I just assumed it was William Dunsford's wife.'

Max frowned. 'Why?'

'Because it was clipped to the photo of Dunsford House. With Tim's shorthand notes.'

She didn't like the way Max was staring at her. She felt herself go hot.

'What?' she said, alarmed at his serious expression. 'You know something. Tell me. What?'

Max rubbed his hand over his face. 'I promise you, Ez,' he said, his face grim. 'I had no idea. Absolutely no idea.'

48

Max resumed his seat on the armchair, insisting Esme sit down too. She perched on the edge of the sofa, her body tense, aware of a hissing in her ears which could have been the sea in the distance or could just as easily be the anguish swirling inside her head. She had no concept of what she was about to hear and yet the associated items – Tim's list, the note of his appointment with Cole, the photograph of Dunsford House – and now the image of the most famous individual associated with typhoid, a subject already buried in the depths of this story, already told her that the trauma ran deep.

'I say again,' Max said, the force of his plea visible in his eyes, 'that I wasn't aware of any connection here. I'd say it was a coincidence but –'

'But you had an inkling. Which is why you sought me out, isn't it?' She was amazed her voice was so calm given the turmoil in her head.

Max scowled. 'I did not set you up, Esme. I knew nothing about that.' He waved his hand in the direction of the table. 'And if I'd come across it myself–'

Esme cut him short. 'Max, please!' she said, all calm lost now. 'Explain, for God's sake. What's the significance?'

Max shook his head. 'To be brutally frank, Esme, I don't actually know the significance. In fact I'm not much further ahead of you at knowing where it even fits in with everything else. Not completely, anyway.' He leaned forward, resting his elbows on his knees. 'Look, if I tell you the background, maybe between the two of us we can work out how the hell it fits together because I'm…damned if I know.'

She was aware he'd curbed his language for her benefit but it only served to illuminate the depth of his shock, which in itself revealed something disturbing.

'OK,' Esme said. 'I'm listening.' She clamped her jaw tightly shut, twitching slightly at the effort.

'A woman got in touch with me,' began Max.

'When?'

'1990.'

They eyed one another at the significance of the date. The year Tim died.

'Go on,' Esme said.

'She was a former nurse in a psychiatric hospital.'

'Dunsford House?'

'I really don't remember.'

'It must be, mustn't it? Why else –?'

'Yes, yes. OK. Given the evidence, it's a logical assumption.' He paused to take a breath. 'It wasn't a story which particularly grabbed me and I think the woman was a bit pissed I wasn't more interested, to be honest. But she ploughed on and I got the gist.'

'Which was?'

'She claimed a number of women had been locked up in solitary confinement for years because they were deemed to be a risk to health, on the grounds they were typhoid carriers.'

'And this was when – the 1990s? How can that happen in this day and age?'

'Ah well, that was her point. The origins of this situation went back years. Some of the women were incarcerated in the 1940s and 50s to protect public safety, before penicillin was freely available to treat such cases.'

'So why not release them once it was available?'

'Because by then it was too late. Her words were, *if those women weren't mad when they went in, they were driven mad by being in there.* And so they were never released.'

Esme shuddered. 'So the list that Tim made...?'

'The women she named, in all likelihood.'

'So how come Tim wrote it and not you?'

'Like I said, it wasn't my sort of thing. And I was up to the ears with something else, I guess. Whatever. When this woman asked whether there was someone else she could talk to...'

'Having realised she'd not found a sympathetic ear.'

Max acknowledged her comment with a sideways nod. 'I put her on to Tim. Never thought about it again, and he never mentioned it. Didn't even know he'd taken it on.'

'Ingrid Cole told me her mother died of typhoid,' Esme said. 'I don't know what's worse. Losing someone to the disease or them being alive but locked away out of reach. At least you had hope, I suppose.'

'From what the nurse said, the families often had little to do with these women and, over the years, lost all contact. Younger family members probably didn't even know of their existence. Older ones were wary of the stigma of both being a carrier and of being in a mental institution and never spoke of it.'

Something stirred deep inside Esme's head but it refused to come to the surface. 'Do you know why this woman came forward when she did?'

'Someone had found some old hospital records in amongst the ruins of the building left behind when it closed down.'

'I'd say that fitted with Dunsford House's history – closing down, building abandoned – but it could be true of many places with the changes in mental health policy over the years.'

She got up and wandered over to the window. Two walkers were standing by the bench above the beach, the wind whipping around their jackets puffing them up so they resembled over-stuffed duvets.

Was Maddy's suggestion credible – that the drugs element of Tim's death could be penicillin and not Class A? But while there may be loose connections, just because Tim took an interest in the story of the enforced incarceration of typhoid carriers, it didn't mean anything. Journalist juggled with stories all the time. And, as she implied, Max hadn't yet proved they were even talking about Dunsford House. It could have been anywhere.

She turned back into the room. Max was staring at the floor, probably examining the same issues.

'Can you establish whether it was Dunsford House, Max?' she asked him. 'We need to be certain.'

Max stood up. 'I'll make a few calls,' he said, pulling his phone out of his pocket. 'I'm pretty sure a similar case was flagged up only a few years ago. There may be some background I can dig up.'

Esme picked up the tray of abandoned coffee. 'I'll make us a fresh pot. I could do with it.' She took the tray through to the kitchen and filled the kettle. As she placed it on the Rayburn and emptied out the cafetière, she revisited Max's story. Could it really be at the heart of a murder – either Gallimore's or Tim's? The practice of isolating typhoid carriers, while harshly judged by today's procedure, was a sound enough motive for circumstances of the time – the protection of the general public at a time when typhoid was feared and untreatable. But where was the motive for murder?

She shook her head. The whole thing was getting out of control. This was never going to be solved by oscillating from one wild theory to another.

The kettle boiled, she set up coffee for the second time. As she carried the tray into the sitting room she saw the list Max had translated that she'd dropped on the kitchen table. She stopped to pick it up and put it on the tray before taking the tray through to the sitting room and setting it back down on the low table as Max ended his call.

'OK,' he said, scrolling down his phone. 'It *was* Dunsford House where the nurse had worked. The records found in the rubble were patients' notes. They were passed to a local record office and this former nurse got to hear about it. Makes you wonder why she never exposed it before, if she was working there.'

'How could she? She'd have had to abide by patient confidentiality. And as you said before, if families were ashamed of the situation, they'd hardly have cooperated in exposing the practice, for that reason.'

'You may well be right. When she came to us she was probably looking for someone else to blow the whistle.'

'So why did Tim visit Cole?' she said. 'For his expertise on penicillin and treating typhoid?'

'Doubtful,' said Max, looking down at his phone. 'It seems Cole worked there briefly in the 1940s.'

'He what?' Esme's mind raced.

'Does that put a different slant on things, d'you think?' Max asked.

Esme exhaled out of the corner of her mouth. 'I'm sure it does, though I'm not sure I know how, yet.' She picked up the list of women's names from the tray and looked at it. 'Do you think he was instrumental in consigning any of these poor souls –' She faltered, blinking as she focused on one name on the list.

'What's up?' Max said, getting up off his chair and coming over.

Esme realised she was shaking. 'If we kidded ourselves that we could dismiss this as a coincidence, we can't now.' She handed Max the list. 'Second one down. Jean Barber. That's the name of Ingrid Cole's birth mother.'

49

Esme sank down on to the dining chair at the table and sifted through the implications of what she'd just read. In her mind's eye, she saw Ingrid, dressed in her green coat, standing amongst the shrubs in the grounds of Dunsford House. Was her interest because of her father's connection? Or because she knew more about her mother than she'd let Esme believe.

'Didn't you just tell me Ingrid's mother died of typhoid?' Max said.

'I did, yes. But in 1943, the year after Ingrid was born. To be on Tim's list she must have been still alive in the 1990s.'

'So she was lying to you?'

'Or someone lied to *her*.'

Have you ever had that feeling that everything you'd ever known was made of sand? Ingrid had said. 'She already knew her father had,' Esme said. 'Though she was talking about his affair with Vivienne, not this. Whether she knows about her mother being in Dunsford House, I wouldn't know.'

'Will you try and set up a meet to find out?'

'I could try. Though I'm not sure she'll see me. Her husband wasn't keen on her digging around in the past. He was worried she might burn herself out, that she was becoming obsessive about it.' She looked up at Max. 'If she doesn't already know, Max, it's a pretty painful truth to discover.'

'Cole would have known.'

Esme nodded. 'Yes, of course. Which will make it even harder to bear.'

'The truth isn't always easy, as we both know.' Max stood

up. 'I should go. Let me know if you get any joy.'

'I will. But she may duck the issue. I can't force her to confront her past and the last time I spoke to her she was on the verge of backing away.' She sighed. 'Her husband might have a point. Maybe it's easier to live with the myth. Neater, that way.'

Max frowned. 'Didn't think you subscribed to that philosophy, Esme?'

'No. Nor me.' She gave him a melancholy smile. 'Just trying it out for size, that's all.'

*

Esme's only contact details for Ingrid were by phone or post. Sending a letter seemed too casual, implying none of the urgency she felt the message warranted. She opted to send a carefully worded text, saying only that she'd discovered something which might be of interest if Ingrid was still keen to find out the truth. If the truth *was* still on Ingrid's agenda, it would generate a response. If she'd decided against pursuing that particular path, Esme would have done all she could. As she'd told Max, she couldn't force Ingrid to go down that route, however much it might benefit others.

She slipped on her duffel coat and walked across the grass to the beach. The breeze was building and clouds were forming in angry shapes on the horizon. She climbed down the stone steps and across the pebbles to the top of the ridge, taking care not to twist her ankle in the gaps between the boulders. At the edge she stood, gazing along the pleats of rock as they stretched out across the cove into the waves, and sifting through all the names they'd encountered since the search for Vivienne's fate had begun. They formed a chain. Gerald Gallimore, Faye Gallimore, Donald Cole, Ingrid Cole, Jimmy Beer and even the abhorrent Viktor Kruger. The only person she couldn't link directly to Vivienne was Lloyd Gallimore who wouldn't have been born when Vivienne returned to the UK in 1946. Lloyd's role in Vivienne's story must come through his father and mother.

The thought of Lloyd led her back to the unfathomable truth of what had happened to Vivienne when she'd confronted Gallimore. She knew enough to know that it had impacted directly on Faye and Lloyd, on Jimmy and, ironically, even on Bea. But was there more to it? Was it tied in to what they'd just learned about Cole and his working at Dunsford House? Was it that link which had drawn Ingrid to the Gallimores' house? Ingrid said Faye had visited Cole shortly before he'd died and it was for that reason she'd wanted to speak to her. Could it have anything to do with Ingrid's birth mother not dying from typhoid but being a carrier? Had Cole lied to Ingrid because he'd seen it as protecting her from the truth?

Esme squeezed her eyes shut. All she was doing at the moment was giving herself a headache. She should be preparing herself to continue the search without Ingrid's testimony. What happened to Vivienne must take priority now and she needed to focus on which direction they should take next. She wondered whether Jimmy had returned to his farm and whether anything had found its way into the press about Lloyd Gallimore, yet. She'd forgotten to ask Max, in all the trauma of their discovery.

She turned back to the cottage, reaching it as the first raindrops landed on the ground around her. She discarded her coat and switched on the local radio station to catch the news. She watched the heavy splashes of rain hitting the windowpanes of the cottage while she washed up the coffee mugs, reflecting on the extent to which the content of local news mirrored its locality. In Shropshire, though a rural county, much of the coverage focused on the urban Midlands. Here in the South West, the items evoked a different life, with stories of the RNLI rescuing stranded beach walkers from being cut off by the tide and the latest distressing figures of the instances of TB in cattle. A police appeal for any sightings of a woman who'd wandered off from a care home made her think of Bea ending up at Jimmy's farm. What did Bea think of Jimmy now? Did giving him a hot meal the other night indicate she still saw him as vulnerable or had it been just a ploy to hold him there until Esme arrived? Esme guessed events of the last few weeks would have changed their relationship dramatically.

There was no mention of Lloyd Gallimore or Jimmy Beer on the news bulletin. Esme dried her hands and picked up her phone to call Maddy.

'D'you think Ingrid will get in touch?' Maddy said, when Esme told her about their discovery.

'I'm not hopeful. I got the impression last time she'd said more than she really wanted to. It's easy enough to delete my text message and pretend it never happened.'

Maddy sighed. 'Well, you never know.'

'Any news on Jimmy?' Esme asked.

'Not that I've heard. I've got his box of photos and stuff here. Just the last few to scan in. I guess I'm best to pass them to Bea for the time being, once I've printed them off. She can hang on to them until he turns up.'

Esme thought back to her assessment a moment ago, as to the changes between Jimmy and Bea. 'Well, most of them relate to Vivienne in some way. You might even make a second copy of those while you're at it. I'm sure she'd like that.'

*

Esme busied herself with household chores for the rest of the day, determined to keep her mind from dwelling on the disturbing aspects of earlier. She was still undecided as to what she should do next in her search. It felt like every route had fizzled out into a black hole. At the moment, all she could think of was what Ingrid could tell her. But although she checked her phone every so often for a message, she found nothing.

The storm raced around the cottage into the small hours, rattling the windows and whistling through every void and cavity within the fabric of the building. Esme snuggled under her duvet and let the sounds transport her into an imagined sea voyage, on a ship with billowing sails. When she woke, all was silent other than the distance hiss of breaking waves.

She lay for a moment, allowing the elements of the previous day to drop into her head, one by one, before throwing back the covers and clambering out of bed. The room was bathed in a muted yellow light, a promise of a brighter day. She went over to the window and pulled back the curtains, pressing her face against the glass to look towards the sea.

At the end of the gravel track, someone was standing looking back at the cottage. A woman wearing a bright green coat.

50

Esme threw on a pair of jeans and a baggy jumper and hurried down the stairs. She slipped on her wellies and, grabbing her coat from the hook by the door, went outside.

Ingrid had turned away from the cottage and was gazing out to sea. Esme walked over and stood beside her.

'Hello Ingrid.'

'I didn't want to come,' Ingrid said, still staring ahead. 'I wanted to ignore your message. Pretend I didn't want to know. But then I couldn't sleep and…'

'I'm so sorry but –'

'Are you?' Ingrid snapped, turning sharply to glare at Esme. 'Are you really? You didn't have to get in touch. You could have left me alone.'

Esme glared back. 'That's not fair,' she said, feeling her face reddening. 'When we met before you were looking for answers. I found some. I thought you'd want to know. Look, I didn't force you to come,' she added. Ingrid didn't respond. 'It's entirely up to you,' she said, turning away.

She strode back towards the cottage, shaking and with the sting of tears in her eyes. Despite her defensive words, the responsibility of churning up truths that Ingrid had no wish to disturb grew like a boulder in her chest.

She'd almost reached the cottage door when Ingrid caught up with her and grabbed her arm. 'OK, OK. You're right. I was being a bitch. It's not you.'

Esme stopped. She took a deep breath and turned to Ingrid. 'I know it's not easy,' she said, sighing. 'Believe me, I've been there.' And fear I will be again, she almost added.

Ingrid bowed her head and nodded.

Esme pushed a strand of hair out of her eyes. 'Shall we talk inside?'

They went into the sitting room. Ingrid declined Esme's offer of tea or coffee and took the armchair by the fireplace, lowering herself down into it as though every muscle in her body was tense to the point of pain.

Although the wood-burning stove was still warm from last night's fire, the room felt chilled. Esme knelt down by the fireplace. She added a few sticks to the embers and opened the vents to rekindle the flames.

'You said this was about my mother,' Ingrid said, leaning forward.

Esme sat back on her knees. 'Yes, your birth mother, Jean Barber.'

'My birth mother?' She blinked, clearly thrown. 'I don't understand.'

Esme brushed off her hands and sat down on the chair opposite Ingrid. 'I think I know why my husband came to see your father. You remember I told you I found Tim's note saying Dr Cole and a date?'

'Wait a minute. You're going too fast. I thought you said this was about my mother.'

'The two things are linked, you see. Tim was following a lead about women being admitted to Dunsford House because they were typhoid carriers. Jean Barber was on the list of patients.'

Ingrid frowned and shook her head. 'No. That can't be right.'

'She'd be considered a risk to public health. While she may not have been ill, she carried the virus.'

'Yes, yes, I realise that. But my father was a pioneer for penicillin. If anyone could treat her, he could.'

'Which is what I thought, too. So did he?' Esme added, a thought coming into her head.

'Why are you asking me?'

'You don't know her medical history?'

'No, of course not.'

'I wondered if that's why you were at Dunsford House that day I saw you.'

Ingrid's expression was disdainful. 'No.'

'But you knew your father worked there?'

'Look, I've already told you. I thought my mother died soon after I was born. I know nothing about this.' She slumped back in the armchair, her face grey. 'You know, of all the things I thought you might tell me, I never imagined this. She pulled a tissue from her pocket and blew her nose. 'So why did he lie?'

'The social stigma of her being held in a mental institution?'

'But he worked there, for God's sake. That can't be the reason, surely.'

'Perhaps he was worried you may want to contact her if you thought she was still alive.'

Ingrid considered and nodded. 'You may have something there. My mother – my adoptive mother, that is – might have struggled with that. I was her manna from heaven. I'd never have searched for information about my past while she was still alive.' She looked down and rubbed her hands down her thighs. 'You're right, of course, about Papa working at Dunsford House. I'd forgotten the name of the place until I saw the name in the local paper. Something about it becoming a hotel?'

Esme nodded, remembering the hoarding around the site when she'd visited.

'It was seeing that which stirred everything up,' Ingrid continued. 'The name triggered something. I'm sure it was part of that argument I told you I overheard between my parents.'

'The one where your mother accused your father of carrying a burden of guilt?'

'Yes, that's it.'

Something crept into Esme's consciousness. 'At the time, you thought it was about his affair with Vivienne Lancaster.'

Ingrid gave Esme a sharp look. 'At the time? What are you saying?'

'What if it wasn't about errant husband and mistress, but about doctor and patient?'

'Meaning?'

'What if the remark about guilt was to do with your father having the ability to cure your mother but couldn't?'

'But why couldn't he?'

Esme shrugged. 'I don't know. I'm no medic. Maybe it's different with typhoid carriers. They don't actually get the disease, only carry it. Maybe penicillin doesn't work for them.'

'Is that possible?'

'Or, maybe he didn't actually have access to penicillin. We're talking 1946, here, don't forget. Servicemen in the field might have got hold of it but I don't know how quickly it would be more widely available to the general public. Do you?'

'But that would mean it wasn't his fault, so why would he talk about carrying a burden of guilt?'

'The irrational assessment of a dedicated man, perhaps?'

'Maybe.' Ingrid shook her head sadly and sighed.

'Does your husband know you've come here today?'

'He thinks I'm somewhere else.'

'Will you tell him?'

'I don't know. Probably. He'll be OK. He might not be happy I looked but he might accept that now I know the truth, I won't need to look any further.'

Esme wondered about Ingrid's questions for Faye Gallimore, still unanswered but she kept quiet. If Ingrid wanted to dig deeper, that was her decision. The truth about her mother must have laid certain ghosts to rest. Perhaps that was enough.

Ingrid stood up. Her face was red and blotchy.

'Are you sure you're all right?' Esme said, getting to her

feet. 'Can I get you a drink or something before you go?'

Ingrid shook her head. 'No, thanks. I'm OK.' She looked around. 'But if I could use your bathroom...?'

'Yes, of course.' Esme directed Ingrid upstairs and returned to the kitchen, mulling over the possible reasons for Cole's lies about Jean Barber. Was it inadvertently to protect his wife, so there was no risk Ingrid would make contact with her birth mother? Ingrid was quite clear on the effect such contact would have on her adoptive mother and why she'd waited until her death before beginning her search.

She heard the sound of a vehicle's engine outside and glanced out of the kitchen window to see Maddy's van pull up in the parking area. Before she was half way across the room to the door, Maddy burst into the room.

'Maddy! What the –'

'Sorry, Esme, didn't mean to freak you out,' Maddy panted, her eyes bright and her face flushed. 'But I just had to show you. I couldn't wait.'

'Show me what?'

Maddy thrust a small card into Esme's hand. 'Take a look at that.'

'What is it?' Esme said, looking at the card. Written across the top of the card were the words CARTE D'INDENTITE and there was a photograph on the right-hand side – the short, dark hair, straight dark eyebrows on a fresh young face. Esme recognised her immediately.

Esme looked up. 'It's Vivienne's French ID card.'

'Yes,' said Maddy, nodding enthusiastically, a child-like look of excitement on her face. 'Isn't it brill?'

'Well, if we'd any doubt she was an SOE, it's confirmed now. In Jimmy's box, I assume.'

'Yes, but there's something else.' Maddy bounced forward, pointing. 'Look at the name.'

'Jeanne Barbière,' Esme read. 'Her code name.'

'Yes, but don't you see?'

'See what?'

Maddy rolled her eyes and laughed. 'You're not usually this slow, Esme. Think! Jeanne Barbière. Jean Barber. It has to be, doesn't it? Vivienne must be Ingrid Cole's birth mother.'

A sound like an animal in pain came from the stairs. They looked round. Ingrid stood on the bottom step, staring at Maddy, her face white and her hand across her mouth.

51

Esme felt as though the connection between her brain and her limbs had been disconnected. She also seemed to have lost the ability to speak, as the implications of what Maddy had found ricocheted around her head.

'Oh, sorry.' Maddy's voice penetrated Esme's befuddled brain. 'Didn't mean to barge in.' She gave Esme a baffled look. 'You should have said you had a visitor.'

'Maddy,' Esme said, finding her voice. 'This is Ingrid. She turned to Ingrid. 'Maddy's been restoring some old photographs for me.'

Maddy's face drained of colour as she glanced between Esme and Ingrid. 'Oh, God. What have I just done? I'm so sorry. What must you think?'

Ingrid stepped down off the bottom step and held out her hand. Esme passed her the ID card. Ingrid snatched it and stared down at it while Esme and Maddy looked on.

'I'll go,' Maddy said, looking at Esme and giving a helpless shrug of her shoulders. She looked close to tears.

'Catch up later?' Esme said.

Maddy nodded and slipped out of the door.

Esme took a deep breath and turned back to Ingrid. A moment ago her head was full of questions. Now it felt so full of mush she couldn't think straight. She couldn't begin to imagine what impact all this was having on Ingrid. As the thought came to her, she realised the wider implications. What about Ruth and Bea? They'd have to be told. What effect would it have on them?

Ingrid put the ID card down on the table. 'I should have

known there'd be more lies, shouldn't I? It seems to be what my past has been built on.'

'Sometimes people lie to protect others.'

'Or themselves.'

'Yes. Usually that.'

'Which makes me as guilty as anyone else, I guess.'

'Oh?' Esme's insides churned as she immediately thought of Tim. Had Ingrid lied about what she knew, after all?

'You asked me once if I knew who my real father was.'

'You said you didn't know.'

Ingrid gave a humourless laugh. 'What I actually said was, what do *you* think? You filled in the rest.'

'So, are you telling me that Donald Cole *was* your father, after all?' Esme said, recalling Ingrid's vehement assertion that she was not the consequence of his affair with Vivienne.

Another snort. 'That would be ironic, wouldn't it?' She shook her head. 'No. It wasn't him. He wasn't able to father children. A situation which almost destroyed my mother and why the opportunity to adopt me was such a godsend.' She took a deep breath. 'I should go.'

Esme nodded. 'Yes, of course. I understand. You need time on your own to take everything in. I'll get your coat.'

She fetched the now iconic green coat from off the hook beside the door and held it open for Ingrid to put on, knowing she had to ask the question and wondering if Ingrid would give her an answer.

'So if Donald Cole wasn't your father,' Esme said, opening the door to let Ingrid out. 'Who was?'

Ingrid fastened the top button of her coat and looked directly at Esme. 'Gerald Gallimore.'

*

Esme wandered over to the window and watched Ingrid walk away up the track back to her car. Ironic that they'd inadvertently hit on the truth when speculating that Gallimore and Vivienne might be lovers, given Gallimore's reputation and Joe Paxton's comments about romantic liaisons being common in the stress of war.

Esme got the impression that Ingrid had always known who her father was. Perhaps she'd suspected it when she learned of his involvement in the adoption process. Esme doubted she knew Gallimore's secret, though – that his credentials were false. Then again, perhaps she did know. But how to find out one way or the other without running the risk of upsetting Ingrid any more than they'd done so already? The poor woman had enough distressing information to process.

Her thoughts inevitably drifted back to Gallimore. If he knew Cole as well as Ingrid implied, he'd have been well aware of the Coles's desire for a child. Had Cole known about Gallimore's relationship with Vivienne? Did he know it was she who was pregnant? Or had he learned who she was much later? Had the circumstances mattered to him? The opportunity to adopt Vivienne's child to satisfy his wife's desperate urge to be a mother must have been compelling.

And now with Maddy's revelation that Vivienne was Jean Barber, Esme wondered how that altered Vivienne's story. Could the secret that Jimmy was so anxious to keep be that Gallimore had fathered Cole's adopted child? Was that likely? Surely such a secret was kept for reasons of sensibility, rather than any dubious motives? And what about Vivienne being held at Dunsford House? Where did that fit in?

The germ of a theory began to grow in her head.

239

52

Esme manoeuvred through the crowd in the pub at Warren Quay to the table in the far corner of the bar. Maddy was scrolling through her phone, a pint of orange juice and soda in front of her and a beer in the empty space opposite. Esme slid on to the bench as Maddy looked up.

'I got the drinks in,' she said, slipping her phone in her pocket. 'It was filling up and I thought there might be a wait. There's a birthday party in.'

'Yes, so I see,' Esme said, glancing back at the bar which was rapidly becoming crowded as more people pushed in through the door. She picked up her pint. 'Cheers,' she said. 'I need this.' She took a long draught before replacing the glass on the beer mat. 'Thanks for coming.'

'No worries.' Maddy leaned towards Esme, her face anxious. 'Are you sure Ingrid was OK? I felt so bloody stupid barging in like that.'

'You weren't to know.'

Maddy shook her head. 'Even so.'

Shrieks of laughter came from over by the bar as the noise level grew. Maddy leaned in closer to make herself heard. 'Anything Ingrid told you bring you any closer to knowing what happened when Tim visited Cole?'

'Not specifically but something Max said a while ago keeps chasing around my brain.' She gave Maddy a wan smile. 'I think we've jumped to the wrong conclusion.'

'About what?'

'About Vivienne. And it goes right back to Gallimore and

240

Jimmy's claim that Vivienne went to tackle him about his betrayal.'

'Not connected with her being admitted to Dunsford House?'

'Yes – that's the whole point.'

Maddy shook her head. 'You've lost me, Esme.'

Esme glanced across at the party goers. 'Let's adjourn outside, shall we? I can hardly think in here.'

They downed the rest of their drinks and squeezed their way between the revellers to the outside door. Esme pulled her coat around her as the chill of the evening air hit her after the warmth of the bar. They wandered along the terrace, stopping at the top of the ramp to the beach and leaning on the wall to look over the harbour. Esme gazed into the semi-darkness, listening to the sound of cables tapping against masts echoing across the water as she marshalled her thoughts.

'OK,' Esme said. 'Take this scenario. Jimmy said Vivienne came to see him as soon as she got back home which was in 1946. He maintains that after she went to see Gallimore he never saw her again.'

'Do we believe him?'

'Let's just say we do, for now. The thing is, Cole was working at Dunsford House in 1946. Ingrid told me about a row she'd overheard her parents have about the burden of guilt. She'd assumed they were talking about Vivienne being Cole's mistress. When she was here earlier, we speculated whether it was about the circumstances between patient and doctor, rather than mistress and lover.'

'Meaning what?'

Esme took a deep breath. 'I think Cole admitted Vivienne under false pretences, to get her out of the way.'

'Bloody hell!' Maddy turned to face her, dropping her elbow on to the top of the wall. 'You mean Gallimore used Cole to get rid of Vivienne after she saw him with Kruger?'

'That was my first thought, yes. But now I'm having my doubts whether it *was* Gallimore.'

'It's got to be, hasn't it?' Maddy said, standing upright and looking at Esme as though she'd lost her mind. 'Vivienne would have been horrified to discover Kruger had been recruited by the British, when they knew full well he had blood on his hands.'

'Of course she would. But while she would have been incensed – justifiably so – she was an SOE. She'd have signed the official secret act, something I'm sure she would have taken very seriously. Wouldn't a more likely scenario be that, she'd be forced to accept that it was not her place to question a decision made for the so-called "greater good"? Gallimore would know that.'

Maddy pulled a face. 'Mmm. I'm not sure I go along with that. Even if it was true, she may have *threatened* to kick up a stink to make her point. Gallimore couldn't be sure she wouldn't go through with it. He would know she'd been through a lot. He might not have been able to take the risk.'

'So they both had a motive.'

'Both? So who else wanted her out of the way?'

'I think it was Cole himself.'

'Cole? Why him?'

'For a start, he should have been able to treat Vivienne and yet it seems he didn't. I speculated maybe there was a medical reason why he couldn't. Also, I knew QA nurses were always vaccinated against typhoid, so why not SOE agents? Then I realised I was missing the point. It wasn't about treating Vivienne at all. I think he arranged for her to be falsely admitted as a typhoid carrier – but only as a temporary measure. He'd have expected her to be released soon afterwards once it was established she was clear and was horrified to discover years later that she hadn't been.'

'That's horrible. But why? What was his motive?'

'Ingrid's adopted mother was desperate for a child, apparently, and saw Ingrid, to use Ingrid's own words, as *manna from heaven*. Ingrid told me Gallimore helped in the adoption

242

process, which perhaps makes sense, as we now know that Gallimore was the father.'

Maddy turned and stared out into the darkness. 'Everyone thought Vivienne had died in Germany. And then she lands on Gallimore's doorstep. Not sounding off about Kruger, you think, but demanding to know what happened to her baby.'

'If Cole's wife was expecting to adopt Ingrid and then, out of the blue, her real mother turns up, wanting her back…

'They couldn't afford Vivienne putting a spanner in the works. They had to keep her out of the way until the adoption became official. Then she couldn't do anything about it.'

'Well, it would be difficult, certainly. Involve a long legal battle, probably.'

'Then in 1990,' Maddy said, picking up with Esme's theory, 'Tim went to challenge Cole about the women on the list.'

'Yes. Cole would have seen Jean Barber's name and realised what had happened, that his action had resulted in Vivienne being incarcerated for all those years. He did the only thing he could and rewrote his will with her as sole beneficiary. Maybe he thought it would at least ensure her comfort for the remainder of her life.'

'And then killed himself in remorse.' Maddy shook her head. 'It's a credible theory, if a chilling one. But how do we establish if it's true?'

'It might be credible but it doesn't explain everything.

'No,' Maddy agreed. 'We're still no clearer about what Jimmy's hiding and what happened the day he and Bea went to the Gallimore's place.'

Esme put a finger to her scar and looked down into the black water below. 'And I still have no idea who needed Tim out of the way.'

Maddy put her arm round Esme's shoulder. 'Aw, come on. It's not too late. We may yet solve that particular mystery.'

Esme gave her a sad smile. 'You reckon?' She shook her

head. 'Those who really know, Gallimore and Cole, are no longer with us. The truth died with them.'

'Not everyone's gone. You're forgetting someone who must have known exactly what was going on.'

Esme turned to Maddy. 'Who?'

'Faye Gallimore. Why else would she go to such lengths to avoid talking to you?'

Esme thought back to the reception she'd had when the well-meaning Magda had invited her into the Gallimore's house. Did she still work there or had the Gallimores since sacked her after what happened? 'Even if you're right, I can't see how I'm ever going to get across the threshold to find out. And if I did, I doubt she'd tell me.' She gave Maddy a sad smile. 'But there is something we can do. And that's to update the others caught up in this sorry tale. We have to break the news to Bea and Ruth.'

53

They decided it would be Esme alone who would tell Bea of what they'd learned about Vivienne's past. She would go the next day, taking Vivienne's ID card with her to show Bea and help explain the significance of their finds.

'Will you mention Ingrid?' Maddy asked, as they walked back to the car park.

Esme shook her head. 'Not by name, no. There'll be more than enough for Bea and Ruth to process as it is. Besides, it's Ingrid's call. I have to know whether she wants to make contact with her birth family. And you know what her feelings are about Vivienne.'

'Yes, but that was when she thought Cole and Vivienne were having an affair.'

'True enough. But we'll see.'

*

Bea was on the phone when Esme arrived the following morning, talking to Ruth by the sound of the conversation. Bea beckoned Esme inside, gesturing for her to take a seat while mouthing she'd not be long. Ideally, Esme would have liked Ruth present so she could tell them both together. Perhaps she should ask Bea to invite Ruth to join them.

She sat down at the table and focused on the breakfast television programme, trying not to eavesdrop on Bea's conversation. There was another appeal about the woman missing from the care home and some footage of the coastguard rescue of the two walkers who'd got into difficulties. An RNLI spokesman came on camera to remind people to check the tide tables before going on to the beach. She watched without focusing, as she played over in her mind how to open the conversation with Bea.

'Not the brains they're born with,' said Bea, dropping the telephone handset back on its cradle. 'Surely they realise that the tide comes in as well as goes out, for goodness sake?' She clicked the remote to turn off the set and sat down at the table. 'This is a nice surprise, Esme,' she said. 'Just passing were you?' She cocked her head in question, her smile fixed as though trying to refute the anxiety which was clear in her eyes.

'You're wondering why I'm here,' Esme said.

'*Worrying* why you're here would be closer to the truth.' Bea's face twitched in the effort of trying to make light of what was clearly terrifying her.

'You might want Ruth to be in on this,' Esme said.

Bea pursed her lips. 'If you've got something to say, let's hear it,' she said. 'Ruth'll be here in her own good time.'

'Then I'll get to the point.' Esme laid her hands palms down on the table, her thumbs touching, and looked up at Bea. 'Yesterday, Maddy and I discovered something about Vivienne that's going to come as a shock.'

Bea pressed her lips together and nodded. 'I knew you would eventually,' she said, quietly.

'You've probably already speculated why Vivienne didn't come home, since you found out from Jimmy that she'd survived the war.' She wondered if Ruth had shared with her their theory about a GI bride which had ended in a dead-end. 'And the truth is, she had a child. A daughter.'

Bea gasped and leaned back in her chair. 'She thought she couldn't come home because of that?'

'I don't know. Might she have been concerned at the reception she'd get?'

Bea frowned, presumably thinking back, imagining what

her parents' reaction might have been had they known. Had they been the kind of people who'd turn their daughter out on the street, accused of bringing disgrace on the family? Bea shook her head. 'But she would have at least tried, wouldn't she?'

'Test the water, you mean? Perhaps. But unfortunately, it's more complicated than that simple fact. Apparently she had the baby in occupied France, or possibly Germany. At some point after that – I'm afraid details are sketchy so I don't know exactly how it happened – she was captured and put into a prison camp.'

Bea's face drained of colour. 'What happened to the baby?'

'She was adopted by a German family.'

'A little girl.' Bea reflected on this for a moment. 'And what about Vivienne?' she said after a while.

Esme took Vivienne's ID card out of her pocket and slid it across the table. 'The next thing we know is that she was admitted to Dunsford House under the name Jean Barber.'

'Jean Barber?' Bea stared down at the card. 'Why not use her real name?'

Esme hesitated. 'There are…irregularities about her admission. The Anglicised version of her code name may have been deliberately chosen so she wasn't traceable under her own name.'

'What sort of irregularities?'

'She may have been admitted under false pretences – that is she was deemed to have been a typhoid carrier at a time when typhoid was untreatable. She was put away for public safety.'

'But that wasn't true? Is that what you're saying?'

'That is what I'm saying, yes.'

'But why?'

'I'd be lying if I told you I knew for certain why that was. But unfortunately, I only have theories.' She leaned forward and laid her hand on Bea's. 'It's at this point, Bea, that Tim becomes part of the story.'

'Oh Esme, this is awful. For you, I mean.' She took hold of Esme's hand in hers. 'Tell me about Tim.'

Esme explained about the former nurse, about the list of names and the realisation as to its significance. 'Tim went to see Dr Cole because he'd worked at Dunsford House in 1946, the time Vivienne was admitted.'

'And did he explain himself?'

'We just don't know. But it's somehow tied up in whatever Jimmy knows and probably what secrets he's keeping and the deal he spoke about.'

Bea pulled her hands free and stood up. 'Damn Jimmy and his misguided sense of honour,' she said, pulling her cardigan around her. 'He's to blame for the mess we're in here.'

Esme conjured up the image of Jimmy in the Home Guard photograph, standing beside his father, along with Pete's words about the auxiliaries being trained killers. *And you don't lose that skill. Especially someone like Jimmy.* She thought again of the knives she'd seen at Mel's. The prong of a pitchfork. The smaller dagger. Double bladed and lethal. She raised a hand to the scar on her cheek. Jimmy didn't want the truth to come out. He'd struck a deal to keep quiet, accusing Esme of putting it in jeopardy. Had he killed to keep the truth hidden? Could it have been him who'd rushed past her, slashing at her face, moments before she'd discovered Tim's bloodied body?

'Where *is* Jimmy?' Esme said, swivelling around to address Bea who was standing at the kitchen sink, looking out of the window. 'Have you seen him since that night?'

Bea turned round and folded her arms. 'No. Pete went to check out the farm yesterday. Wouldn't let me or Ruth go. Found junk mail behind the door where it'd fallen. Reckoned Jimmy hadn't been there in days.'

Esme's mobile buzzed. She took it out of her bag and checked the screen. It was Maddy. Odd for her to call. The arrangement was that Esme would phone her after the visit.

She glanced up at Bea. 'Sorry, Bea. It's Maddy. She'd only phone if it was important.' She connected. 'Maddy. Is everything –'

'Have you seen the local news?' Maddy interrupted, her voice breathless.

'Well, I did earlier –'

'Put it on now. You'll just catch the headlines.'

Esme looked up. 'Bea. Can you put the TV back on, please? Maddy says there's something we should see.'

'What's it about?' said Bea, picking up the remote and switching on.

'I've no idea,' Esme said, as the screen flickered into life. 'She just said –' She stopped as she recognised the images from a news item she'd seen before. The reporter handed back to the newsreader in the studio who concluded the report with, 'The Police ask that if anyone knows the whereabouts of the missing resident, Jean Barber, to contact them or the care home immediately.'

54

Esme stared at the screen, oblivious to the remaining news items as questions circled inside her head. Jean Barber. Vivienne. Surely it couldn't be a coincidence? Vivienne was still alive and living here in the South West. Did Jimmy know? Was this part of the secret deal with the Gallimores? And what had prompted Vivienne to walk out of the care home?

'Are you still there, Esme?' said Maddy.

'Yes, yes, sorry,' Esme said, giving her head a shake. She glanced over to Bea who was looking back at her with a bewildered expression. 'Look, I'll get back to you. Bea and I need to bring Ruth up to speed.'

Esme cut the call. 'Are you OK, Bea?'

'That is the name you've just told me, isn't it?'

'Yes. I don't know what to say. I'm as shocked as you are. I had no idea.'

Bea dropped down on to a chair. Her face darkened. 'Jimmy knew, didn't he? He knew my sister was alive but he never told me.'

'I can't answer that one, Bea,' Esme said, shaking her head. 'But it's possible. He did talk about protecting Vivienne so he might think –'

'Protecting her from who?' Bea spat, jabbing a thumb into her chest. 'Me? What threat is her own sister? He has no right to make that sort of decision.'

'No, I agree. His perspective on this seems to be completely skewed. We need to talk to him and find out what's going on. But first, we need to speak to Ruth and tell her what we've found out. Are you up to that?'

In answer, Bea strode across the room with a determination which belied her age and snatched up her coat.

*

They found Ruth in the garden, pegging out washing. She peered at them over the line.

'Hello?' she said, taking two pegs out of her mouth and frowning at them. 'You two look a bit glum. Is everything all right?'

'It's that Jimmy Beer,' Bea said, waving her fist in the air. 'He's duped us all these years, Ruth.' Her anger evaporated into despair and Esme detected a sob in her voice.

'Hey,' Ruth said, going over to Bea and putting an arm around her. She looked over at Esme, her expression troubled. 'What's going on, Esme?'

'It's about Vivienne and what Jimmy did or didn't know. It could be that he knew a whole lot more than he's ever let on to Bea. Let's go inside and we can explain everything properly.'

*

Pete was hosing down the yard as they came round the corner of the farmhouse. He looked up, puzzled.

'You'd better bring Pete in on this, too,' Esme said. She pulled out her phone. 'I'll be with you in a sec. I need to make a couple of calls, first.'

Pete had already turned off the tap before Ruth reached him. He listened, glancing across at Esme as she tapped in the numbers, before following Ruth across the yard to the back door.

'What's up?' he said, as he reached Esme.

'Come on inside,' Ruth said, steering him into the boot room. 'Mum'll explain. Esme's going to join us in a minute.'

Esme called Maddy.

'It's got to be her, hasn't it?' Maddy said. 'It can't be a coincidence.'

'I guess we won't know for certain until we speak to Jimmy.'

'And where the hell is he likely to be?'

'I'm working on it. Maybe Bea might have some ideas. Meanwhile, can you go through Jimmy's box of mementos again? See if anything jumps out at you as more significant now we know what we know. And if you find anything, bring it over to Ravens Farm. We're just having a pow-wow to bring Ruth and Pete up to speed.'

'OK. On it.'

Esme disconnected. She then called Max and brought him swiftly up to date. He offered to find out everything he could about the news story and get back to her as soon as he could. She cut the call and headed inside to join the others.

They were already sitting around the kitchen table, Pete at the head with Ruth and Bea together on one side. Esme sat down opposite. Bea had already launched into her story, peppering it with jibes at Jimmy and citing his betrayal of her trust. When she'd finished, Esme added what she'd learned in the past twenty-four hours which she'd conveyed to Bea earlier.

'I can't believe it,' Ruth said. 'I have a cousin out there somewhere?'

'So what was this deal all about, then?' Pete asked.

'Exactly!' Bea said, jabbing her finger on the table.

'Keeping a secret in return for something, we assume,' Esme said.

'Is the fact that Vivienne's still alive the secret?'

Esme looked at Bea and back at Pete. 'We don't know anything for sure about the whys and wherefores. A lot of it's guess work. We really need Jimmy to come clean with us.'

'You think he'll let on?' Pete's tone was dismissive. 'He's lied at every turn so far. Can't see him being cooperative now.'

'I'm hoping he'll see there's no advantage in keeping quiet about it any longer, now we know. He does have a soft spot for Bea. He might realise he's reached the point where not to speak out will only cause her further distress.'

Pete snorted. 'You've got more faith in him than I have.'

Esme gave him a weak smile. 'Or I'm just over optimistic.'

'So why's she upped and gone now?' Ruth said. 'Coincidence?'

'I did think that,' Esme said. 'Perhaps it's got nothing to do with what's going on. She's just confused and gone wandering off.'

'What I don't get,' Ruth said, 'is why she needed to stay incognito for all these years?'

'If we find Jimmy's known where she is all along,' Esme said. 'He can answer that one.'

Ruth stood up and went over to the window, folding her arms and peering out, her back to the room.

'What if she's not upped and gone of her own accord at all,' Pete said. 'What if someone's taken her?'

Ruth spun round. 'Who?'

'Whoever wanted her silence in the first place.' Pete caught Esme's eye and she guessed what he was thinking. Now that everything was unravelling, they wanted rid of her.

Esme thought of Jimmy jabbing his finger at her, declaring Esme's meddling had created a problem, how he'd insisted his only aim was to protect Vivienne. What did he mean by that? Had they put her in danger?

Her phone rang. She glanced at the screen. 'It's Max,' she said, standing up. 'I asked him to see what he could find out. I thought it might help us decide what to do next.' She put the phone to her ear. 'Max. Hi. Thanks for getting back. Get anything?'

She listened and nodded, aware that the others were fixed on her, waiting, concern etched on their faces. She thanked Max and finished the call.

'Well?' Ruth said.

Esme glanced at Pete. 'You were right, Pete. Looks like Vivienne didn't abscond of her own volition. Someone came to pick her up but never brought her back.'

Bea whimpered.

Esme wanted to reassure Bea that Vivienne would be fine but Pete's unspoken concern a moment ago checked any words of comfort she might have voiced.

'Someone's coming,' Ruth said, straining to see out of the window. 'Looks like Maddy's van.'

They all looked in the direction of the yard and waited. Footsteps sounded in the boot room. Ruth strode over to the door and pulled it open. Maddy stepped inside, looking round at everyone as they stared back at her, waiting for her to speak.

'You found something?' Esme said, breaking the spell.

'Come and sit down, Maddy,' Ruth said. 'Sorry. Us all gawping at you like that.'

Maddy shook her head and took a seat. 'No, don't be silly. I can't imagine what a horrible shock this is for all of you. Bea, you especially.' She pulled a small book from her pocket and laid it on the table. 'I didn't realise what this was before but now I do, it might be important.'

'So what is it?' Ruth asked.

'It's called *The Countryman's Diary*. It was in Jimmy's box.'

'I never saw that,' Pete said, pulling it towards him and flicking through the pages. 'Bloody hell, I've never seen a genuine one before.'

'Thing is, I didn't take much notice of it before, as there was nothing written in it,' Maddy said.

'Will someone tell me what's so special about it,' Ruth said.

Pete glanced up. 'It's a World War Two saboteurs' handbook. In disguise, if you like. So as not to attract attention if it was spotted. As an auxiliary, Jimmy would have had a copy.'

'Someone's sketched something inside,' Maddy said, pointing. 'There, on the next page.'

Pete opened it out, rubbing his finger down the centre line so the book lay flat. Everyone strained forward to peer at the selected page. Esme looked over Maddy's shoulder. In faded pencil, she could just make out a rectangle drawn in the centre of an irregular shape shaded in hatched markings. Two sets of parallel lines ran from the middle outward, one to the left-hand side, the other to the top.

'What is it supposed to be?' Bea said.

'It's the plan of a hideout,' Pete said. 'See? That's depicting it's underground.'

'You told us there were hundreds all over the country,' Esme said, an idea growing in her head, 'ready for the British resistance to hide out in the event of an invasion.'

'Operation Bases, they were called, officially.' He tapped the diagram. 'Their entrances were hidden, for obvious reasons. Biggest problem during the digging process, Granddad said, was getting rid of the spoil without anyone noticing what was going on. You couldn't pile it up anywhere or someone would see it. Round here they used to tip it into local streams.'

'And Jimmy could have been a part of that?'

Pete sat back in his chair. 'I know where you're going with this Esme. You're thinking Jimmy could be keeping his head down in one of these.' He nodded at the diagram. 'While I can well believe Jimmy would love the idea of re-living some sort of World War Two fantasy land, it doesn't stack up.'

'Why not?'

'Because they don't exist anymore. They were all destroyed after the war.'

'How d'you know? What if some survived?' She nodded to the book. 'That one, for instance. If he was involved in building it in the first place, he'd know where it was.'

'So what if he does?' said Ruth. 'It's not much help to us. We have no idea where it is.'

'*We* don't, no. But Mel does, at Bleakmoor Airfield. She's got maps marking all their locations.' Esme stood up and looked at Maddy. 'We need to see them.'

55

Mel pulled out a heap of folded maps from her bulging cabinet and dumped them on the worktop. She sifted through the pile, checking the scribbled notes on the face of each fold until she found the one she was looking for and put it to one side. The remainder she returned to its home. Esme watched her, conscious of the twisted knot in her stomach – a cross between anxiety and anticipation.

Mel opened up the plan and flattened it out. 'This what you mean?' she said.

'I think so,' Esme said as she and Maddy leaned over to take a closer look.

Mel traced her finger over an area on the left-hand side. 'These would have been arms caches,' she said, indicating a series of dotted lines and blocked areas in red. 'And those are the hideouts where agents would have hidden in the event of an invasion. Estimates reckon to above a thousand countrywide by the time the auxiliary unit patrols were disbanded.'

'Pete said the hideouts don't exist anymore,' Esme said.

'Yes, that's true. After the war, a team of Royal Engineers went round and destroyed them so they didn't get used for criminal activity or become a danger to the public.'

'All of them?' Maddy said.

'Some on private land survived, though they've probably caved in by now.'

Not if they'd been maintained, Esme thought. 'What were they like?'

Mel wrinkled her nose. 'Apart from being cold, damp and smelly, you mean?'

Esme smiled. 'Yes, apart from that. How big were they?'

'Big enough for a group of people to live down there undetected, at least. Which was the whole idea, of course. Somewhere for the British resistance to lie low and observe the occupying enemy and plan their sabotage operations.'

'A sort of glorified Anderson shelter, then?' Maddy said.

Mel nodded. 'Some were pretty basic, not much more than foxholes with a log roof and poor ventilation, at least at the outset. At the other end of the scale, some were quite sophisticated with running water and rudimentary drainage. But they all eventually had bunks, a stove for cooking and a supply of food and water.'

The perfect place for Jimmy to hole up until the crisis passed. Though Esme wondered if he realised it was a crisis which wasn't going to pass. Not now. Not after so much had been revealed.

'So how did they access these places?' Maddy asked. 'Some sort of trap door?'

'In some cases,' Mel said. 'Any entrance that was easy to disguise in the undergrowth from anyone walking past or from aerial surveillance. They made use of whatever the landscape offered, as well. Tunnels or mine shafts could be useful.'

'The coast round here has plenty of caves and old smugglers' tunnels,' Maddy said. 'Did they use those?'

Mel shook her head. 'Too risky. They'd be too well known. They needed places few people knew about.'

Maddy leaned over and studied the plans. 'Esme, look, there's one here right on the edge of Jimmy's farm.'

Esme nodded. 'Good as place to start as any.'

Mel furnished them with copies and wished them good luck. 'Let me know what you find, won't you?'

Esme nodded. 'We will.' She looked at Maddy. 'OK, let's go.'

56

Esme and Maddy arranged to meet Ruth, Pete and Bea at Crossways Farm. There seemed little point in trawling the land surrounding Jimmy's farm before checking he wasn't ensconced in his own kitchen, innocent of everything they suspected.

But the kitchen appeared as unused as when Pete had visited earlier in the week and Ruth's search of the rest of the farmhouse told no different a tale.

Ruth cleared the kitchen table and Esme laid down the copies of the plans so they could study them.

'They're not maps as such,' she explained. 'So their accuracy isn't brilliant. But it gives us a vague idea of the area we're looking in. Mel gave us a crash course in what to look out for. We'll just have to see what we come up with. If Jimmy *has* been using it recently, we should see the evidence in the surrounding undergrowth.'

After a heated debate, it was decided that Ruth and Bea would remain at the farmhouse while Maddy, Pete and Esme searched. The lack of mobile phone signal was a concern until Pete pointed out that they'd be on higher ground so they should be able to keep in touch. As Ruth and Bea had access to the farm's landline, they agreed to check in every ten minutes. Ruth said if she didn't have contact from anyone after that period of time, she intended to phone the police so warned everyone not to be complacent.

'Come on Mum,' Esme heard Ruth say as the rest of them went out of the door. 'No point in sitting here chewing our fingernails. We might as well keep ourselves occupied and tidy up this hellhole.'

Pete, Maddy and Esme trudged up to the higher side of the farm and climbed the hill overlooking the yard. There was a small scruffy copse running along the higher side of the meadow, ankle deep in dead leaves and broken branches.

'God, we'll never find anything under this lot,' said Maddy, kicking at the debris.

Pete peered down at his map and looked around. Not many landmarks to go by.'

'Maybe the first thing to look for is evidence of recent disturbance,' Esme suggested.

Pete looked down at his phone screen. 'At least I was right about there being a signal up here. It means we can split up and report in if we come across anything interesting.'

They set off in different directions, Esme heading westward. According to the plan, there was an entrance close to the bank, just before the wood petered out and became scrub and gorse. She walked alongside the bank, head bent, looking for signs of upheaval of the woodland floor.

Her phone rang. It was Maddy. 'Pete's gone up to the far end of the site,' she said. 'I'm now concentrating on the middle section. Call me when you've finished your end and we'll decide on where next.'

'OK, fine. You don't think we're wasting our time here, do you? I'm beginning to have doubts that my idea wasn't just wishful thinking. Mel agreed with Pete that they'd all been filled in long ago.'

'Well Pete said so too, and he's happy to look. We may as well now we've started. At least we can cross it off the list of possibilities.'

Esme disconnected and continued on, scrunching through the dried leaves. The path came to an end and she looked around for another route to follow. Going back the way she'd come but at the level below seemed the best option. She grabbed hold of a young elderflower tree and lowered herself down the slope. As she turned round to set off, her foot caught something and she almost fell.

She crouched down and shoved the leaf litter away to one side. Underneath was an area of stony ground out of which looped a tree root. It must have been that which had caused her to trip.

As she stood up, she saw a sharp edge – very straight and definitely not organic. With a sense of excited anticipation, she scraped away the rest of the leaves to reveal a rusted hatch. But despite the glint of metal around the framework, she couldn't decide whether it had been opened recently. She reached for her phone.

But perhaps she should check it first, see if it opened. She slipped the phone back into her pocket and grabbed the edge of the hatch at the point which appeared to be opposite to the hinges, wincing as the metal cut into her fingers. Pity she'd not thought of bringing gloves. She pulled the sleeves of her jacket down as far as they'd go and used the cuffs as padding. She grabbed the edge again and pulled.

For a moment she thought it would yield but her optimism was short lived and her efforts came to nothing. It wouldn't budge.

She sat down on the ground and pulled her phone out of her pocket again, eying the hatch warily. It probably didn't matter that she hadn't been able to open it. She had no desire to descend into the abyss. A memory flooded into her head of another anguished search, on that occasion for her niece. She could still taste the dank, acrid smell as on that day and which was certain to permeate the bottom of the shaft in front of her.

She shuddered and scrolled down to find Maddy's number.

'Got anything?' said Maddy, when the call connected.

'Found a hatch but I can't shift it,' Esme said. 'Can't decide whether it's me being weak or that it hasn't been opened for decades.'

'Sounds promising. I'm on the far side of the wood. Where are you? I'll come over.'

Esme dug out the copied map from her pocket and shook it out, laying it across her lap. 'Follow that embankment until you get to –' she scrambled to her feet and looked around for a suitable landmark. As she peered down from the platform where she'd been sitting, she noticed that the ground fell away, revealing a fissure in the rock wide enough to walk in. 'Hang on, I think there's something down here. I'll call you back when I've had a look.'

She disconnected and clambered down the slope into the channel, slowly making her way between the rock slabs which formed walls either side. As she reached the end she saw a narrow opening, half obscured by a broken door, hanging off one hinge. She peered inside but it was too dark to see anything. She activated her phone and held it up to use as a torch. The passageway disappearing away from her seemed to have been hewn out of the rock. The light from her phone only reached a few yards inside but as she had no intention of going any further she pulled back and put the phone to her ear.

It was then that she heard a sound in the undergrowth above. She slunk back. It couldn't be Maddy; she'd been too far away to get here that quickly. Perhaps it was a pheasant picking over the leaf debris. Or it could be Pete. He might be closer than Maddy.

Or it could be Jimmy.

She shrank into the entrance, stepping over the hanging door into the dark, her back against the rock face, out of sight. Her breathing seemed unnatural and alarming in the gloom. But as long as she kept that chink of light in view, she'd be fine.

And if Jimmy appeared? It was all very well ducking out of sight but he'd see her anyway, the minute he came inside.

She reminded herself that Maddy was heading her way. And she may have already phoned Pete. Jimmy may have seen them and realised his secret hideaway had been discovered.

He may have even been watching them from a vantage point somewhere else on the farm. While the image of Jimmy in retreat was a comfort, it wouldn't solve any problems. The whole point of the exercise was to talk to him. She sighed. This was a fool's errand.

Her eyes were becoming more accustomed to the low light now. She took her phone out of her pocket and shone it behind her down the passage. There was some sort of junction up ahead. She thought of what Mel had said about there being bunks with an area for cooking, of space for several people to hole up. Had Jimmy really set himself up like that? It wasn't far. She could just take a quick look.

She inched her way along until the passage opened out, revealing two rooms, their doors ajar. She slid along the wall and peered round the first doorway, holding the phone up in the air to survey the room.

In the corner was a single bed, iron rails at its head and base. The bed was made up with sheets and blankets. A pillow with a crisp white cover lay at the top. Beside the bed was a small wooden chair and on the floor was a rag rug. On the opposite wall stood a narrow table and a camp stool. If this was Jimmy's hideout, he took a lot more care of it than he did the farmhouse.

A noise from behind startled her and she turned, stumbling back against the door jamb. She fell, dropping her phone with a clatter, as the image of two frightened eyes flashed on to her retina. Then everything went black.

57

In the oppressive darkness, Esme suddenly became aware of the damp acrid smell inside her nose and mouth. It invaded her throat, nausea adding to her sense of disorientation. For a few seconds she was transported back to another time and place before she forced herself to face what was happening now. She pushed the memories away and propped herself into a half sitting, half lying position against the wall.

She heard the sound of a match being struck. The flame flickered in the narrow passageway, throwing shadows around the walls and revealing Jimmy's silhouette. He lit a small gas lamp and blew out the match. He picked up the lamp and held it up, peering down at her. The light emphasised his deep eye sockets, making him appear ghoulish and surreal.

'For God's sake, Jimmy,' she said, trying to bank down the panic rising in her throat. 'What do you think you're doing?' She tried not to think of the display of knives in Mel's would-be museum, praying that the lamp was all Jimmy had in his hands, and that there wasn't a knife secreted in a scabbard strapped to his leg.

'You shouldn't have come 'ere,' he said.

Esme peered up at him from her slumped position on the floor. 'Oh, leave it out, Jimmy,' she said. 'Bea was right. You can't pretend everything is going to go away. You owe it to her, after everything she's done for you over the years, to tell her the truth.' She wished he would move back but he seemed determined to corral her against the wall. 'And you do know the truth, Jimmy, don't you? So why won't you tell us? Is it because of the deal? Is that it?'

'What you talking about, woman? Riddles, that's all you ever say.'

'So put me right, then. Is the deal to keep it secret that Vivienne's still alive? And I know she is, Jimmy. I know about Jean Barber. We all do.' She waited for a response but got none. 'Come on, Jimmy. It's over. The secret's out now. But I want to understand. Why couldn't Bea know? Why didn't Vivienne use her real name?'

'He said it wore best.' Jimmy thrust his face towards her. 'There wore no shame in it! Not after everything she'd been through.'

'Shame?'

'She couldn't cope. She tried but it wore too much. As it'd be for anyone who'd survived what she had.'

'I know, Jimmy. You told me. Which is why she was so upset to see Gerald Gallimore with the man who'd been in charge of the prison where she'd been held.'

'Reckon that was the start of it.'

'The start of what?'

Jimmy tapped the side of his head. 'Played on her mind, see. Not surprising it did for her.'

Esme wriggled into a sitting position, against the wall. It was cold against her back but it was more comfortable. 'What are you trying to say, Jimmy?'

'Months in a prison cell, beaten up, half drowned to get her to talk. Leaves its toll. Tis no wonder it did her head in.'

'You're telling me that Vivienne had a mental breakdown?'

'Yes, woman. For pity's sake. Thought you were supposed to be the clever one.'

Esme's head spun in confusion. 'When? When did Vivienne have a breakdown?'

He flapped his hand. 'Years ago.'

'Yes, but when exactly. You mentioned her not being able to cope.'

'With the baby. Though her would've been a little girl by

then, mind. Bout five or six, I reckon.'

'Who told you all this, Jimmy? Vivienne?'

He glowered. 'What's that to you?'

A thought gripped her. 'It was Gerald Gallimore, wasn't it? The day you went to Gallimore's house, demanding answers?'

Jimmy scowled. 'What if it wore?'

'Is that what he said – that Vivienne was in a mental hospital, having suffered a breakdown as the result of her wartime experiences?'

'But she did. I know.' He jabbed himself in the chest with his thumb. 'He told me where she were and I went and saw her and...' He sniffed and wiped his nose with the back of his hand. 'Pitiful it was. I hardly knew her. She knew me, though,' he added, his voice cracked. 'I was a comfort for her.'

'I'm sure you were, Jimmy. But why didn't you tell Bea? She was desperate to know.'

'Couldn't.'

'Lloyd Gallimore?'

A nod.

'Why?'

'Can't say.'

'Oh, yes. Your deal. Trouble is, Jimmy, I'm not sure Gallimore told you the truth that day. You see, I've tracked down Vivienne's daughter.'

Jimmy's mouth dropped open, then closed. She fancied she saw tears in his eyes.

'Gallimore lied to you, Jimmy,' Esme continued, aware of the rapid pace of her heartbeat. 'If Vivienne did suffer a mental breakdown, it wasn't because of her struggles as a mother, it followed her being admitted to Dunsford House hospital as a typhoid carrier in 1946.'

Jimmy narrowed his rheumy eyes. 'No,' he said, shaking his head. 'You've got that wrong. You're twisting things. I don't believe you.'

'You don't have to believe me, Jimmy. Believe Vivienne's

daughter. I've met her. She doesn't remember her mother at all. She grew up in Germany for the first few years of her life, until she came to England when she was adopted by Donald Cole and his wife. What Gallimore told you wasn't true.'

Jimmy looked around, as though the answer was posted on the wall somewhere, if only he could find it. 'He wouldn't do that. It dun't make no sense.'

'Perhaps he made it up in the heat of the moment? To pacify you, standing on the doorstep, threatening him? You do know he was the father of Vivienne's baby?'

Jimmy looked at the floor. 'I didn't care about that. I just wanted to know where her was.'

Esme slumped against the wall and closed her eyes. Gallimore had played on Jimmy's concern for Vivienne, using him for his own purposes. But if it had been so easy to convince Jimmy that Vivienne was in Dunsford House because of her mental health without revealing the true circumstances behind her admission, why insist she hide her real identity? Was she missing something here?

Her eyes shot open. Of course she was. This didn't involve Gerald Gallimore at all. She already knew that. The deal was with Lloyd Gallimore, made after Gerald Gallimore's murder, not before it.

Esme shifted her position. 'What happened that day at the Gallimore's, Jimmy?'

'It's nothing to do with you. I told you afore.'

'But the secret's out, now, isn't it? I've told you we know Vivienne's alive. If keeping that quiet was the deal you had with Lloyd...'

'Who said it wore?'

Esme closed her eyes and shook her head. It was hopeless. 'Well, I can't force you to tell me but if you think you're protecting Vivienne, as you claimed that night at Bea's house, then you're wasting your time. Vivienne's gone missing. Someone's taken her. Who, Jimmy? Is it Lloyd? Is he worried you'll break your silence? Or does he think you already have?' She scrambled to her knees. 'Help us, Jimmy. The police are out looking for Vivienne now. You could help instead of skulking about here.'

Jimmy glowered at her. She stared back, searching for a hint of how strong his determination was or how close he might be to surrendering what he knew. As she did so, an image of two eyes flickered in her head.

It all happened at once. A voice echoed down the passageway, calling her name. Maddy. Jimmy's head shot round towards the sound and back to Esme. He lifted a fist and growled.

Esme scrambled to her feet. 'No, Jimmy,' she shouted as he stepped towards her. 'I'm not your enemy.'

But it wasn't Esme's caution which stopped him. It was a cry from behind. Jimmy turned and Esme saw again the frightened eyes blinking in the light of the lamp. And the terrified face of an elderly woman.

58

The ambulance pulled out of Crossways Farm and on to the lane, heading off to North Devon District Hospital. Inside was one frail old lady, confused by her experience of being removed from the comfort of her care home, a confusion compounded no doubt by being referred to as Jean by the emergency services and Vivienne by another elderly lady who insisted she was Jean's sister. That the older woman had responded with obvious joy to being reunited with her sibling had persuaded the ambulance crew to allow Bea to accompany them to the hospital.

'What are the police going to make of everything, d'you think?' Maddy said, as the vehicle pulled away.

'Can't see Jimmy giving much away,' Esme said, looking across at Jimmy sitting, head bowed, in the back of the police car. From what had emerged so far, Jimmy was a regular visitor to "Jean" and all that was alleged was that he'd failed to return her to the care home after he'd taken her out, or to inform them she was safe and well.

'What was he thinking?' Maddy said.

'He thought he was protecting her.'

'So Lloyd Gallimore's still a threat then?'

'Well, it's his secret he's keeping?'

'But the secret's out now. Vivienne and Bea have been reunited.'

Esme shook her head. 'There's another layer. And it's all tied up with Gerald Gallimore's murder.' And, she knew, with Tim's, too. What had he stumbled upon when he went to question Donald Cole?

'Any idea what?'

'I wish I did.'

Ruth and Pete were deep in conversation with a police constable beside their Land Rover. Esme saw Ruth nod and glance across to Esme and Maddy before hurrying over.

'Everything OK?' Esme said.

'Yes, fine. We're going to follow the ambulance so we can bring Bea home.' She hesitated, her face grim. 'I can't believe he's never told Mum.'

'I think he thought she'd be taken away from him if he did. He walked right into their trap that day at the Gallimore's and he's been dangled on the end of a piece of string ever since.'

Esme and Maddy watched until all the vehicles had departed and silence fell in the yard.

'Maybe Jimmy will change his mind when he's questioned,' Maddy said.

'Perhaps.' Esme recalled the determined look on his face, the fury at realising he'd been tracked down. 'But he's kept the secret for so long, I'm not sure he'd be able to explain everything if he wanted to. He must still be wary of what he still has to lose.'

'Which might be more than we know.'

Esme frowned. 'What do you mean?'

'We don't know what price he had to pay,' Maddy said, her expression sombre. 'His silence may be as much to cover up his own crime as to protect Vivienne.'

Again, Pete's words ricocheted around Esme's head, *auxiliaries were trained killers. And you don't lose that skill. Especially someone like Jimmy.* Had Lloyd Gallimore's deal involved murder?

*

By the time Esme got back to her cottage, her head was thumping. But she still had an important call to make. Ingrid needed to know her mother was still alive. Perhaps she'd already realised? She may have seen the news item herself. She had the same information as they had – would she fit the pieces together?

Esme guessed that if she had, she'd have already been in touch and there was no message from her. There was one from Max, however, looking for an update. She sat down on the sofa and scrolled down her phone to find his number. He listened attentively as she relayed everything that happened, interrupting to ask questions now and again.

'I don't know whether to feel sorry for Jimmy or mad at him,' she said, leaning back into the sofa cushions and putting her feet up on the coffee table. 'But Maddy's worried I've got a blind spot and that I'm not seeing how he could be responsible for what happened to Tim.' Even after everything, she still had to speak of his death in couched language. It was too difficult to be more direct.

'She has a point,' Max said.

Esme rubbed her eyes. 'Am I ever going to know, Max?' she said. 'I said to Maddy the other day that maybe there wasn't anyone left alive who knew the truth. She said there was – Faye Gallimore. But you and I both know where she stands. We've both tried and failed. Ingrid the same. I can't see she's going to change her position anytime soon, not with Lloyd being so implicated. And I can hardly go in hard, demanding to know the truth, can I? Vulnerable Old Lady Bullied by Researcher. I can see the headlines now.'

'Ah. See where you're coming from. Leave it with me. I've an idea.'

'What sort of idea?'

'I'll be in touch.' He disconnected.

She frowned at the blank screen before taking a deep breath and trying Ingrid's number.

*

Esme sat in the cafe window, gazing out across the street to the river, her view broken regularly by shoppers hurrying along on the pavement on their way to the high street. Vehicles flowed continuously across the Old Bideford bridge, slowing to a crawl as they turned on to the quay and filed past the cafe. She spotted Ingrid waiting on the opposite side of the road, looking for a gap in the traffic. As she crossed over, she saw Esme and waved.

Inside, Esme gestured Ingrid to take a seat at the table and went to the counter to order their coffees.

When she returned, she took a photograph out of her pocket and slid it across to Ingrid. 'Maddy thought you'd like this,' she said, sitting down. 'It's Vivienne when she was a Land Girl in Devon. It was amongst Jimmy Beer's photos.'

Ingrid picked up the photograph and studied it. 'I still find it hard to think of her as Vivienne. She's still Jean in my head.'

'She's been living under that name for more years than she was Vivienne, bizarrely. Not for her family, though, of course.'

'No, of course.' She handed the photograph back to Esme.

Esme held up her hand and shook her head. 'No, that's yours. Maddy made you a copy especially.'

Ingrid smiled and nodded. 'Thank her for me, will you?' She took another look at the image before storing it in her bag.

Their order arrived and they sat in companionable silence, sipping coffee. Esme thought of all the photographs she had of her own late mother, some in albums, some tiny snips, others more formal portraits at key stages in her life, all to be brought out and browsed through any time she wished. One picture slyly copied from Jimmy's collection seemed the least she could pass on to Ingrid.

'I tracked down the nurse who your journalist friend got his information from,' Ingrid said, breaking into Esme's thoughts.

'Oh, well done,' Esme said. She frowned. 'How was it? Was she forthcoming?'

'Yes, very. We had a long chat on the phone. She said how she and Jean used to have discussions about news items in the papers and TV programmes. She seemed pretty lucid most of the time, apparently.' She replaced her cup in its saucer.

'I asked her if she thought Jean would have survived in the outside world.'

'What did she say?'

'She said that, in many ways, Jean gave the appearance of being in full control, but having known only the inside of a small room for years, she thought it doubtful. In fact, she was concerned for her when the hospital closed and the patients were moved. She thought it might be too much for her. But by then an old friend had started to visit her regularly and she seemed to respond to that.'

'Jimmy Beer, I suppose she meant,' Esme said. 'At least she had someone – even if the circumstances were totally dishonest.'

'What's happening with him? I assume he's the man they arrested?'

'Yes, but he's been released now. He's no fool, is Jimmy. He played the "confused old man", claiming not to understand what all the fuss was about. Ruth's been deliberately cagey about what she told them, even though she'd been calling Jimmy every name under the sun earlier in the day. But she accepted that Jimmy had been deceived as much as anyone. At least finding Vivienne had been the result, at the end of the day.' Despite the outcome, Esme was still wary of Jimmy's part in the saga. She couldn't rid herself of Maddy's fear that he had more to hide about his obligations to Lloyd Gallimore than she'd so far uncovered.

'Ruth,' Ingrid said, picking up her cup reflectively. 'Seems odd to think I have a cousin. Does she know about me?'

'She knows you exist "somewhere out there". But I've not told her or Bea yet that I've contacted you.' She hesitated. She'd told Jimmy in order to convince him that Lloyd Gallimore had lied to him about Vivienne's past. She wondered whether he'd tell Bea. She might need to own up sooner than she planned. She turned to Ingrid. 'When and if you want that to change, just let me know.'

Ingrid nodded. 'So,' she said, looking round at Esme.

'What about you and your search?'

Esme shrugged. 'If you don't know what happened when Tim came to see your father –'

'Which I don't. You can trust me on that, Esme.'

'Then it seems there's only one person left who does and hopes in that direction are feeble to say the least.'

'Faye Gallimore.'

Esme nodded. 'Max thinks he's an idea how to get her to talk to me but I can't see it, myself.'

'She's a cold bitch,' Ingrid said, her mouth set in a hard line. 'She was up to something that day in my father's office, the day before he killed himself.' She gave Esme a weak smile. 'Seems she sways power over us both, Esme, eh? Another coffee? On me this time.'

As Ingrid went to the counter, Esme reflected on Ingrid's observation. Was it about power? She thought back to when Lloyd walked in the room when she'd visited Faye. At the time it seemed to be Lloyd throwing his weight around, accusing her of being "that Cole woman" but Faye had already instructed Magda to show her out and Faye had interrupted Lloyd, as though to emphasise she had already taken control of the situation. So had it been Faye who'd instructed Lloyd to strike up the deal with Jimmy? And what was her interest in keeping Cole's secret from being exposed? It had to be connected to her visit to Cole that Ingrid had witnessed. But what could it be?

Her phone buzzed and she picked it up automatically, her mind still sifting through her muddled thoughts. Max's voice at the other end of the line made her jump and for a moment, she couldn't register what he was saying.

'What?' She looked at her watch. 'Today?'

'Three o'clock sharp. Can you make it?'

Esme's mouth gaped for a second before she put her brain in gear. 'Yes, yes. Of course I can.'

'Right. Catch you then.' And he was gone.

Esme dropped the phone on the table top and replayed the brief conversation in her head, suddenly aware that Ingrid had sat back down and was staring at her.

'Max,' Esme stammered. 'Seems to have hit the jackpot, though God knows how.'

'Jackpot?' Ingrid said, head cocked.

'Faye Gallimore has agreed to meet. I've got to be at the Gallimores' place at three.'

Ingrid narrowed her eyes. 'I want to come too.'

59

As Esme drove up the M5 towards Taunton, she deliberated whether she should warn Max about Ingrid coming too. But she couldn't risk it. Faye may use it as an excuse to cancel the meeting. She reasoned that a fait accompli had more chance of success.

Esme had suggested they park their respective cars in the quiet streets near the Gallimores' house and walk round together. She arrived only a minute or two ahead of Ingrid. They got out, acknowledged each other with a nod of determination and strode along the pavement to the end of the road. As they rounded the corner, Esme stopped, Ingrid careering into her.

'What the hell –?' began Ingrid, until she saw what Esme'd seen. They retreated back round the corner.

'Press have clearly got wind of something,' Esme said, chewing her lip. 'There's a proverbial posse of reporters out there.'

'Complete with camera crews too, by the looks of things. What do you reckon?'

'Don't know,' Esme said, with a shake of the head. 'But I don't fancy running the gauntlet, do you?'

Ingrid shook her head. 'No, definitely not. Is there a back way in?'

'There's a garden gate, I think,' Esme said, remembering Bea's story of the day she came with Jimmy and how she'd run away across a lawn. Esme dipped into her bag for her phone. 'But I ought to warn Max of the change of plan.' She found his number and made the call. Max said he'd meet her on the boundary. She almost mentioned Ingrid but decided he'd find out soon enough. And too late, hopefully, to do anything about it.

They hurried back down the street along the stone wall which surrounded the garden. A wooden door set within the stonework was almost lost in the shade of a large cedar which towered above creating a canopy over the pavement. Esme glanced around before thumbing the latch and pushing open the door. They stumbled through into the garden and straight into Max waiting on the other side.

'Who the –' he began, seeing Ingrid.

'Max, this is Ingrid. And before you say a word, you can't deny that she has as much right as I do to hear the truth from Faye Gallimore.'

'It's not what I think that's relevant here, Ez. I've swung this for you, not –' He jerked his thumb in Ingrid's direction.

Esme shrugged. 'Tough. She's here now.'

Max scowled. 'She's not going to like it.'

Esme scowled back, thrusting her arm out, indicating the direction from where they'd come. 'I could, if she'd prefer, go and throw some meat to the baying wolves out the front, if you like?'

Max narrowed his eyes. 'You wouldn't.'

'Wouldn't I?' She put her hands on her hips and glared at him. 'Try me. I've buried this truth for years, Max, you know that. But having braced myself to face it, I'm not going to back down now. Not when I've come this far.'

Max turned and stomped off across the lawn.

Esme felt Ingrid beside her. 'That told him,' Ingrid said in her ear.

Esme nodded, not trusting herself to speak, aware she was shaking. She stood up straight and breathed in. 'Come on. Let's get this over with.'

They caught up with Max as he arrived at the impressive

and elaborate conservatory Esme had seen on her last visit. They followed him along a path which ran around the side where he stopped at a glazed door in the gable end of the building. He snatched open the door and ushered them inside.

Palms, banana plants and a collection of giant spiny cacti lined the glasshouse in gravel trays. The floor was laid with brick paviors, arranged in herringbone rows, on which stood a number of basket chairs with damask cushions. Waiting at the other end of the room, smartly dressed as before and erect in her wheelchair which was parked beside a cast iron French cafe-style table, was Faye Gallimore. Behind her, arms folded and wearing what Esme guessed was a habitual expression of disdain, was her son, Lloyd. When he saw Ingrid, he dropped his arms and took two strides towards the new arrivals.

'What the hell's going on? There was only mention of Mrs Quentin.'

Ingrid marched over to one of the basket chairs and sat down. 'I'm not going anywhere,' she said, crossing her legs. 'So you better get used to the idea.'

Max walked past Ingrid and addressed Faye. 'This is Ingrid Cole, Mrs Gallimore. Mrs Quentin is perfectly willing for her to be present.'

Lloyd threw a sneer at Esme. 'It's not for Mrs Quentin to declare her willingness for or against,' he said.

Faye lifted her chin. 'It hardly matters to me one way or the other, Lloyd,' she said. 'So please stop making such a fuss.'

'I think it's time we learned the truth,' Esme said, addressing Faye. 'And I suspect you think so too.'

'Oh, very commendable,' Lloyd snapped. 'Forcing your way into people's houses and making demands.'

Faye shot Lloyd a withering look. 'Enough. *Servo tu.*'

Lloyd hobbled across the room and threw himself down on a well-worn faded leather chesterfield armchair in the corner, leaning back, his arms draped across the sides and his ankles crossed.

Faye sneered at Max and Esme before turning her head towards the garden. 'I expected to take the secrets of that time to my grave.'

Esme glanced at Max and lowered herself down on the chair next to Ingrid, a whooshing sound of blood pulsating in her ear drums.

'It was all for Vivienne's sake, of course,' Faye continued.

'Vivienne's?' Esme said, scornfully. 'I'm sure having discovered your husband's affair and a baby the result of it, you'd have your own reasons for burying the truth.'

Faye pressed her lips together and gave Esme a contemptuous stare. She turned to Ingrid. 'You may have barged your way in here, my dear. But you'll very soon wish you hadn't when you hear the truth. My husband's misdemeanors pale into insignificance compared to the evil of Celia Cole.'

60

Ingrid shot out of her chair. 'You bitch!' she yelled Faye recoiled and Lloyd got to his feet.

Esme stood up and laid a restraining hand on Ingrid's arm. 'Come on, Ingrid, sit down,' she said. 'Let's hear what she's got to say.' Why had she not known Cole's wife was called Celia and why did the name resonate with a memory in her head? She guided Ingrid back to her chair and sat down beside her. Lloyd backed off and returned to the chesterfield.

'Well?' Esme said, turning to Faye. 'Perhaps you'd like to explain yourself.'

Faye looked at Ingrid. 'Surely you already know how obsessed your mother was with Gerald?' she said. 'Of course he had not the slightest interest in her. Gerald and I were already engaged when the war started. But she disregarded all that. She set her sights on him and dogged his every footstep. It was why she joined the SOE in the first place.'

'Celia Cole was an SOE?' Esme said. She glanced at Ingrid. Had she known? Ingrid's expression suggested she hadn't.

'Oh, didn't you know?' Faye said, tipping her head to one side and taking pleasure in knowing facts that Esme didn't. Esme ignored the taunt, her mind too busy recalling their conversation with Joe Paxton. She shot a glance at Max, who was leaning against the back wall, arms folded. His expression told her he'd realised the same thing. The SOE Joe had mentioned, code name Yvette, the woman who'd been close to Gallimore. *Her* name was Celia – Celia Bradshaw. Her surname before she'd married Donald Cole? Esme tuned back into Faye's voice.

'Whether she had some romantic notion,' Faye was saying, 'that the two of them would be drawn together because of their joint struggle or whether she thought she could impress him in some way, I have no idea. Of course, her whole plan rebounded on her in the most horrific way.'

'How?' Esme asked.

Faye faltered at the question, as though she'd forgotten she had an audience. 'Because of the torture she was subjected to in that dreadful prison camp, obviously. It's why she couldn't have children.'

'No,' Ingrid said, shaking her head. 'That was because of Papa. Not her.'

'Utter whitewash,' Faye said. 'Celia was too ashamed to admit she was at fault.'

Esme scoffed. 'Hardly *her fault* if it was the result of what she suffered at the hands of –' A sudden thought. 'Where was she held? Which prison camp?'

'What difference does it make which prison –?'

'Which one?'

Faye threw a glance at Lloyd. 'Jurgenbrück, I believe. But I don't see –'

'Did Vivienne tell Celia what she'd seen?'

Fay scowled. 'I have no idea what you're talking about. How could I possibly know what went on between Celia and Vivienne? They were rivals. I very much doubt they even spoke to one another.'

'Vivienne saw Kruger and your husband together,' Esme said. 'She believed he'd betrayed her. And his country.'

Faye tossed her head dismissively. 'That's quite ridiculous.'

'No, it's not. She told Jimmy Beer about it.' Something stirred in the forefront of her brain. The memory of Bea mentioning a woman other than Faye being present when she and Jimmy had confronted Gallimore. She cried out. 'No, of course she didn't hear it from Vivienne,' she said. 'She heard it from Jimmy.' She glared at Faye. 'Celia was there that day, when Bea and Jimmy came, wasn't she? She would have heard Jimmy hurl Vivienne's accusations at your husband, how she'd seen him and Viktor Kruger together. What must Celia have thought when she found out the man she'd idolised all those years was a traitor?'

Faye sneered. 'Stupid, stupid woman,' she said. 'She was never the most stable person. Gerald thought it our duty to support her. I should never have allowed her into my house, let alone befriend her.' She glowered at Esme. 'You talk about betrayal but that woman betrayed me that day and I never forgave her for it.'

'Betrayed you?' Esme said.

'It was bloody Beer's fault,' Lloyd snapped, sitting up straight now, leaning forward, face flushed with anger. 'Ranting on while that infernal woman wailed next to him to come away. What she was doing there, God only knows.'

'She was hoping Jimmy would see sense,' Esme said. 'That your father would convince him that he'd imagined it all, as she thought was the case. But he couldn't, could he, because everything Vivienne had told him was true.' She turned back to Faye. 'Jimmy brought a gun with him, didn't he?'

Faye looked away. 'Gerald and Lloyd managed to disarm him,' she said, staring out into the garden. 'He wasn't much of a match, against the two of them. But we underestimated Celia and her reaction to his histrionics.'

'Father brought it on himself.' Lloyd's agitation was clear now and it seemed to be aimed at his mother. 'He shouldn't have left the bloody gun on the table.'

'That will do, Lloyd,' Faye snapped.

It took a moment for Esme to grasp what he'd implied. 'It was Celia who shot him?' Behind her she heard a quiet gasp from Ingrid.

Faye turned away, signalling Esme had guessed right – Celia, horrified by Jimmy's damning account of what Vivienne had witnessed, had picked up the gun and killed

Gerald Gallimore for betrayal and treason.

Esme stared at Faye, unable to comprehend her concealing the murder of her husband and the perpetrator. Her bitterness towards Celia was evident. So why would she sanction Celia evading justice?

But as Esme grappled with the fusion of hate, dishonour and motive before her, she began to understand. It wasn't about shielding Celia from facing criminal charges. That was a price Faye was prepared to pay. It was about Faye protecting herself. Involving the authorities risked exposing everything the Gallimores had covered up in the last forty years, including her husband's fraudulent identity and Vivienne's false incarceration. Reputation was everything to a woman like Faye Gallimore.

When Jimmy turned up, exposure was threatened once more. They'd had to find a way of keeping him quiet.

'You traded Jimmy's silence for a pack of lies,' Esme said. 'A cock and bull story of Vivienne's breakdown from her wartime traumas. But it was never that which sent her over the edge. It was what *you* did to her.'

'He got what he wanted,' Lloyd spat at her. 'And more. He was well paid for his trouble. He had no complaints.'

'That's before he found out the truth.' Esme glared between Faye and Lloyd. 'So, what other hold do you have over him?' she added, her voice rising as the fear she'd been suppressing for so long found its outlet. 'Oh, of course. The gun with his fingerprints all over it. Threatened to use it against him, as evidence that he killed Gerald, did you, unless he'd rid you of anyone who got too close to comfort?' She exhaled, shuddering, her hand to her mouth, unable to continue.

'You do realise who she's talking about,' Max said, speaking for the first time. 'Tim Quentin. He found out about the women typhoid carriers and came asking questions.'

Faye hooted with contempt. 'Are you seriously suggesting we engaged Jimmy Beer as some sort of hired assassin?'

'You must have worried he'd expose what you'd done to Vivienne Lancaster,' Max said, mildly.

Faye laughed out loud and looked across at her son. 'We should have thought of that, shouldn't we Lloyd?' Lloyd clearly didn't share his mother's amusement and glowered back at her without answering.

Faye's gaze returned to Esme. 'I never saw your husband, Mrs Quentin. It wasn't me to whom he addressed his questions. It was Donald Cole.'

Esme swallowed and reined in control of her emotions. 'But you knew what was at stake. Gerald was party to the adoption.' She eyed Ingrid who was rocking gently in her chair, her expression reeking pain. 'He was well aware of Celia's need for a child.'

Faye snorted. '*Need* isn't nearly strong enough. It was like a hunger with her, a craving.'

'And when Vivienne returned before the papers were signed, the pressure to keep her from discovering where her child had gone was crucial.'

'It would have given the Coles complications, certainly.'

'So whose idea was it to falsely incarcerate her in Dunsford House?'

Faye shrugged and looked away. 'I really have no idea.'

'Oh, really.' From everything she'd seen and heard, Esme was convinced it was Faye herself who'd hatched the plan, desperate to keep her husband's wartime lover out of the way. How fortunate that there was a child involved and a willing victim like Cole to manipulate to do her bidding, twisting the circumstances so he believed she was only concerned for him and his childless wife. 'But you must know what happened when Tim turned up,' Esme said, a quick check at Max. 'Or we wouldn't be here.'

Faye gripped the arms of her wheelchair. 'If only Celia had just kept quiet. But she couldn't, could she? Oh, no. Not Celia. She imagined everything falling apart around her ears and she panicked.'

'Imagined?' Esme said, latching on to a word which seemed out of place.

'Yes,' Faye snapped. 'It was all in her head. Like I said, she should have kept quiet. No one would have known.'

Esme stared. Tension in the room intensified. It was as though fear and dread had slipped in through the open window, joined forces and curled around her throat. 'Tim knew, though, didn't he? He found out somehow. Did Cole tell him when he realised Jean Barber was still where he'd put her all those years before?'

Faye trained her eyes on Esme. 'I have already said, Mrs Quentin. He did not address his questions to me.'

'To Celia then?'

'I don't think so,' Faye said, shaking her head. 'D'you know the most absurd thing? Celia expected *me* to do something about it.' A humourless laugh escaped her lips. 'Me. What did she imagine I could do? I told her straight. You're the one with the necessary skills, Celia. You do it. Who's going to suspect you?'

Esme went cold. *Who's going to suspect you?* Her fingers flew to the scar on her face. *No one saw anyone suspicious in the pub. No one who looked handy with a stiletto, anyway.* Celia Cole. At the time she was a woman in her sixties. *We're fooled into thinking they're harmless*, Maddy had said. But Celia Cole wasn't harmless. She was a trained killer.

She heard Max, distant and muffled as though at the end of a long tunnel. 'Are you telling us that Celia Cole killed Tim Quentin?'

The rush of blood in Esme's ears drowned out Faye's answer. But she must have said yes, because Esme heard Ingrid cry out.

'Oh, she was so proud of herself,' Faye was saying. She was staring at Ingrid now. 'Proud to have saved your father from the ignominy of his medical colleagues discovering that he'd broken the Hippocratic Oath.'

Esme imagined Cole's reaction. Already struggling with

the knowledge that Vivienne had not been released as he'd assumed, he now discovered his wife was a murderer. No wonder he rewrote his will and found he could no longer live with the consequences of his actions.

'In fact she was so pleased with herself,' Faye added, 'that the stupid woman went home and boasted to your father what she'd done.'

Ingrid jumped up, her chair clattering to the floor behind her. 'No!' she shouted, approaching Faye, her arm outstretched, her finger jabbed towards her. '*She* didn't tell Papa what she'd done. You did.'

'Don't be ridic–'

'I saw you. I saw you come to our house. You told him everything and he killed himself.'

Lloyd was up on his feet now. He grabbed Ingrid and shoved her aside. 'Enough,' he said, turning to Max. 'Get them out of here. Now.'

Esme steered the now sobbing Ingrid out of the conservatory and out into the garden, Max following behind. They hurried across the lawn to the exit gate in the wall, Esme still holding on to Ingrid, encouraging her on. When they reached the boundary, Esme turned to Max, shaking. 'So, what happens now?' She surprised herself that she could still speak coherently. Inside her head she was screaming.

Max shrugged. 'Like what?'

'What do you mean, *like what*?' She jerked out her arm and pointed back towards the house. 'Like, false imprisonment, perverting the course of justice, concealing a crime, accessory to murder. That not enough for you?'

'Cole was responsible for falsely imprisoning Vivienne, and his wife for murder. They're both dead, Ez.'

'And the rest?' She looked beyond the bows of the cedar tree to the house across the lawn. 'Faye and Lloyd Gallimore are culpable, Max. How can you not see that?'

Max shook his head. 'Forget it, Ez. There's no evidence.

D'you think they're going to repeat what they've just said back there and incriminate themselves?'

'But we've just heard them confess! You did, I did,' she glanced around. 'And Ingrid did.'

'Sure. But that was the agreement. You wanted the truth, didn't you? Well, you just got it.' He jabbed himself in the chest with his thumb. 'And *I* got it for you. Just like you asked.'

Esme's eyes narrowed. 'In return for what?'

'It's no big deal, Ez.'

'In return for what?' she repeated, louder this time.

'Look, I've earned it, with all the work I've done.' He swallowed. 'An exclusive to write Gallimore's story –'

'The sugar-coated version, of course. Missing out the criminal elements.'

Max scowled. 'What is it with you? You got what you wanted, didn't you? Isn't that enough?'

'No,' she snapped, her voice breaking. 'It's not enough. That's not justice for Tim.'

He shook his head. 'The woman's dead, Esme. There never can be justice for Tim. Get real.'

She glared back at him, tears spilling down her cheeks. She wanted to scream that she'd tell the authorities anyway, that Ingrid would back her up. But she knew it would be futile. The Gallimores would never make a formal confession. They'd deny everything and she had no evidence of their involvement. They didn't really believe they'd done anything wrong. Even Cole's actions, which might be unpicked from medical records, didn't tell the full story.

Unable to find the words to express her disgust for his attitude, Esme turned her back on Max. Taking Ingrid's arm, she stumbled through the gate and out on to the street.

61

The hangar at Bleakmoor Airfield resounded with vintage songs from the 1940s courtesy of an enthusiastic trio of harmony singers. Their audience, equally enthused and dressed in clothes from the period, danced, sang or tapped their feet along with the music, cheering wildly at the end of each track.

When the singers took a break and the chair of the Bleakmoor Wartime Museum fund-raising committee took to the stage to make the obligatory speech of thanks and draw the raffle, Esme slipped outside for some air.

She wandered to the edge of the tarmac and gazed out from the hazy pool of light spilling from the building's outside wall lamp into the semi-darkness. A faint grey line beyond the expanse of moorland marked the point at which land became sea. She imagined the silhouettes of the planes of the Black Squadron flying in from their secret missions overseas, precious cargo of agents returning to be debriefed at HQ, as circuits were discovered or betrayed to the Gestapo. How many times was the success and failure of those courageous individuals finely balanced? She thought of Vivienne, of Celia Cole and of every other captured serviceman or woman who suffered as a result of the task they'd taken on. Did they ever regret their choice?

Ironic that Vivienne and Celia, rivals for Gerald Gallimore's affections, might have been a support and comfort to one another in their shared traumas, under different circumstances. As it was, they became as bitter enemies as any in the field of war. A remark by Joe Paxton niggled in her memory. When he first arrived in France, he said, a female SOE had just been arrested, having been betrayed to the Gestapo. Esme wondered who'd betrayed her. Someone local, possibly, having seen something suspicious and reported it, perhaps in return for extra rations? But it was something Faye Gallimore had said of Celia Cole that kept coming back to her – that her whole plan had rebounded on her in the most horrific way. Was she simply referring to Celia joining the SOEs or had she meant more by it? Had it been Celia who had alerted the Gestapo, to get Vivienne out of the way so she'd have Gallimore all to herself, only to suffer the same horrific fate?

Esme shivered. Maybe. If that was true, Vivienne had survived her treachery and ultimately been reunited with her sister, albeit with many years lost to her. Celia, on the other hand, had been broken, losing her precious Gerald to Faye and being renounced by her husband when he discovered what she'd done in his name. Had that been what had finally pushed her over the edge? The analogy Ingrid had used, prodding certainties to discover only sand beneath, must surely have developed from experiencing the shock of having both her parents take their own lives. Esme hoped she'd find some solace in becoming acquainted with her family at Ravens Farm.

Max's book had been fast-tracked for rush publication to coincide with Lloyd Gallimore's selection to stand as an MP. She'd seen it displayed in high street bookshops, advertised on the Internet and reviewed to glowing acclaim in the Sunday papers. She had no desire to read it. Maddy had offered to get a copy on her behalf and report back what was in it to "save her the pain" but Esme told her she'd rather not know. Maddy said it would never become a best seller and Max was kidding himself he'd get rich on the proceeds. Esme had smiled sweetly and said the thought had never entered her head.

Cheers and applause carried out of the hangar and the band struck up once more. Esme turned to see a figure walking towards her.

'For you,' Ruth said, handing Esme a Champagne flute half-full of sparkling wine. 'You missed the toast celebrating the first thousand pounds raised.'

Esme raised her glass. 'To the first thousand pounds.'

They clinked glasses and sipped the fizzy liquid in silence.

'How's Bea –' Esme said, and laughed. 'Oh for goodness sake, how many times have I asked that question over the past few weeks? Your mother has a lot to answer for. I hope she realises.'

Ruth chuckled. 'I think I may have told her something along the same lines.' She took another sip. 'How is Ingrid? Yes, I know she's keen to meet us all, as we are her I just wondered how she was dealing with everything since, you know, she discovered such shocking things about her adoptive mother.'

Esme put her arm across her waist. 'I *think* she's OK. Her husband's been very supportive, despite his initial wariness of her starting her search in the first place. That must help.'

'She must feel a bit disorientated – no, that's not quite the right word – I don't know, bewildered, about Cole leaving all his money to Vivienne and nothing to her. I mean, it was hardly Ingrid's fault, was it?'

'I imagine he thought the truth would out and Ingrid would be reunited with Vivienne.'

'Happy ever after? Surely he wasn't so naive. Neither could be certain that's what would happen.' Ruth looked at Esme. 'Is that why he used her real name in the will? He hoped it would trigger something?'

'I assume so. Still a long shot, though, I agree.'

'But he must have realised that he risked Ingrid learning everything – and I mean, everything. Didn't he stop to consider what that would be like for her to find out what Celia had done?'

'A decision made under pressure, perhaps? Maybe he never really thought it through. There's no way he could ever have guessed that she'd find out in such a dramatic fashion.'

'I can't imagine Celia would have ever confessed. Which makes you wonder why she didn't contest the will.'

Esme hesitated, fingering her glass, thinking of what Frank Crombie, the probate researcher, had told her about Celia's reluctance in pursuing her claim. Now she knew why. 'There was a letter,' she said. 'Written by Cole and lodged with his solicitor, to be opened should Celia mount a legal challenge.'

'A letter? Saying what?'

'Detailing everything that had happened – his guilt in Vivienne's story and what his wife had done to keep his role secret.'

Ruth gasped. 'So you have a written confession – that she killed Tim?'

'It's not *her* confession, though. It was written by Cole after Faye Gallimore came to see him and told him what Celia had done.'

'What Faye Gallimore had coerced Celia to do, you mean.'

'That's certainly what Ingrid believes, yes. Not that it's much comfort to her.'

'Well, it's all very well fretting about everyone else's state of mind,' Ruth said, laying a hand on Esme's arm. 'But what about you? Has finding out about Tim been the catalyst you'd hoped for? You haven't really spoken about it.'

Esme's mind drifted back to the past when she'd spent so much time and energy keeping herself in a world devoid of reality. She knew she didn't want to go there again. She couldn't allow it. She'd fought hard to be where she was. And now she'd faced what she never thought she'd have to, and survived – not the discovery of Tim's assassin, she'd been prepared for that – but that he'd been murdered despite being no threat to his killer. Tim had never uncovered the whole truth. Celia, as Faye had so crudely assessed, had panicked. And Faye had exploited that panic for her own insurance.

'Max seemed to assume it would be all so simple,' she

said, after a while, swivelling her glass by its stem. 'Find out the truth. Tick. Done. Sorted. He seemed to think I should be more grateful that he'd swung it for me.'

'Oh, come on. He can't really believe it would be that simple, can he?'

Esme sighed. 'Probably not. Probably just feeling the pressure of the situation. It was pretty intense.'

'And Tim was his colleague and friend. Maybe there was a fair bit of flustering going on to cover up his own distress.'

'You may be right.' As she thought about it, she realised that part of the reason she'd been so upset with him was that Max seemed to have forgotten that very fact – that he was more driven by pride about the deal he'd swung than touched by the shocking truth of Tim's death. She thought back to what he'd said about Cole and Celia being dead, as though it somehow diminished the magnitude of the crime. 'At least I've learned who Tim's attacker was and the motive,' she added. 'Unlike those who lost loved ones in wartime. They had no identifiable assailant, other than a generic *The Enemy* and precious little understanding of the circumstances.'

'I suppose that's why those letters from commanding officers were so important, to try and put the dreadful news in context.'

Behind them the music started up again. 'Come on,' Esme said, draining her glass. 'Let's get back inside. It's chilling off out here.'

As they walked back across the tarmac, Esme thought of Gallimore's letter to Vivienne's parents. When he wrote it, did he really believe she was dead? Or did he take a greater part in her disappearance than it presently appeared? Did he know of her suffering in Jurgensbrück camp? Did he lie about that to protect her family? There must have been many families who were lied to in order to protect them from the harshest of truths.

And what of Jimmy, and his claim that he'd done what

he did to protect Vivienne? Was it true? Or was he merely protecting himself? Perhaps he really believed he was acting in Vivienne's interest. It was impossible to unravel fact from fiction when it came to Jimmy.

They reached the half open door of the hangar and looked in at the sea of happy faces and gyrating bodies. Maddy waved to them from the dance floor and hurried over.

'There you are,' she said, flushed and breathless. 'Everything OK?' Her smile faded.

'Of course,' Ruth said, linking Esme's arm. 'Just putting the world to rights, weren't we, Esme?'

Esme nodded and held up her glass. 'Top up required, I think,' she said, taking a breath and lifting her head. 'I feel like celebrating something. And I really don't mind what.'

Author's Note

If you've not yet read *The Malice of Angels*, I'd urge you to STOP and come back when you reach the end of the book, as what you read here may give away too much of the story!

I became interested in the subject of Special Operations Executives, or SOEs, when our local news reported the death of an elderly lady in Torquay. She was described by neighbours as a polite, but private, individual. What stunned everyone was the discovery that this unassuming woman had a hidden past. Her name was Eileen Nearne and she'd been a secret agent involved in highly dangerous missions in occupied Europe during World War Two. Subsequent reading about Eileen's experiences and those of other SOEs set my writer's brain ticking and I knew I wanted Esme to investigate someone who'd served in this way.

A few years previously, in 2008, I'd heard the shocking revelation by BBC reporter Angus Stickler concerning the incarceration of typhoid carriers during the 1940s and 1950s. At least 43 women who'd recovered from typhoid but been found to still excrete the bacterium of the disease, were condemned to a life of isolation due to an over exaggeration of their risk to public health. The image stayed with me and, merged with my research into SOEs, found its outlet in the plot of *The Malice of Angels*.

SOEs were often 'head-hunted' and invited for interview where they were told recruits were being sought to take on dangerous work, vital to the war effort. If they responded positively, they underwent rigorous training which assessed their suitability as candidates. If successful, they progressed to the next stage, where they learned "the art of silent killing" – a practice seen by some as dishonourable and undermining the integrity of the British Army. As a result it became known as "ungentlemanly warfare".

If selected, SOEs would be dropped behind enemy lines by parachute where they would be involved in acts of sabotage and the gathering of intelligence which would be relayed back to HQ in London by wireless operators. The chances of being betrayed were high, either from locals earning food or favour by exposing suspected agents to the Germans, from infiltration by double agents or from fellow SOEs being captured by the Gestapo and tortured into revealing what they knew.

To reduce the risks, agents were known to one another only by their code names and told to operate alone whenever possible. The life of an agent was not only hazardous and stressful but lonely, too.

In France, men of working age were rounded up by the German army for war work, meaning male agents were more likely to attract unwanted attention. Women, on the other hand, were able to blend into the community as "wives and mothers". It was for this reason that it was decided to recruit female agents, a policy not without controversy.

The character Viktor Kruger was based on a German counter-intelligence officer called Horst Kopkow who was deemed to be responsible for the deaths of many Allied agents. While in custody for war crimes, he was reported to have died of bronchopneumonia and a death certificate issued. But he hadn't died and was subsequently released to work for British and American intelligence. Perhaps unsurprisingly, the files surrounding this scandal were only released by the National Archives in 2004. Ironically, Kopkow did eventually die of pneumonia. But not until 1996, at the age of 85.

Bleakmoor Airfield, so named in the book, was modelled on a real airfield further inland, near the village of Winkleigh.

Few know about the crucial wartime role it played alongside better-known air bases in eastern England. Here the secret Black Squadron was based, flying perilous missions behind enemy lines taking agents to, or retrieving them from, war torn Europe in its distinctive Lysander aeroplanes. So secretive was the squadron that the authorities didn't even acknowledge its existence. Planes were painted black, with no insignia, a camouflage which would have disastrous consequences. On 4th August 1944, two of the squadron's planes were caught on radar as they returned to Winkleigh. An RAF Mosquito night fighter was scrambled and intercepted them over Brittany. Believing them to be enemy aircraft, the pilot attacked, hitting one of them. The fuel tank exploded and the Lysander crashed to the ground in flames, killing everyone on board.

While reading about the auxiliaries – the clandestine 'home' army, ready to become a thorn in the side of the enemy should there be an invasion – I discovered there had been one of their concealed tunnels not far from where I used to live. Also, barely a few hundred metres from my house, a small, unassuming building, clad in corrugated iron and used as a chapel, had been a secret ammunition store.

Further Reading

The RAF Winkleigh Story can be found on the website of Devon photographer, Jackie Freeman: http://jackiefreemanphotography.com/.

Bernard O'Connor's book *Churchill's Angels* gives an account of every female SOE agent, the work they did and what became of them.

A Life in Secrets by Sarah Helm tells the fascinating story of Vera Atkins, a British intelligence officer who made it her mission to discover what had happened to those agents whose fate remained uncertain at the end of the war.

Angus Sticker's report on the "typhoid women" can be found on the BBC news website: http://news.bbc.co.uk/1/hi/uk/7528045.stm.

Thank you for reading *The Malice of Angels*. If you enjoyed the book and have a moment to spare, writing a short review on your favourite site would be greatly appreciated. Authors rely on the kindness of readers to spread the word.

To sign up for updates on giveaways, special promotions and new releases, please sign up for my newsletter on my website: www.wendypercival.co.uk.

You can also visit me on Facebook: www.facebook.com/wendypercivalauthor and on Twitter: @wendy_percival

I look forward to hearing from you.

Printed in Great Britain
by Amazon

67830445R00180